"I'm trying to do the right thing, Jenny...."

"But sometimes I wonder...."

"I wonder, too," Jenny replied. "I wonder why you broke our engagement. And now I wonder why you're trying to pretend it was a big deal for you."

"Please, Jenny. In spite of what you think, I want what's best for you." He reached over, tipped up her chin and looked her in the eye. "I mean that. I was convinced I'd made the right decision for your future, and for mine." He paused and cleared his throat as his fingers drifted to her cheek and slowly began to outline her jaw. "I—I only want what's best...."

Jenny stood as if paralyzed as all the old sensations burst inside her like roman candles. It was always the same. The minute he touched her, reason fled.

"Jenny," he whispered huskily, "the truth is that all I really want is you." Then his lips closed over hers...

ABOUT THE AUTHOR

"I enjoyed writing this story," says Megan Alexander, "because I lived in the redwood country for four years. My husband owned a sawmill, and I taught in a one-room schoolhouse exactly like the one my heroine teaches in. I'll tell you, after working in one of the largest schools in Los Angeles, that little school hidden away among the big trees seemed like heaven." Megan currently lives in Santa Rosa, California, and writes full-time.

Books by Megan Alexander

HARLEQUIN SUPERROMANCE

Words of Wisdom

MEGAN ALEXANDER

Harlequin Books

TORONTO • NEW YORK • LONDON
AMSTERDAM • PARIS • SYDNEY • HAMBURG
STOCKHOLM • ATHENS • TOKYO • MILAN

For June and Phillip Campbell
and in memory of Bertha Ohlson
and Maria and Ray Barney
whose warm hospitality and friendship
made our years in the redwoods
a high point in our lives.

Published October 1989

First printing August 1989

ISBN 0-373-70377-5

ACKNOWLEDGMENTS

My thanks to Pat Patterson for lending her talent as a poet for the words of Robbie's song.

GLOSSARY

The following words used in this novel are from a genuine American lingo documented by linguists and historians. The jargon was deliberately contrived in order to confuse outsiders and was widely spoken by the close-knit inhabitants of a small northern California lumber town during the early years of this century. Remnants of this language can still be heard in the speech of some of the local inhabitants. I have used the crafty device in WORDS OF WISDOM, which is set in a fictional lumber town in a similar redwood area.

airtight: a lumber mill
codgy: senile or feebleminded
featherleg: an impudent person, a know-it-all
highpockets: a man of authority
jimhead: a perplexed or stupid person
lizzied: pregnant
schoolch: schoolteacher
serowlsh: of no account
shark: trick or defraud or to get the best of another
squirrel bacon: a derogatory term
teebowed: deaf

CHAPTER ONE

THE SECOND TUESDAY in August Jenny's calico cat disappeared, she lost her cashier's job at Andy's Little Supermarket and Luke's letter arrived. She wasn't too worried about Fat Cat. He had always been able to take care of himself and had the battle scars to prove it. And when Andy apologetically told her he had to let his part-time help go, she said not to worry. Luke was already working at his new job in Otter Bay, so they would be moving north as soon as they got married.

But the letter was a different matter. She'd pulled it from the mailbox and opened it with eager fingers. At last. Luke had left six weeks ago with his Uncle Charles to establish a branch office for Beaumont Business Services in Otter Bay, a north coast California lumber town. When they'd finished their business, their plan had been to unwind for a day or two of fishing. Luke was no letter writer. He'd called twice and sent a couple of postcards. "Miss you, Jenny" was scrawled across one, and on the other he'd described the various sites he and his uncle were considering for the new office.

"The Chamber of Commerce has been very helpful," he'd added. "Their city hostess knows the area like the back of her hand and has been showing us around." Then not a word since. A scant month to accomplish their business and do a little fishing seemed reasonable. Visualizing Luke flipping his line into some mountain stream, she'd been unconcerned about not hearing from him. But by the end of last week she kept reminding herself that Luke was a poor correspondent, and by the sixth week she'd had to restrain herself from calling Uncle Charles's San Francisco office.

She opened the letter with eager fingers. A breeze playfully wrapped her skirt mummylike around her slender figure and pulled strands of blond hair from a knot, streaking them across her face. She brushed the hair from her eyes and read expectantly. Shock turned her rigid as she raced to the conclusion. Luke's handwriting blurred in and out of focus as she read it again. Slowly.

Somehow she managed to remain standing, hanging on to the wrought-iron support of the mailbox as fear sapped her strength. There had to be some mistake. Luke didn't write this. He couldn't have. He would come home soon to reassure her and declare it a misunderstanding.

She trudged into her apartment, cautiously now, as if she were walking in darkness and each step might plunge her into some unknown chasm. She dropped the letter on the desk. *Ignore it for a while. Eat. Do some chores, then read it again objectively.* She'd probably missed something or misinterpreted. She put the kettle on for tea and set up the board to do some ironing, but the letter was like a scream in the room. She couldn't function. She had no tenacity. The kettle boiled dry, and the kitchen windows grew opaque with steam. She picked up the letter, read it again, then tossed it aside and threw herself down on the daybed. She felt as if she were dying. And in her mind she heard Luke's words echoing over and over again: "So in the final analysis it's best if we part now. Our marriage would end in disappointment and heartbreak for us both."

Shock, pain, disbelief all flailed her at once every time she recalled his words. Her sense of self-worth, her ego, her future—everything seemed to shrink into a wraithlike creature and fade into nothingness. If only she could embalm the day and bury it forever.

Reasons? Oh, he had several. His job encompassed far more than he expected—travel among his uncle's various firms, becoming active in community affairs and long, long hours, just to mention a few. Most important, he'd learned that his uncle was grooming him to take over the business on his retirement—an exciting prospect, but it meant that Luke would have to dedicate his life to the business for at least the next ten years. This job opportunity was beyond his wildest dreams, and the early years were crucial to success.

Jenny pounded her fists on the bed. Hadn't he any more faith than that in their love? Toughing out difficult times together was what marriage was all about. What had happened to the strong, loyal Luke she knew?

Jenny had no doubt that his Uncle Charles had put in more than his two cents' worth. "So this is your fiancée," Charles had said when they'd first met. He'd acted as if he might soil his pale fingers if he shook hands with her.

Well, she didn't approve of him, either. He was pompous and arrogant and a snob. She had been immediately concerned that Luke was going to work for such a man.

She wondered if the real crux of the matter was children. Luke had been less than enthusiastic whenever she'd brought up the subject. In her own joy of looking forward to a real home at last, she knew she'd talked endlessly about having the family that, as a foster child, she had never experienced. Did the thought of supporting a family appear that overwhelming to Luke? Was that what had made him back off? She didn't believe it for a minute. After all, he'd helped to support and bring up his own five brothers and sisters.

Actually, in a strange way, Luke had made her responsible for his breaking off their engagement. "Darling, you've been sacrificing all your life," he'd written. "I won't ask you to sacrifice your dream now. I know how much you want children right away, but that won't be possible with this new blueprint for my career. After my own upbringing, I'm all too familiar with the heartbreak an absentee husband and father can cause. I will not ask a woman to share my life until I can first provide a home, financial security and quality time to spend with her and our children."

Nonsense! How many couples waited until everything was perfect before they started a family? Anyway, she and Luke could have waited a year or two if he was so concerned about the new state of affairs. Her biological clock still had some time to run. No, that wasn't his real reason, though she had no doubt that he'd used these arguments to convince himself.

She stared at the ceiling and tried to corral her wild emotions. *This can't be happening! I'm caught in some merciless nightmare!* Had the loving support they'd offered each other these past months, the hard work, the shared dreams, all been a sham?

Not for Jenny they hadn't. She'd entered into the relationship with caring and commitment, and she had been convinced that he had, too. Naive Jenny Valentine had been manipulated into the same tired old scenario experienced by countless other gullible souls. She was good for a whirl on the merry-go-round and a few laughs, but unsuitable for the long haul, for commitment, children, marriage.

She'd better face the truth. Luke had never really loved her. Now she could see circumstances that showed he'd felt no commitment to their relationship. No wonder he'd wanted their engagement kept secret. No wonder he hadn't been in any hurry to introduce her to his relatives. Their relationship had no roots. It was like a passage from a book taken out of context.

But for Jenny nothing had been detached. Everything was still relevant. A loneliness more poignant than she ever dreamed settled as a deep chill into her heart. *Oh, God, Luke! How could you do this?*

Why hadn't she seen through his duplicity? Easy. She'd fallen hard for a pair of warm brown eyes and the kind of loving words she'd longed to hear all of her life.

She felt the emptiness of their house settle desolately around her. Luke's presence was tangible: his tennis racket in the corner overlapping hers, an old brown sweatshirt on a hook by the back door. She could see him sitting at the table, his head propped in his hands as he studied, his thoughts seemingly miles away, but still not so distant that from time to time she caught him watching her as she worked at her own desk across the room.

She wiped her eyes and recalled the first time they met. It was last February just as spring classes started at the University of California at Berkeley. . . .

JENNY ARRIVED from tennis five minutes late for her statistics class. Fortunately the professor was talking to a tall young man who looked a little too well dressed and much too mature to be a regular student. But then students came in all varieties these days.

She watched idly as the two continued their conversation for a few minutes longer. Then the tall young man moved with an athlete's ease to a seat in the adjacent row. Surreptitiously she admired the strong lines of his jaw and the steady alertness of his dark eyes. But then she became engrossed in the lecture and forgot all about him until later when she was sitting in the campus coffee shop, a book propped in front of her, making do with a cup of coffee for lunch because of her tight budget.

"Hello, Jenny Valentine," he said, his voice a pleasant baritone.

She looked up and recognized him. "Hi. Statistics 370, right?"

He made a circle with thumb and forefinger. "I'm Luke Beaumont, and if you'll turn on at least a twenty-five-watt smile, I'll feel a lot more comfortable. May I join you?" She nodded, and he sat down opposite her arranging his legs with difficulty under the skimpy table.

"And how do you know my name?" she asked, not hiding her surprise at his sudden appearance.

He leaned forward as if to share a secret. "After class I sneaked a peak at the seating chart."

"Oh, you're with the CIA!" He smiled, and Jenny decided she liked his smile. It was a little shy.

"Yeah, well sometimes my intelligence training comes in handy. For example, I spotted you right away. Did you know that you're an anachronism? I said to myself, 'Beaumont, that girl with the unbelievable blue eyes and gorgeous blond hair has just stepped out of the last century. Grab her before she steps back.'"

Jenny straightened the full skirt of her checked gingham dress and rolled her eyes. "Heaven help me. I'm not sure I can digest all that corn."

"Hey, don't get me wrong. I aim to please, honest. I assure you that underneath my brassy exterior I'm shy as hell and scared stiff that I'm turning you off." His hang-dog expression appeared real enough. She couldn't help but laugh.

"Okay. Your perception of me is not too far off at that. I was raised on a farm in a little town in Montana that no one ever heard of. I came to California when I was in high school and earned a partial scholarship. I used to teach classes for blind children, but now I work at a day-care center. End of biographical excerpt."

"But you've left out the relevant part."

"Well, I'm almost twenty-seven years old," she added.

"You look more like seventeen, but I'm not talking about age."

She shrugged. "Well, I don't smoke pot. I'm terribly sentimental. Someday I want a big, lively family and I talk too much," she finished breathlessly. *And you, Luke Beaumont, dazzle and terrify me!*

He shook his head. "You know, I have this crazy feeling that I've known you somewhere. Maybe we were married in some former life."

A terrible line, she thought. Couldn't he do any better than that? Still, there wasn't an ounce of guile in his earnest expression. She tucked a curly wisp of hair behind an ear. "I was wondering how long it would take you to recall our past. Well, what have you been doing in *this* life, Mr. Beaumont, of the socially prominent San Francisco Beaumonts, no doubt?"

"Charles Beaumont is my uncle," he said with a sudden frown, and she wondered if she'd offended him.

"Actually, I'd have thought you were more closely related to the defenders of the Alamo," she said. "Don't I detect a certain Texan flavor in the accent? I suspect you were recruited by the athletic hierarchy to shore up our faltering basketball team."

"Well, you all," he drawled, "You're right enough. I'm from the Big D—that's Dallas to you Californians—but I'm not into basketball. Tennis is my game. At this late date—I'm thirty-one—I'm here finishing up my master's in business administration. Expect to complete it in June.

I happened into your class today to chew the fat with a former college classmate, your instructor. My uncle has offered me a job in one of his branch offices when I graduate in June.'' She raised an eyebrow. Beaumont Business Services was a prestigious firm in San Francisco.

"Marking time, then?"

He made a wry face. "Hardly. I'm working full-time for a local accounting firm, traveling among several interstate branches. In my spare time—what there is of it—I'm writing my thesis. This is my first day off in ages."

As they'd talked, the noon crowd had been slowly reaching its peak. Around them the room resounded with voices and clattering dishes. Just then a busboy spilled an entire tray of cups and saucers on the floor next to them.

"What a madhouse!" Luke said. "Look, now that we've each presented our credentials, why don't we go to some civilized place and talk? I live only five minutes away. We could go there."

Disappointment stung her. Why did he have to be one of *those*? She would have wagered he wasn't the type. "Or we could go to the library or the student lounge," she said, "but unfortunately we can't listen to your newest album or find my favorite white wine chilling in the fridge."

His grin was undeniably winning. "How did you guess?"

She gathered up her books. "Whatever happened to the grand old pastime of plain old getting acquainted?" she asked bitterly. "Everyone around here thinks he's a jet-setter—move fast, a few slick words and hop into the sack. Shove off, Texas boy, I'm not interested."

Color flooded his face, and he looked genuinely embarrassed. "I apologize Jenny. I didn't mean it that way. Honest."

Puzzled, she studied him for several minutes.

"Okay," he said, finally breaking the silence. "Have you tallied up my score? I seem to be adept at putting both feet in my mouth. I hope you found a few sterling qualities to add along with the obvious."

The obvious, Jenny decided, was that Luke Beaumont thought he was a lot smoother than he was. "Excuse me, but I have a class."

He reached over and took her hand. "Don't go," he said quietly. His brown eyes were warm and pleading.

I refuse to be taken in by this character. I simply will not. She rose. "I'm not in the habit of cutting classes," she said as stiffly as she could manage, then inhaled the exquisite aroma from a passing waiter's tray and sat down again. "Well, okay, if you buy me a hamburger, a double order of fries and a pineapple shake. I'm starved."

"All that?" he asked in mock amazement. "Aren't you worried about your figure?"

"No way. I'm hungry. At least I can teach you one thing, Luke Beaumont. Treating girls with cornflower-blue eyes to lunch can be mighty costly."

JENNY KNEW AT ONCE that she was in love. She reveled in the magic and excitement of it and at first tried to sort out what had happened to her, then decided it was absurd to analyze something that wasn't meant to be analyzed.

Their busy schedules allowed her and Luke little time together, although they had dinner at one of their apartments whenever possible. As the semester reached midterm, she watched the circles under Luke's eyes grow darker and the spring go out of his step.

"You've got to slow down," she told him one rare Saturday evening in her apartment. "Working full-time and studying half the night is turning you into a zombie."

"Don't worry. In a few months it will all be over, for better or for worse."

"For better. There's no way you're not going to meet the deadline for your thesis," Jenny insisted, as always supremely confident regarding Luke's abilities.

Luke slumped on the sofa, mumbled something about perennial optimists and instantly dozed off. Jenny sat on the floor with Fat Cat in her lap and looked at Luke's weary face.

Jenny wished he didn't have to work such long hours, but he'd explained that his father had a compulsion for dabbling in high-risk investments that habitually turned sour. It was years after his death, but Luke was still paying off his debts—a fact he preferred to keep from Uncle Charles.

Jenny reached over and gave Luke a gentle poke. "Listen, Rip Van Winkle, I'm tired of seeing you only one point zero times a week, and I'm even more tired of watching you kill yourself for lack of sleep."

Fat Cat stretched languidly and gave a massive yawn. Luke followed suit. Then his face took on an earnest look, and his mouth set in a way that always exposed a dimple in his left cheek. Whenever he looked like that, she wanted to hug him. He reached for her hand.

"Well, Jenny girl, I just happen to have a solution."

She caught her breath. As if the moment demanded privacy, Fat Cat hopped off Jenny's lap and padded with dignity out of the room.

"Oh, yes?" she said.

"Move in with me. Then at least we'll be together. We're practically married now. All we need is that piece of paper, right? Besides, my apartment is closer to the university and to your job at the day-care center, too."

Jenny swallowed hard. They planned to marry as soon as Luke graduated. A live-in arrangement wasn't in the script as far as she was concerned. She thought of her early years when she'd been shuttled from one foster home to another, always seeking but never finding the security and love she craved. She'd had enough of that. No way did she plan on half a loaf in her future. Luke, who had grown up among a host of adoring relatives, could have no conception of the lack of security a person felt from truly belonging to no one.

She entwined her fingers with his in a tight grip. "I can think of five reasons against your offer—two psychological, two ethical and one rather personal."

He looked up sharply. "Personal? What do you mean by that?"

"I'd kind of planned on the long white gown and veil, a bouquet of white roses and at least one attendant before we share an apartment."

"Good Lord! We can't get married now. My Texas relatives would never forgive me, especially my mother. They're a close-knit bunch, Jenny. They arrive en masse for weddings, funerals, christenings, you name it! I practically signed my name in blood, promising my mother to let her know if I ever planned to get married. You have to understand how it is with a big family."

She didn't know how it was with a big family, but regardless, the decision didn't seem complicated to her. "Well, what's stopping us? Why not go ahead and tell her?"

"Lord, no! We can't have visiting relatives and all that hoopla now. I can't afford time away from my studies. At this point it could make the difference between getting my degree or waiting another six months. Uncle Charles is holding a job for me contingent on finishing this June."

The silence stretched overlong as she considered the situation. Commitment meant a wedding ring. Still, he'd given her an engagement ring several weeks ago. That stood for commitment, didn't it?

He reached over and tipped up her chin. His expression softened as he looked at her solemn expression. "Hey, remember me?" Caring shone in his face as tangible as sunlight.

"Okay, let's do it," she said finally.

"The minute I graduate we'll head for Dallas and get married. Prepare yourself for a true Texas-style bash. I can't wait for you to meet my mother. She'll be crazy about you, Jenny girl. But we better keep our plans under our hats until June. My family, including Uncle Charles, has a way of taking over. Okay? Okay!" he said, settling the matter, then leaped up to rummage in the refrigerator. He found a half-empty bottle of wine, poured out a couple of glasses and handed her one.

"Not exactly Dom Perignon, but this occasion demands a toast. Here's to us," he said, and they touched glasses. Their eyes locked and their expressions grew solemn. "Forever," Luke said softly, as if repeating a vow.

"No matter what," Jenny pledged.

They finished the drink and set down their glasses. Luke put his arms around her and pulled her close. "I love you, Jenny," he said.

Tears stung her eyes. The words always seemed such a miracle. Her arms went up around his neck, and she leaned her head against his shoulder. "And I love you, too," she said.

He kissed her gently, then again with deepening ardor, and her response rose in a pure assured flow. Moments later they silently folded out the daybed, then helped each other undress. He unpinned her hair and let it flow through his fingers as it fell about her shoulders.

"You're so beautiful," he whispered, and again pulled her to him.

Luke's large hands were always gentle, and she nestled against his firm body in awe that their intimacy remained always new, always exquisite. She'd known little tenderness in her life. Always she'd longed for the physical reassurance and nourishment that touching could bring, and now that she had such abundance, she could never quite believe her riches.

In his arms she wondered if such magic could last, if anyone deserved such perfection. But the thought vanished as she soared with her love to a realm that belonged only to them.

"Oh, Luke, my dearest Luke," she said at last when she was able to speak.

THE NEXT MORNING Jenny rose early as was her custom, sat in a chair with one foot tucked under her and watched Luke wake up. He came out of sleep in slow motion as though dragging himself down from another planet, then lay painfully staring at nothing, no doubt waiting for his batteries to recharge.

Morning sunlight slanted through the window, stretching a golden shaft between them. His eyes focused on her slowly, as if she were a stranger.

"Say something, Luke. You're so far away. I can't stand the way you lie there looking like some combination of Heathcliff and Rochester."

He muttered something that could pass for an oath in any language.

"Wake up! Now that you've sweet-talked the fair maiden into sharing your abode, there's a little matter of moving over her dowry and closing her apartment."

He groaned. "How come your realities are always so real?"

She stood quite still and shed her flippant manner. "My reality is you, Luke," she said quietly.

"You know something? It's dangerous to look at a man with such solemn devotion," he muttered. Fully awake at last, he got up and caught her in his arms, hugging her hard. "I don't deserve you, Jenny girl. And where did you get that crazy dress?"

She twirled away, her skirt billowing. "At a rummage sale, and the salesgirl said, 'It's very trendy, dearie!'" She preened and wrinkled her nose at him.

"It looks like three-fourths of your grandmother's patchwork quilt!"

"My, aren't we full of compliments!"

"Yes, I are, but I'm fresh out, so let's get moving."

FROM THEN ON the single phrase, "When Luke graduates," expressed Jenny's every hope for their future.

Because she wanted to pay off her school loans before they were married, Jenny found a part-time cashier's job three evenings a week at Andy's Little Supermarket in addition to her afternoons at the day-care center. When Luke discovered her action, he was furious, stomping around the apartment and bellowing in a manner quite unlike him.

"Idiot! Do you have to be so damn independent? I'm not entirely broke, you know. As soon as I start my job, I'll take care of your loans."

"Cool it, Luke R. Beaumont, M.B.A. I love teaching at the day-care center, and besides, all this experience will look good on my résumé. As for working at Andy's, what with you away half the time, I need something besides studying to fill my lonely hours." She knew Luke would take care of her debts, but he'd been doing just that for his own family for a number of years. She wanted to start out with a clean slate. Besides, something compelled her to earn her degree all on her own.

The additional work made for a long day, and there were times when she questioned the wisdom of taking it on. Her college classes lasted until noon. There was no bus to reach the day-care center, so she hiked the two miles, eating her bag lunch as she walked. On the evenings Luke was home, they concentrated on their studies. June was the light at the end of the tunnel.

Her own graduation would have to be delayed until she finished another semester of practice teaching, but she could easily do that after she and Luke were married.

The longed for day of Luke's graduation arrived at last, and Jenny sat in the stadium audience proudly watching a solemn Luke, sunlight glancing across his dark hair and the strong planes of his face. He strode with confidence to the podium to receive his diploma. For a breathless instant he paused to scan the audience as if searching for her to share in his elation. The glistening moment wound another loop around her heart.

Afterward she waited for him by a fountain where they'd planned to meet. Soon he ran across the grass, and they rocked for a few moments in each other's arms, unable to speak.

"Hey, we can't just stand here," he said finally. "Let's celebrate. You name the place. I'll take you there. Hang the expense!"

Jenny spread her arms to indicate the abundance of blue skies and sunshine. "Anywhere. Just don't coop us up on a day like this. I'm positively exploding with happiness!"

So they stopped at Andy's to share the good news. He presented them with a bottle of champagne, and they brought Brie, sour French bread and some of Andy's homemade salami, then headed for the park a few blocks away from their apartment.

It was a brave little oasis wedged between encroaching high rises. Pink floribundas bloomed with abandon against a fence. The sycamores were scarred with initials, and in more than one place the grass was worn thin. But bathed in bright sunshine and saturated with their exuberance, the park became Elysian territory.

As giddy as children, they raced across the grass, allowing the long months of tension to drain away. Exhausted at last from their high jinks, they spread out their food under a willow whose green skirts offered a modicum of privacy. Pouring champagne into paper cups, they joyously toasted their future.

"Jenny, Jenny, sweet as sugar candy," Luke sang out, and kept the champagne flowing. "Get out Robert's Rules or Miss Manner's handbook or something. It's time to set the agenda!"

"What agenda?"

"I seem to recall I promised you a giant spectacular after graduation, you little knothead."

No, she hadn't forgotten, but the traditional wedding she'd wanted so much didn't seem to matter anymore. It was time to let go of one period of her life and leap happily into the next. She reached for his hand and laid it against her cheek. "I don't need a big wedding, Luke. Why don't we have a small, private service in a chapel and just concentrate on the honeymoon? I'd love to go to Texas and meet your folks."

Luke whooped his agreement. "Prepare yourself for an extravaganza. I'll never be able to restrain my mother."

They planned to call her the minute they got home, and settled on a week from Tuesday to fly to Dallas after the ceremony. She felt enormous relief at the change of plans. A private wedding in Berkeley and a reception in Texas would eliminate the embarrassment of not having a single relative of her own to present. She looked forward with a kind of wonderment to at last being embraced by Luke's large clan.

A little lost boy suddenly ran up to them, wailing pitifully. Jenny put an arm around him and calmed him, found a ladybug and allowed him to watch in wonderment as the insect "flew away home." Then, with the child calmed down, Jenny walked him across the park to find his mother. In moments she ran back, sat down on the grass and pulled Luke's head into her lap.

"You have a way with kids, all right," Luke said. "No wonder you want a passel."

"Six. Remember?" She'd probably told Luke a hundred times she'd never marry a man who didn't want children.

"Why six?" he asked.

"I like even numbers."

"Ye gods, didn't they teach you anything in that statistics class?"

She feigned a pout. "You're a drag, Beaumont. Okay, I'll settle for five, all boys, a basketball team."

He groaned. "It's about time someone clued you into the population explosion."

"Oh, I'll just be having a few extra to make up for persons who can't have any."

"Precarious logic, my girl. How do you propose we support so many kids, much less send them to college?"

"No problem. I'll be married to a rich and prosperous business executive, and anyway, children with parents who get four-point averages are bound to be scholarship material.''

Luke closed his eyes and placed his hands in an attitude of prayer. "Oh, Lord," he intoned, "grant thy humble servant five winning lottery tickets and one oil-rich Arab godfather for each of my children."

She chuckled, rumpled his hair, then grew serious. "Oh, Luke, I can't imagine myself not having children. I mean, I've dreamed about it all my life. I can hardly wait to become a mother. I want to feel everything! Everything!" she cried, opening her arms wide to the skies. "Can't you imagine how I'll look?"

"Yeah, like a full-blown steamer with calico sails," he teased, and pulled her head down to kiss her hard on the lips. "You're really serious, aren't you?"

"Of course," she said, surprised that he would ask. "No way I would ever marry a man who didn't want a family. Can we start right away?"

He plucked a blade of grass and crumpled it in his fingers. "Surely you don't mean that! Having kids that soon is the last thing I want. Don't you think we deserve a little freedom before we take on more responsibilities? This past year has been tough for both of us. Speaking for myself, I want to get settled into my job first, find a house and let you furnish it—have a little fun before we tie ourselves down."

Jenny felt puzzled by his attitude. Now that she thought about it, he'd shown this same reticence every time she brought up the subject. Having a family had always seemed such a marvel to her that she never thought of it as being in any way restrictive. But life was too wonderful to argue about that now. Jenny was pretty sure she could change Luke's mind when the time came.

They spent the rest of the afternoon passing judgments on all aspects of life, admiring the pink roses and agreeing their beauty was enough to break one's heart.

Luke helped her pack up the remains of their picnic. "Five kids," he said with an exaggerated sigh. "And will you still love me after I grow bald and paunchy supporting that brood?"

She stood motionless and stared up at him, incredulous that he'd even consider such an idea. Then she kissed him in a way that left no doubt of her loyalty. "Forever, Luke, no matter what," she said, breathless from the satisfying kiss. "No matter what!" she repeated, and fitted the words rhythmically into a traditional wedding march, singing lustily.

They had barely arrived home when a call came from Luke's Uncle Charles. Luke mouthed bits of the conversation to her as it progressed.

"Congratulations, Luke. Pleased to hear you graduated magna cum laude," Charles began. "Although I expected nothing less from a Beaumont."

"Thanks. I'm glad it's over."

"Now hear this," Charles said. "The board of directors has decided to open a new branch in Otter Bay. According to my recent survey, Otter Bay is one of the few West Coast cities of its size that provides no comprehensive business services such as ours. Believe me, Luke, they're ripe for the picking and you've been elected head honcho. I want you to join me immediately to look over prospective locations. Setting up the office and hiring personnel will take at least a month. If there's time afterward, we can knock off for a couple of days' fishing, maybe on the Klamath, for trout. I belong to a hunting and fishing lodge in that area. You deserve a little fun and relaxation, my boy."

The conversation ended with Luke agreeing to drive the two hundred miles up to Otter Bay the next morning.

After he hung up, Luke looked at Jenny with shining eyes. "I can't believe this! I'm going to be the boss of a new branch in Otter Bay. The head honcho. It's incredible, Jenny!"

"It's wonderful, but did you say right away, Luke? What about a week from Tuesday?" She tried without success to keep her voice steady.

"What *about* a week from Tuesday?"

"Oh, nothing. I thought we had a wedding on the agenda."

"Jenny! My God! Do you realize I'm in charge of the new office? I hadn't expected that. I thought I'd have to spend at least a couple of years as low man on the totem pole. We'll tie the knot and take off for Texas the minute I return. That's a promise."

Jenny hid her disappointment, and the next morning helped him pack his bag and later waved a smiling good-bye. For Luke to go was the sensible choice. After all, she'd waited this long to get married and to meet his family. What difference did another few weeks make?

She'd watched them drive away in Charles's maroon Mercedes until it disappeared in the distance, determined not to allow disappointment to edge into the high joy of the day....

That had been six weeks ago. Today she'd received Luke's letter.

CHAPTER TWO

LUKE SAT at the desk in his new office, staring at his full appointment calendar, willing himself to concentrate on the tasks he must accomplish within the coming months. He'd managed to beat the days into tight agendas, but his body ached with the need for sleep, and his head felt as thick as if he'd been on an all-night drinking binge.

He reached for the telephone to dial Jenny's number as he had hundreds of times during the past week since he'd sent the letter that had gutted their world. But once again his hand froze, as if all neural connections had been severed. The call wouldn't go through anyway; she'd had her phone disconnected.

He stared down at the neat reminders on the pad in front of him, bird tracks across the Sahara of this new existence, then held his head in his hands and once again tried to recall why breaking up with Jenny was the only honorable thing he could have done.

The doubts that had surfaced to shatter their upcoming marriage had been totally unexpected when he'd bid her goodbye and had driven up to Otter Bay with his uncle. During the long ride Charles had filled him in on the dimensions of his job, spreading out for the first time the panorama of his future with all of its wonderful and terrible implications.

Luke was amazed to learn he would have to do a lot of traveling among the branch firms and attend numerous conventions, as well as be present at the biweekly meetings of the managers at the main office in San Francisco. Moreover, he was expected to attend organizational meetings of the local lumber industry as well as join just about every damn organization in town. Why? In order to keep Beaumont Business Services before the public, of course.

Charles also made it plain that Jenny should make an all-out effort to become a leader in Otter Bay society, to become active in women's groups, charity functions and the like. Luke was amused. Uncle Charles could forget that. Jenny had her own priorities, and women's clubs weren't even in her vocabulary.

"And find out at once if and where important timber owners go to church, then you put in an appearance once in a while," Charles added. Luke couldn't believe his ears. If he accomplished everything Charles was asking of him, he'd never be home. He'd be a carbon copy of his father.

Through the years Luke had seen his uncle at infrequent family gatherings, and from his teenage vantage point had admired him in an almost worshipful manner. Charles appeared to be the ultimate man—handsome, self-assured and successful. Luke often wondered how his own father, Charles's brother, could have been so different.

Luke and Charles hadn't been on the road an hour before Luke realized their association would be far more complicated than he'd ever imagined. From his ramrod-straight posture to his perfectly tailored suit and his well-toned mid-fifties body that spoke of regular visits to an athletic club, there wasn't an undisciplined thing about Charles, Luke decided.

"Now is the time to dig in and learn this business inside out," Charles told him. "I intend to retire in about ten years, and I want you at the helm. Someday it will all be yours, you know. Don't look so surprised. You're my sole heir."

Luke Beaumont, head of Beaumont Business Services? Luke allowed the beautiful words to wash over him. It was a heady thought. "I'm overwhelmed," he said, swallowing against the sudden huskiness in his voice. "To run a chain of firms such as yours is beyond my wildest expectations. I can't tell you how much I appreciate your faith in me. You won't be sorry."

"I know that, Luke. I have excellent judgment and a talent for picking the right person for the right job. I always wanted a son. For years I've wondered what would happen to this empire of mine after I'm gone. You can't imagine what it means to me to know that you're going to carry on." With a quick gesture he seemed to brush moisture from his eyes.

"And that's not all I have up my sleeve," Charles continued. His expression suddenly turned roguish and he bathed Luke in a benevolent grin. "You and I are going to be quite a team. Would you believe my secret dream has always been to see a Beaumont in the U.S. Senate? And now it's possible. I've got a nose for politics. I have the connections as well as the means, and you, son, have the charisma and intelligence for it. Once you get this business under your belt, we can turn it over to a board of hand-picked directors, and then we'll go for it!"

Luke stared unbelievingly. What was Charles saying? Pride at his uncle's faith in him tangled with the gnawing fear that Charles was taking charge of his life. "Hey, slow down. I want to be totally involved with the business, but I'd like you to know right now that politics isn't my bag. Not interested."

Charles leaned back in his chair. Under emphatic dark brows his eyes narrowed and grew unreadable. This is what a poker face looks like, Luke thought.

"I think you'll change your mind when the time comes," Charles said at last in a tone edged in steel.

Luke hid surprise at his uncle's imperious tone. This man he had admired so much was quickly taking on other dimensions. *He acts as if he considers himself master of the universe,* Luke decided, and wondered if he ought to let Charles know that he had no intention of becoming a slave.

Luke recalled a remark his father had made years ago when the two brothers had quarreled. "Charles devours people!" he'd said with bitterness. Luke had dismissed the words as just an emotional outburst, but now he knew his father was right. He knew something else, too. *I won't let him devour me!*

They turned their attention for a while to matters they would have to accomplish during the coming weeks. "I'm beginning to see that this job is going to be mighty time-consuming," Luke said.

"Glad you understand that. It's a demanding mistress, all right, but you'd better believe it's worth it in the long run." Charles gave him a challenging look. "You might as well forget any kind of family life for at least ten years. Maybe longer."

"That long?" Luke felt as if a load of bricks had been dumped on him.

"Absolutely. You're going to be more thoroughly married to this job than to any woman. At this point you have to be at the beck and call of the business twenty-four hours a day. I mean that, Luke. Frankly, under the circumstances, maybe you ought to consider delaying your marriage. You'll be taking on a lot and won't even have any spare cash until you finish paying off your dad's debts. I realize how much it means to wipe that slate clean. Yes, I know all about it, and I admire you for it. A Beaumont has too much pride in his name to default, right?''

Thanks to his position in the Otter Bay firm, Luke figured he could clear up the debts in months rather than years. "I don't consider that a problem, considering the salary I'll be earning."

Charles nodded approval. "Good, but something else worries me about your coming marriage. I guess you don't have to be reminded about how your own father affected your home life with his continued absence. Put your mother through hell. I shouldn't think you'd want to subject your wife to that kind of life. Are you certain she understands what's going to be demanded of you? What's expected of her?''

For a moment the old loneliness washed over Luke as he recalled how as a boy he'd waited in vain for his father to take him on a long-promised fishing trip, how after repeated promises, his dad never showed up for Luke's high school graduation, and most heartbreaking of all, how his mother had tried to hide her tears. "I'm certain Jenny has no idea of what this job encompasses, but truthfully, neither did I."

"This is no nine-to-five job," Charles said, emphasizing each word. "You're being groomed to head the business, and don't you forget it. It's a whole different ball game."

Luke tried to take in this new concept of his job. After the long years of struggle, he'd been so ecstatic about his good fortune that not once had he considered how it might affect Jenny. He recalled that glorious day in the park after his graduation. Fragments of their conversation still rang in his mind. "Oh, Luke, do you realize how much it means to me at last to have a family?'' Jenny had asked, her eyes shining. ''I'd never marry a man who didn't want children.''

But ten years! Could he ask Jenny to wait that long? Surely it would be worth it. By that time their future would be secure for life. But until then, how could he father children knowing he'd rarely be around for them? He and Jenny had argued a lot about starting a family right away, but nothing he'd ever said had convinced her to wait even a year or two. He didn't blame her, not with the bleak childhood she'd experienced. But the specter of his father would never allow him to become an absentee parent and husband. Never would he do that to Jenny. When the time came, no ifs, ands or buts about it, he intended to be a reliable provider and a full-time father.

During the first couple of weeks after they arrived in Otter Bay, Luke took the initiative in searching for a location, tending to permits, interviewing prospective personnel. Meanwhile, Charles occupied himself with what he characterized as ''advance marketing.'' This seemed to consist of lunching with the mayor, seeking out important timber owners and chatting with members of the Chamber of Commerce, with Stacy Adams in particular, the efficient and attractive Chamber of Commerce representative and city hostess. Stacy assured them that she would be happy to introduce them to every VIP within a hundred-mile radius.

As Luke forged ahead with his work, he was continually amazed at the way Charles questioned even incidental decisions, always seeming to act the devil's advocate. Was this part of the grooming process, he wondered? He recalled the matter of choosing a desk for his office. Charles took one look at the compact, sturdy piece of furniture Luke had ordered and insisted he exchange it for a massive walnut desk they'd seen earlier.

"I disagree," Luke said. "Besides costing five times as much, it's far too large for this office. It would intimidate clients."

"Precisely the point. This piece has no class. Get rid of it!"

"It suits me," Luke said firmly, and decided the switch would be over his dead body.

Luke had the feeling the small episode had become an important test of wills and didn't know what to make of the faintly amused glint he'd caught in his uncle's eye.

Then there was the matter of leasing a suite of offices. Several days spent with Stacy Adams along with the Realtor she recommended failed to turn up a single appropriate location. "We may have to build our own offices. Believe me I've looked at everything!" Luke said, hoping it would be a long time before he'd have to trek through so many buildings again.

"Nonsense. In a town this size there has to be something. What about that business complex just being completed at the south end of town?"

"I happen to know about that one," Stacy Adams said. "My office is just across the street from it. Every suite was leased over a month ago."

Charles impatiently dismissed the information. "Call the Realtor. I'd be interested in having a look anyway."

Fifteen minutes later they met the manager of the complex. "Too bad you missed out on this place. There's not a single vacancy. Tenants will be moving in next week," he said with an apologetic smile, but showed them through at Charles's insistence.

Office spaces were smaller than they would have liked, but the suites were well arranged, and the building had a

classy exterior, professional landscaping and an unob-
structed view of the bay from most units.

Undaunted, Charles asked to read the contracts and
immediately pointed out a loophole concerning one of the
lessees who hadn't met the deadline for the closing payment. The Realtor waved a hand. "Oh, I think he'll come
through."

Charles's face flattened coolly, but his tone was sympathetic. "A contract is a contract. May I point out a
clause in the second paragraph? Obviously this tenant isn't
able to meet his responsibility. I'll gladly put up the fee to
find another place for him," Charles said. Then he wrote
out a check for a five-year lease of the suite, plus a good-
will bonus of a thousand dollars, and the deal was con-
summated.

Everyone shook hands and waltzed through a set of
amenities. Luke felt remorse for the hapless tenant and
wondered at still another facet of his uncle's personality.
As far as Charles was concerned, it appeared that business had nothing to do with moral values, with right and
wrong. It had to do with winning. How did it feel to be so
nervily sure of one's self? "No man is an island," to quote
John Donne's poem, but Charles came close. Luke decided that if his uncle returned to his San Francisco office
that afternoon, it wouldn't be too soon.

Luke's worries multiplied as he thought about bringing
Jenny into this new situation. He knew how much she
looked forward to at long last establishing a home and
starting a family. With the blueprint Charles had laid out,
it looked impossible. He thought about it continually.
During dinner with a couple of attorneys one evening,
Luke felt so overwrought he couldn't even hold up his end
of the conversation. Later, back in the hotel room, Charles
confronted him.

"All right, let's have it! You're not with it, are you? What's the problem?"

Luke mumbled something about a sore throat, but under relentless prodding, he finally poured out his concerns about Jenny.

"Listen, son," Charles said, placing a hand on his shoulder. The word *son* flowed easily from Charles's tongue nowadays, and he never bothered to correct anyone who assumed the relationship. "I don't blame you for being concerned. It would take a mighty special woman to adjust to these beginning years. Are you worried that it will be too much for your girl?"

Your girl, Luke thought angrily. Charles knew her name. Why couldn't he say it? "Jenny has energy to burn," Luke said evenly. "It's just that things are going to be much different than we expected. As I told you, Jenny and I are planning on a family."

"A family!" Charles pronounced the word as if it were an eccentric condition, or at least something that had slithered out from under a rock. "My dear boy, surely you realize you can't afford to get bogged down in domesticity at this point!" And as Charles enumerated one reason after another, Luke deliberately tuned him out, hoping to keep his mind in focus.

Charles slammed a fist on the table, effectively recapturing Luke's attention. "My God, but you're self-centered! Damn it, can't you see how selfish it is to drag this girl into our situation? How unfair can you get?"

"Jenny and I love each other. Doesn't that count for something?"

"Maybe not as much as you think. Sure it's a difficult decision, but consider her, for God's sake. From what you say, she'll sacrifice anything for you. Tell me, if you ask her to relinquish her right to have children, what do you think she'll say?"

"I know Jenny. She'll agree to it."

"Exactly. *If* you ask her, you already know her answer. *If* you ask her to, she'll sacrifice her God-given right to have children, because she loves you. Do you *want* Jenny to be unhappy?"

"That's the last thing I want!"

"Then don't ask her to sacrifice this passionate dream of hers, because she will. Just let her go, Luke."

Charles was right in that respect, Luke thought, contrite at his tunnel vision. How could he ask Jenny to sacrifice her dream? And if he did, would their marriage survive? Could he ask her to wait five or ten years—until her biological clock was ticking into the danger zone? Oh, God, he couldn't do that.

"And take it from me," Charles added. "You can count on her regret and resentment poisoning your marriage. You're not the only man in the world, you know!"

As the weeks slipped by, Charles kept returning to the point. "Pretty hopeless, isn't it?" Charles said brusquely one evening, sensing Luke's dejection. "But breaking an engagement isn't the end of the world, my boy."

"A breakup would kill Jenny," Luke insisted, and he knew it would devastate him, too.

"A momentary pain. You're both young."

Weights pressed on Luke's chest. "How can I do that to someone I love?"

"If you *really* love her, let her go. Consider the consequences. What makes you think you can have your cake and eat it, too? Damn it, Luke. End it quickly. Write her a letter."

"I can't do that," he said quietly. "While you hold down the fort, I'll drive to Berkeley for a couple of days and talk things over with her. I want us to decide together. Besides, I need to pick up some insurance papers. I'll go tomorrow."

Charles shrugged. "Suit yourself. But when you're in this kind of emotional quagmire, a lot of talk will only confuse the issue. Take it from one who has been through it."

Luke looked at his uncle's cold gray eyes, and his stomach churned. He rose abruptly and put on a jacket. "I'm going for a walk. Don't wait up for me."

CHARLES WATCHED Luke stride out the door. Young love! Thank God he was beyond it. He wondered actually if he'd ever experienced it. Oh, he'd had plenty of women, still did when he found one who amused him, but he was an expert at bowing out before involvement set in. His three-year marriage had been a disaster and had cured him from ever taking such a step again. His wife had spent her time collecting vague illnesses like some women collected antiques, keeping to her bed and rarely in his. The divorce provided deliverance for both of them.

Charles peered out the window through the early darkness, catching a final glimpse of Luke as he passed under a streetlight, shoulders hunched as he fought his private battle. Charles felt his throat contract and knew it defined elation. Luke would become his son, the one his wife had refused to give him.

He'd watched Luke grow up in a kind of time-lapse sequence of intermittent family visits, always noting the boy's quiet determination to succeed at everything—from winning a place on the junior soccer team to earning a Phi Beta Kappa key.

This crush Luke had for that girl had worried him at first. Thank God he'd managed to pull a rabbit out of the hat. So what if he'd lied a little or a lot about what Luke's job would encompass. Such lies added up to real favors in this situation.

The girl had no-win credentials. Charles pictured her leaning on a broom with a couple of frowzy kids hanging on to her skirts. She'd be Luke's ticket to oblivion, as far as any upward mobility went. Her unreasonable nesting urge would have split up the relationship anyway.

Charles glanced at his watch. He'd better get out of here. Everything was going to work out. He felt it in his bones. Matters usually did for Charles Beaumont.

LUKE WALKED the few short blocks to the bay, then trudged along the beach that bordered it. There was a wild and primitive feel about the loneliness here, the hostile, gravelly pound of the surf a few yards away, the forlorn cry of some distant gull, the amorphous swirls of mist that tasted of salt and seaweed.

Without breaking his cadence, he kicked aside pieces of driftwood and the occasional skeletal remains of some luckless sea creature, each step measuring the labyrinth in which he found himself.

Far ahead he knew the beach ended where a cliff jutted out into the ocean a few miles away. He determined to get his head on straight by the time he reached it.

"Marry me, Jenny. We'll work something out," he said to the wind. Was that such a selfish plea? He felt certain of her answer, which would come wrapped in her heart. But surely such asking and answering would create a warp that would soon turn them against each other.

Would he be able to live with himself if he asked her to sacrifice her own needs and desires? She'd been doing that all her life. Surely she deserved better now.

"Oh, God, what shall I do?" Luke cried aloud, but heard no answer. He was no phantom creature hovering in the mist. He was flesh and blood. He wanted to shake his fist at the starless sky and curse the unmindful moon.

Once he passed a night fisherman casting his net with rhythmic persistence into the frothy surf, but each man had the grace not to violate the other's privacy. A rogue wave soaked his shoes before he could stride away, chilling his feet. His hands tightened in his pockets, and his breath came hard, making his throat ache.

Hours after midnight, drained and numb, he made his way back to the hotel room. At once he saw his uncle's note propped on the table, no doubt full of needless reminders all in alphabetical order—a gun aimed at his future. He picked it up and read it.

Dear Luke,
Just received a call from the main office. Something vital has come up and I'm needed in the San Diego firm, so I'm taking off immediately. Sorry, but guess you'll have to postpone your trip south. I won't be able to get back for at least six weeks. You have my sympathy in your dilemma, but just keep in mind that the only way you can keep Jenny from making a terrible sacrifice is not to ask her. I'll pick up the papers and mail them to you. Keep in touch.

Charles

It seemed that fate had clasped him in a firm grip with no intention of letting go. With a heavy heart he read the note again. Then he sat down and wrote Jenny a letter.

CHAPTER THREE

CHARLES BEAUMONT WAITED for the valet to bring his Mercedes from the underground parking facility adjacent to his San Francisco office. He'd verified that Luke's former fiancée would be home after five. She'd had her telephone disconnected, so he'd had to track down the landlord to give her the message. He could have sent one of his secretaries to pick up Luke's papers, but he wanted to have another look at the girl who had sent his nephew into such a spin. It had both surprised and annoyed him that Luke would succumb to so much turmoil, especially over someone like that Valentine woman.

From their brief meeting the morning he'd picked up Luke to go to Otter Bay, he'd found her somewhat of an enigma. He supposed she had to have something to attract an intelligent man like Luke. And he had to admit she had a certain indefinable air about her in spite of her old-fashioned hairdo. He was aware that young people dressed casually in today's world, but certainly this girl had never been near Saks Fifth Avenue! He prided himself on being able to evaluate people, and it seemed pretty obvious the Valentine woman had neither the class nor the background to fit into the kind of life Luke's future held for him.

Charles had felt a distinct sense of relief at Luke's decision to break off his engagement. For a while he'd been afraid it would never happen. He had been sympathetic concerning the problems an inexperienced young wife would have to face in the small coastal city, gently dropping any number of facts that would give Luke pause for thought. He complimented himself now on his subtlety. Oh, he didn't take all the credit. With the facts before him, how could Luke have decided otherwise? But Lord, the agony the dear boy had put himself through in coming to such a logical conclusion. Some day he'd learn that no woman was worth all that fuss. This Valentine girl with whom he'd had the bad judgment to fall in love had served her purpose. It was time Luke moved on.

Charles smiled. Luke would have plenty of assistance, if Otter Bay's city hostess was any example. Her help had been invaluable in clueing them in to the background of the town and its inhabitants and the way she promptly set about introducing Luke to the right people. Already she'd sponsored his membership in the local country club.

Stacy Adams. Now there was the kind of woman Luke needed, someone who would be an asset to his career. An affair with the attractive Otter Bay woman, with her ability to speak in public, her poise and her charm when meeting people, would soon show him the folly of a liaison with someone like Jenny Valentine. *Jenny,* for God's sake! What kind of name was that? Yes, a clean break was best. He'd learned that when he'd divorced his own wife.

Charles could hardly restrain his satisfaction and delight at the way his nephew had taken charge of establishing the new branch. Watching the way Luke grasped the reins filled Charles with bright visions of their future together. Luke had everything he'd ever wanted in the son he'd never had: intelligence, purpose, discipline and charisma. Charles would allow him a few years to mature in his job as head of the Otter Bay office, then the sky would be the limit. Yes, a Beaumont in the U.S. Senate was an exciting and viable possibility.

He drove across town to the slightly run-down area where Luke's apartment was located. He'd been shocked when he'd seen where Luke had lived. Couldn't the boy have afforded a better neighborhood? He must have been more strapped than Charles realized, not that Charles hadn't done some behind-the-scenes investigation, discovering that Luke had spent years paying off his father's considerable debts, in fact, was still paying.

Charles never had any use for his Texas brother, hadn't spoken to him since long before his death. The man had no self-discipline. Thank God Luke didn't take after him. Considering character and ability, almost anyone would agree that Luke should have been Charles Beaumont's son.

Charles parked his car near the gray stucco dwelling. He got out and started up the walk. Someone was washing the windows. Such industry! He could use some of that vigor in servicing his own buildings. Help was downright inferior nowadays.

He walked up the steps and knocked. The ragtag girl in jeans and T-shirt climbed down from the ladder. She looked wan, but her blue eyes were clear and steady.

"You're Uncle Charles, aren't you? Come in. I have Luke's papers ready for you."

He pretended surprise. "You're Jennifer? I didn't recognize you."

She shrugged as if to dismiss her shabby clothes. "I don't wonder, in this outfit, but it suits the chore, and the name is Jenny."

He lifted an eyebrow ever so slightly. "Perhaps it's an idiosyncrasy, but name contractions bother me. *Jennifer? Jenny?*" he said slowly, pronouncing the shorter form as if it curled his tongue.

She lifted her chin. "I was never Jennifer. Jenny is on my birth certificate. Jennifer wouldn't suit me."

"Ah, yes, I see what you mean," he said, checking the slender girl with a spray of pale freckles on her nose and wisps of blond hair escaping the bandanna. "But you'll surely have to agree that nicknames lack dignity."

"I don't agree at all. I figure either you have dignity or you don't. I can't see that it has anything to do with a name," she said quietly.

Damn. What was there about her manner that irritated him? Still, he'd have to grant the girl spirit if nothing else. He frowned and decided to try to intimidate her again. "Valentine? I'm not familiar with that family name. Are you a native of this city?" He knew she was from some farm in Montana, but he wanted to hear her say it. It annoyed him that this feisty young woman wouldn't assume the station to which he'd assigned her.

She gave him the unwavering look. "I'm surprised that Luke hasn't told you. I have no pedigree, if that's what you're interested in. I was abandoned as an infant and raised as a foster child. I was born on February the fourteenth, so Valentine seemed a natural, and the nurses chose Jenny because they thought I deserved something prettier and more unusual than Jane Doe."

My God! A Beaumont's wife a foundling! Yet there was no apology in her tone. Where did she get all that self-assurance? "Very interesting," he said dryly.

She gave him a searching look. "I can't help but wonder why you're so curious about my background. I get the feeling that I'm being weighed and measured and have come up wanting. Is it because you're afraid Luke and I might settle our differences after all?"

"My dear girl, I certainly am not involved in Luke's personal affairs, but I do have his welfare very much at heart. Permit me to give you some words of wisdom. Count your short relationship as a pleasant interlude and let go. I'm very perceptive in such matters. It's best to part while you're still friends. Isn't that so?''

Her eyes were bright with either tears or anger, but she held her head high. "Sir, I believe you are very much involved in Luke's affairs and will become even more so. Permit *me* to give *you* some words of wisdom. Butt out. Luke is the deliberate sort. You can shove him around for just so long. Best to loosen the reins now while you're still friends." She rose and handed him the manila envelope holding the papers.

He was being dismissed, damn it, and by this impertinent little nobody. He gave her a curt nod and walked out the front door.

Jenny watched him get into the car and heard him rev the engine. Good. She'd gotten under his skin. Hateful man! She had no doubt that he'd influenced Luke against her. The thing that hurt was that Luke had allowed it. She'd believed him to be strong enough to be his own person.

Now, despite her brave advice to Charles Beaumont, she wondered if Luke would fret under his uncle's manipulations. This new Luke wasn't the same person she'd known these past months. Well, Charles was accurate in one piece of advice. "Let go," he'd said. Yes, she could do that with the new Luke. He no longer shared her values. He wasn't the man for her. Concerning the old Luke she knew and loved, it was a different matter.

She walked over to the window and looked out into the twilight. The muted transition from daylight to darkness ordinarily never failed to intrigue her, but tonight she felt smothered by the dusky curtain, reduced to an anonymous figure, lost and forgotten.

A swallow made soundless arcs around the oak tree. Jenny fixed her attention on the bird as if it might carry some universal truth. When it disappeared into the leaden sky, her body tightened. She leaned against the window frame and sobbed.

SHE MUST HAVE FALLEN asleep after all. The last time she'd checked the luminous dial on the bedside clock, it was 3:00 a.m., but now gray light filtered into the room. Everything looked very still, like a stopped movie frame. The squarish, trendy furniture bought by the landlord with an unrelenting eye for durability, diminished to a few surrealistic blobs on a canvas, and the oak tree just outside the window seemed to have rigid painted-on leaves.

Something hammered away in her head. Someone's birthday. That was it. Luke's? No hers. Then the whole devastating state of affairs washed over her like an icy shower and she came fully awake. They'd celebrated his birthday a scant month after they'd first met. What was the matter with her?

During that time their incompatible work hours had allowed only a rare evening together, but making chili on Saturday nights in her apartment had soon become a ritual whenever he was in town.

On the weekend of his thirty-first birthday, she announced there would be a special celebration. Her finances were at a low ebb that month—not an unusual state of affairs—so she robbed the quarters she'd been hoarding in an old peanut butter jar and plotted the occasion.

She bought a fresh crab, a few prawns and clams, a bottle of chardonnay and found a bargain remnant of red-checked cotton, which she fringed and made into a table-cloth. A bowl of red geraniums and a candle in an empty wine bottle formed the centerpiece. Then she baked a chocolate cake and prepared the rest of the dinner. Later she planned to take him to a free concert at the college.

"Wow!" Luke cried when he arrived home to candlelight and the aroma of crab cioppino. "I'm not sure I can stand all this atmosphere, and am I imagining what I think I smell or did you strike oil?"

"Ways and Means Department," she said with a smile, which she hoped was both brilliant and devastating.

"Yeah, I know about bureaucracy. Now fess up! Where'd the money come from?"

"Stop looking like the kind of banker who forecloses at the drop of a hat. Don't worry. I haven't gone into debt for this display of affluence, so enjoy," she said as she ladled out the cioppino. "In case you haven't noticed, I'm one of the world's best cooks."

They ate like gluttons, meanwhile polishing off the chardonnay, toasting everything from the topic of his thesis to the Muppets and the four-letter word that spelled *love*. Sublimely satiated, they forgot about the concert, found an old Humphrey Bogart movie on TV and curled up to watch it on the hard studio couch.

"Hey, there's a movie on," Jenny protested some time later as Luke persistently nuzzled her cheek.

"So what, Julia Childs, Jr? And you're a lousy dissembler."

"Don't pin any of your fifty-dollar words on me."

"That's exactly what I'm doing, so pay up." He pulled her into his arms and kissed her hard. Their eyes, luminous in the half darkness, met and held, mirroring their feelings without evasion. The moment seemed charged with something too strong to ignore.

He kissed her gently on the lips, then drew her down on the couch. Her mind reeled. His eyes, usually so warmly brown, now smoldered with amber lights, and his tenderness, at which she'd always marveled, gave way to passion as he crushed her against him.

"Oh, God, Luke! What are we doing?" she cried as she struggled out of his arms. "Remember me? I'm that calico kid who got caught in the last century, one of those conscionable country girls. Listen, until I met you, my life was quicksand. You're my rock, Luke, solid and wonderful. I don't need any guilt feelings to clutter up things."

Luke sat on the edge of the bed and put his head in his hands and his elbows on his knees.

"Please don't be angry, Luke," Jenny said. "You know how much I love you." She leaned her head against his shoulder.

He'd picked up her hand and kissed her fingers. "Darling Jenny. Also proper, crazy, wonderful Jenny," he'd said with a rueful grin. "How did I get so lucky?"

Too bad she hadn't maintained that attitude, she thought now. After they became engaged they'd often made love. She supposed she had been naive or perhaps merely arrogant to think that somehow *they* were different, that for Luke, the declarations of love had something to do with commitment. Would she ever find a meaning for it all?

She glanced at her watch and saw it was already noon. Her afternoon class at the day-care center began at one o'clock. *Okay,* she told herself. *Stop remembering. Stop questioning and trying to figure things out. Keep the mind locked up. Give it only enough leeway to handle the basics.*

Throughout the rest of the afternoon, the demands of her class of four-year-olds kept her reasonably anesthetized. Later, after the last few children had been picked up by the usual quota of tardy parents, Jenny straightened her desk and made ready to go home. Lisa, the teacher in the next room, stuck her head in the door and asked if Jenny had heard from Luke yet—a perfectly natural question. After all, Jenny had blabbed endlessly about their plans.

Jenny looked up with what she hoped was an undisturbed expression and tried to remember the artful reply she'd prepared for just such times, but for a moment all she could do was stare blankly.

"I guess you could say that Luke has dissolved out of my life—like a pinch of salt in a lot of water," she said at last. "Luke's idea. Not mine. I mean, you don't have to be a Phi Beta Kappa to get the picture. It's the tired and true plot A for the typical class B soap opera, and if you don't mind, I'd rather not talk about it now."

Lisa mumbled something vague and hastily retreated. On the way home Jenny walked three blocks out of her way to shop at another grocery store in order to avoid any conversation with Andy. Explanations, explanations! Maybe she ought to make a tape and run it off for the whole darn nation.

That evening as she ate a bowl of soup she formed some plans. First priority, pack up Luke's books and the rest of his things and get them out of sight. Then she'd look for a full-time job, and when she got one, she'd hoard every penny so that she could devote all her time to her practice teaching during the following semester. Next, she would move out of this apartment and find a room somewhere. It would help not to have to deal with the painful memories conjured up by the apartment.

She found some cartons in the garage and carried them upstairs. After packing Luke's things, she set his tennis racket on top of the boxes and covered them with an old sheet. She'd worry about sending them later.

"All right!" she said aloud, as if commenting on a successful operation, and felt better for saying it. She heard a familiar scratching at the screen door and ran to open it.

Fat Cat shot in and gave a raucous yowl. Jenny poured some food into his dish. "If you can't think of anything pleasant to say, sit down and be quiet. I'm in no mood for complainers," she said, just as the doorbell sounded.

"Never a dull moment," she muttered. It was Joel Spencer, who lived down the street. He was an aspiring attorney who'd recently passed the bar. Short, stocky, with a beacon of red hair and an open, cheerful face, Joel's appearance could supply a long list of contrasts to the tall, dark, thoughtful Luke. Joel and his wife had become Jenny and Luke's good friends, and Jenny adored their three small boys.

"Come in, Joel. What's up?" She indicated a chair.

"Luke's new job, what else? Isn't it outrageous? I just heard. I'm still sending out résumés and driving a taxi to keep bread on the table."

And you don't have a rich uncle, Jenny thought. "Coffee?" she asked carefully.

"Maybe later. Luke called and asked me to pack his things and express them up to him."

"Oh? Do you know his address? I don't have it."

Joel shot her a surprised look, then fished in his pocket. "I've got it here somewhere." He handed her a crumpled card.

"That's the office in Otter Bay, right?"

"Well, sure. Has he found a house for you yet? I guess you'll be moving as soon as everything gets squared away."

So Luke hadn't told him. "That isn't likely, Joel."

He looked startled. "Would you care to explain that?"

"Why not? It won't take long. In that esoteric vernacular of yours, you might say he took a detour and a frolic."

"I don't get it, Jenny. Are you telling me things are washed up between you two? And what do you know about detours and frolics?"

"Oh, I've thumbed through law books now and again. Actually, as you may remember, he left over a month ago. I haven't seen him since."

Joel ran his square hands through his hair, then jammed them into his pockets as if he needed to get rid of them. "He never said anything to me. He's so busy getting organized, he probably hasn't had time to write."

"Oh, he took time to write, all right. I got the Dear John letter a few days ago—or Dear Jane, if you're fussy about gender."

Joel stared at her for a moment, probably noting for the first time that her eyes were still a little swollen. Even without that clue, her face was always as easy to read as the top row of letters on an eye chart.

Joel twisted uncomfortably in his chair. "Oh, hell, Jenny, I don't know what to say. The last thing I heard, you two were all set to get married and take off for Texas."

She nodded. "Interesting, isn't it? That was my impression, too."

"But he was crazy about you, Jenny. I'll swear to it. I can't believe he'd do a turnabout like this."

"Well, it's taken me a while to get used to the idea myself, but I think I'll survive. As a matter of fact, your timing is perfect. I've just now finished packing the stuff he left here."

With a deep scowl, Joel pulled out a roll of nylon tape and set about strapping the boxes. Jenny found a black marking pen and started to print the address, then abruptly handed the pen to Joel. They worked in silence, which stretched overlong, and she knew they were both searching for a safe topic.

Joel viciously yanked off lengths of tape. "There has to be an explanation."

"Oh, he explained all right, but he failed to mention the real reason. No-pedigree Jenny Valentine doesn't have the credentials to keep up with that Beaumont bunch."

"That's a lot of bull!" He glowered at the finished boxes as if they were a group of nasty thugs who had just barged into the room. "Nothing adds up, but so help me, I'm going to do so some figuring."

Jenny managed a thin smile. "Be my friend and forget it. I mean that, Joel. Anyway, a few things have finally started to make sense."

"What, for instance?"

"Do you mind if we delay the postmortem? Come by in a week or two. By that time I should have it all together."

He gave her a brotherly hug. "Take care. Call me if you need a shoulder to cry on."

"Don't make any foolish offers," she said and wiped her eyes with a quick brush of her hand.

Joel mumbled a goodbye and left, carrying the last of the boxes out to his car.

Then, just as Jenny felt a new wave of tears coming on, Fat Cat chose that moment to point his whiskers up at her and began weaving in and out between her ankles in an uncharacteristic burst of affection.

"Oh, come off it," Jenny said. "How come you're not your usual beastly old self? All this charm will get you nowhere. I've had it with charm, my friend!"

CHAPTER FOUR

AUGUST WAS ALMOST OVER and Jenny still hadn't found another job. At the end of the month she'd have to give up her apartment and find a room to rent. But even rooms were expensive, and if she was going to finish her remaining college units this fall, she'd need more money than she could earn at the day-care center. Since she could work evenings only, her job possibilities were limited. She'd spend all her free time tracking down want ads. Not having a car made matters even more difficult.

The quarters she'd hoarded in the peanut butter jar were almost gone. Joel and Beth had offered her the tiny studio apartment Joel was building over his garage, but it would be several months before he finished it. Anyway, if she didn't find another job, she wouldn't be able to afford it. It had been a long day, and she was weary and discouraged as she climbed the stairs to the apartment.

The telephone rang as she let herself in. "Women's Resource Center calling. Miss Valentine?" asked a pleasant feminine voice. Jenny had applied at the center only last week. The administrator had been sympathetic and not the least encouraging.

"A position for a long-term substitute teacher has opened up. It will last for only the fall semester. It's a one-room school in Woodhaven, a little lumber town. Are you interested?"

Was she interested! "But I still lack a few units for my credential. I thought I made that clear."

"Yes, we know that, but this is a special circumstance. Dr. Erdman, the superintendent, will explain it to you. He's reviewed your qualifications and believes you can handle the job."

Jenny's hand trembled, and she breathed hard as she wrote down the time for the interview. Her voice grew husky, and she had to swallow so frequently that it was a wonder the woman understood her. She put the phone down and danced around the room, then stopped abruptly in front of a mirror and tried to assume a demeanor more becoming to a neophyte who had just landed her first interview. She didn't succeed. Her collar was awry, her hair was in disarray, an unsophisticated flush reddened her cheeks and her mouth twitched, ready to break into a radiant smile any second.

A one-room school! Hadn't that gone out with the horse and buggy? In the back of her mind she'd imagined it survived as a historical monument. Well, that was fine with her. The present hadn't earned many raves recently.

She called then to get someone to cover for her at the day-care center, managed to force down half a bowl of soup, washed her hair and then went to bed. For the first time in weeks she dreamed of something other than a tall young man with deceptively warm brown eyes.

The next morning she skipped breakfast in order to spend time on her appearance. She brushed her thick wavy hair, doing it over three times, striving for a smart coiffure. But in spite of all her effort, wispy curls escaped to frame her face. She ought to have it cut and styled. Luke had teased her often enough about her old-fashioned hairdo.

Maybe she should complete the picture and appear in shirtwaist and long skirt, she thought capriciously, but settled for her one good suit, a lively blue wool that matched the color of her eyes. She added a touch of lipstick, then knotted a flowered scarf around her neck and decided she would do.

It was noon when the bus pulled up to the county offices. Good. She liked to arrive early. It would give her time to compose herself. In any case, mornings were her best time. She'd always risen long before Luke.

"What are you doing up at this ungodly hour?" he'd complain grumpily. "I'll bet in your next life you'll return as an alarm clock set for dawn."

But for her there was something breathtaking about the early hours before the day was invaded by people harassed by busy schedules. It was a time of special awareness. The oak tree's limbs just outside their apartment window spreading elegantly against the morning sky; a bowl of apples on the kitchen counter highlighted in a pod of sunshine, or Luke still asleep, his boyish head buried deep in his pillow—all had an aching beauty when viewed in quiet and solitude.

Her appointment was at one, so she had time for lunch. But on checking her purse, she found only enough change for return bus fare. So instead she sat near a fountain and kept one eye on her watch, meanwhile holding imaginary interviews in which she stunned the superintendent with insightful answers.

At exactly one o'clock the secretary ushered her into the superintendent's office. Her first impression after she took the proffered chair was that he looked like a benign old cormorant, if such a contradiction was possible. He hunched over his desk in a dark suit that was much too ample, and his lips moved continually as though he were either chewing something or about to start speaking. But the most prominent feature in his craggy face was a huge nose, which seemed designed for sniffing out unqualified candidates who dared to apply for a position in a one-room school.

The end of her own nose developed a persistent itch, but she forced her hands to remain in her lap. Dr. Erdman sat back in his chair and laced his fingers together. She felt no coolness here, only a steady measuring. At last he nodded as if he found her satisfactory.

"Well, Miss Valentine, you seem to have some excellent qualifications. I see you've maintained a four-point average. The day-care center as well as the school for the blind seems addicted to superlatives. An impressive background."

Jenny watched him thumb through her folder. "I guess it's all there but the credential. I lack nine units," she said smoothly.

"Yes, I expect you're wondering about that. Well, to be perfectly frank, due to the remote location of the school and the scarcity of housing, it's almost impossible to find a substitute. No one on our list was willing to take the assignment. Because of your fine record, we can issue you an emergency credential."

Jenny's spirits soared. She could almost taste new beginnings. "Where is the school?"

"Woodhaven is a little sawmill town up in the redwood lumber area almost two hundred miles north of San Francisco and ten miles inland from the coast. There's a general store, a post office, a gas station, the usual bar and grill and a school built over seventy-five years ago. That's all— no library, no theater, no shopping malls and practically no television reception."

"I understand rural areas. I grew up on Montana farms."

"So I've noted, and it's a point in your favor. I won't deny that most of our teachers have found it difficult to adjust to living in this provincial community, in spite of the attractive salary." He mentioned the figure, and Jenny caught her breath. It was double what she'd expected as a substitute.

He caught her surprise. "Forest areas bring generous tax revenues, and good pay helps to attract and keep qualified teachers."

"It must be a beautiful place, and the school is small. I can't imagine it would be all that difficult to teach there."

Dr. Erdman shook a finger as if to cool her enthusiasm. "During winter storms there are power outages, sometimes for a day or more, and the playground turns into a giant mud puddle. Because of road conditions, orders of books and supplies don't always arrive on time from the county office, which can play havoc with your lesson plans. More pertinent is the attitude of the people. You need to know that as far as education goes, the folks in this particular area are leery of change. You may find that your efforts will be judged by how things were done in grandpa's day. What I'm saying is, it takes a resourceful, flexible individual to survive. Are you up to it?"

Such matters seemed trifling. She was certain she could handle it all. If only she could convince this man across from her. Jenny leaned forward as if to lend weight to her words. "I can assure you that I don't let problems throw me. As for supplies, if I have a roll of butcher paper, a marking pen and a stapler, I can provide anything from reading charts to stage sets. I'm handy with tools and have made bookcases and tables from old crates. I can teach music, too. I play the guitar and sing reasonably well." She gripped her hands together and took a deep breath. "Dr. Erdman, I've wanted to be a teacher all my life. You see,

I'm completely nuts about kids!'' She bit her lip at the unprofessional term.

The superintendent stroked his chin, allowing his hand to cover his mouth for a moment. ''Ah, yes. Well, certainly one thing this school can use, and that's a teacher who's nuts over kids.''

Jenny repressed a relieved sigh. ''What happened to the regular teacher?''

''Yes, I was getting to that. Jed Ballard, a retired army captain, was in a serious accident early in the summer and will be in traction for several months. He'll be out the entire fall semester. Won't return until the first day of February. I'm afraid he ran the school like a military institution, but he was very popular with the parents.''

Score one for the negative side. Following a popular teacher was never easy.

They discussed classroom procedures then, and he asked about the day-care center and her experience teaching blind children. She warmed to the telling and he frequently nodded approval. ''Summer vacation will be over the end of this week. Can you start on Monday?''

Jenny's throat contracted so hard that she could hardly speak. ''You mean, I'm really hired?''

''On paper, yes. But according to protocol, the local board must interview you—a mere formality. I can't imagine anything short of finding you were a member of the Mafia that would make them refuse to hire you. They meet seven o'clock Friday evening at the school. They'll expect you. They can assist you with housing, too. I believe there's an old cottage near the school that's available for the teacher, but I don't know what shape it's in.''

''Oh, I enjoy fixing up things.''

''I can believe that. Why don't you go up early on Friday and get acquainted with the place. Steve Douglas is president of the school board and will be delighted to find that the new schoolmarm doesn't need a hearing aid and has all her teeth. You'll find him at his mill just beyond the school. Oh, and Miss Valentine, a couple of pieces of advice. Forget about any educational jargon when you talk to the board.''

She flashed him a reassuring smile. "Oh, I'm nothing if not plainspoken." She'd always believed it was pompous to use professional jargon around people unfamiliar with it. "And, sir, what was your other advice?''

"Just this, smile like that when you meet the board," he said. They rose and shook hands. He wished her good luck and bid her goodbye, and Jenny was astounded to see him suddenly grow two heads and an elongated body. "Thanks again," she said, and her voice sounded hollow and far away. Then she swayed and crumpled into a chair to allow the light-headedness to pass.

"Are you all right?" Dr. Erdman asked anxiously.

"I'm sorry," she said. "I guess cloud nine was a lot higher than I anticipated. The truth is I probably ran out of fuel. I was so excited I skipped a couple of meals."

He was solicitous and wanted her to rest for a while, but she said it wasn't necessary and made a point of striding out with exaggerated vigor to assure him he'd not hired some fragile female.

A few steps down the hall she stopped and swung her purse high. "An honest to goodness teacher! I'm going to be a teacher!" she cried aloud, startling a custodian into stumbling over his broom.

On the bus, in spite of the sign prohibiting such chatter, she shared her news with the friendly driver and later gave a detailed account to an elderly lady who sat beside her.

Home at last she picked up the mail and raced upstairs and in roughly two minutes made a three-decker sandwich. She poured a glass of milk and sat down to her meal, meanwhile thumbing through the mail. Her hand froze as she picked up the long white envelope with Beaumont Business Services on the return address. For a long moment she stared at the envelope, then ripped it open and took out a note attached to a check for six hundred dollars.

Dear Jenny,
I've paid your September rent and will continue to do so. The enclosed check will help with your other expenses, and I'll send one the first of each month. I hope you'll be able to enroll in your required courses, and know things will go well with you.

Sincerely,
Luke

She picked up the check as if it were grimy. Guilt money! She'd starve before she took it. What made him think she couldn't take care of herself?

She wadded the letter and tossed it into a wastebasket, then jammed a sheet of paper into the typewriter. "Dear Luke," she typed, and sat for a moment to stare at the salutation. Then allowing all her bitterness and hurt to spill out, she furiously pounded two full pages at her best fifty words a minute. She jerked out the page and looked over what she'd written.

Valentine, she thought, *you're a prize fool. If anyone wrote all this drivel to me, I'd throw up.*

She tore it into small pieces and scattered it over Luke's note in the wastebasket, then rolled a fresh sheet into the typewriter. No salutation. No accusations. Just:

I'm returning the ring. Enclosed find your check. I'm moving out of the area to take a full-time job.

She signed only her initials. All that blank space on the page ought to pique his curiosity. Good. It was his turn to try to figure out some answers.

CHAPTER FIVE

AFTER ALMOST TWO HOURS of driving, Jenny turned off the coast highway, shoved the car into low gear and prayed. But Joel's ancient pickup took the hill without a whimper in spite of its crotchety reluctance to start that morning. Joel had sold the car to her yesterday for a promissory note of a hundred dollars, plus the tennis racket Luke had given her for Christmas. The truck was one of a battered fleet he was continually restoring and selling to bolster his income.

She'd consulted a map before starting out that morning and saw that she merely had to follow the coast highway north until she came to the turnoff to Woodhaven. She was also stunned to note that if she didn't make the turnoff but kept following the shoreline, after another hour of curving highway, she would arrive at the town of Otter Bay, where Luke now lived. The information cast a cloud on her move. A thousand miles would have been too close. She determined to keep a low profile and never go near the place.

Everything Jenny owned was stored in the truck bed. Fat Cat alternately sulked and snarled in the picnic basket on the seat beside her. She tapped the basket. "Cheer up. We're almost there, and you can stop complaining if you know what's good for you. Some people would have dumped you off at the pound," she said as they wound up the narrow road.

Reforested areas of small, cone-shaped young trees gave way to thick stands of mature redwoods, pines and firs. She crossed a creaking wooden bridge over a river that foamed around rocks and moss-covered logs. Occasionally the forest opened up, revealing green meadows where sheep grazed behind sun-bleached rail fences. Once she stopped for a while to watch a doe and its fawn standing like statues in a clump of sword fern. Strident sounds of the city, the crowds of people, the smell of burning fuel, the crush of tall buildings all faded from memory, and each new scene seemed to be like one enchanting calendar picture after another.

The woodsy scent enveloped her as she drove, and she felt it soothe her battered ego. Even so, her memory of the events that had so precipitously changed her life still lingered near the surface.

The long-ago picnic she'd shared with Luke had been on a day with this same sparkling quality. She allowed the memories to flow around her and recalled the Luke she knew then, the Luke who tucked a rose in her hair and said, "Jenny girl," as if he were really saying, "My darling." For the millionth time she wondered how that outwardly caring, decent man could harbor such deceit.

Instead of driving up into this backwoods country on the last day of August, she had expected to be a new bride in Dallas, luxuriating in the arms of Luke's family.

Suddenly a truck loaded with logs barreled out from a side road in front of her. She cried out in panic and braked to a stop inches from a ditch. The towheaded driver shot her an impudent grin, jerked a thumb toward a sign and continued driving at breakneck speed as if the rutted road were a racetrack. Then she saw the weathered sign almost hidden by a dusty clump of bracken: Caution. Logging Truck Crossing. After her pulse returned to normal, she inched her pickup back from the ditch and onto the road, driving at barely more than crawling speed, alert to further hazards.

She was in deep shade now as she drove, the enormous tree trunks free of branches as they stretched two hundred feet or more to hold their green crowns in the sunlight. Around the next bend she came upon the school—a traditional little red schoolhouse if she'd ever seen one, except that it was painted white.

She pulled into the graveled driveway with the feeling that any minute a flock of little girls in pinafores and boys in old-fashioned knickers would burst through the open door to the play yard.

"Listen, Fat Cat, I simply have to take a look. I'll only be a minute." But the cat snoozed contentedly, a tiger transformed into a kitten, who no doubt dreamed he did nothing but relax on the classiest of cushions.

She ran quickly up the stairway and stepped inside the schoolroom. It looked bare, almost as if no one ever used it. Abraham Lincoln and George Washington stared tirelessly from the front wall out of twin frames. The desks were lined up smartly. Except for the immaculate blackboards, there was nothing in the room to indicate it was a place of learning. Oh, what she would do to this room to make kids love it! It was a canvas waiting to be painted.

"Want something?" a gravelly female voice inquired. A tall, spare woman stepped from the coatroom. She was probably in her late fifties, dressed in what looked like her husband's overalls, as well as his shoes. Her long gray hair was knotted so tightly on top of her head that Jenny wondered that her eyes weren't pulled up at an angle. The woman stood with her mop handle held forward like a bayonet. Her mouth, pinched and small in her long angular face, looked as if it had been hardened into a permanent grimace.

Jenny smiled. "Hi, I couldn't resist the open door. I'm Jenny Valentine, the new teacher. Is it okay if I look around?"

The woman looked Jenny up and down, then fixed her attention on tightening the mop. Jenny grew uncomfortable in the unfriendly silence.

"Etta Mae Coates," the woman snapped finally. "I take care of the building. All set to wax the floor. Plenty to do before school opens."

In Jenny's mind, the name Etta Mae conjured up dimpled smiles and curls, a far cry from the stern-faced woman. "I won't bother you now, but I'd like to come later and get the room ready for Monday," Jenny said pleasantly, and wondered if anything in the world would coax a smile from that uncompromising face.

"Get the room ready!" Etta Mae cried incredulously, flinging an arm out to encompass her domain. "Supplies in the closet. Books in the cupboard. What do you mean?" She had a way of eliminating the first words of her sentences, as if she'd waxed and polished them out of existence. "Captain Ballard, bless him, always said I kept the room perfect. Don't think he'd want *anything* changed." She gave a deep sigh. "School won't be the same without him."

"I'm sure," Jenny said. "And what time did you say you'd be finished?"

"Didn't say. Don't know for sure. Anyway the board hasn't actually hired anyone yet."

Jenny experimented with a smile and hoped she succeeded. "I meet with them this evening, but I wanted to come early and get settled."

Etta Mae took a swipe at some microscopic blemish on the desk. "Well, then, guess you're not official yet, are you?"

"I suppose not if you mean I haven't signed a contract, but I understood there was no question."

The woman's stance stiffened. "Folks here in Woodhaven don't take things for granted, Miss Valentine. Bad practice. Guess you didn't know there's a real smart local girl available right here in town. No one better with kids."

Jenny felt ice slither down her spine. "I had no idea anyone else was being considered," she said. The superintendent hadn't mentioned another candidate. In fact, she'd gotten the idea she was the community's last hope. Heaven forbid she'd landed in the middle of a squabble.

"I suppose you're one of those who'll start promotin' that fancy dan unified school district truckin' our kids forty miles down the coast. We're just fine up here. Been fine for the past seventy-five years," Etta Mae continued, her voice shaking with emotion and rising almost an octave as she railed about the virtues of the local people versus that of ignorant flatlanders.

Abruptly the woman ran out of words and stalked back into the coatroom where, with a series of bangs and swishes, she let it be known that she earned her salary and then some.

The woman didn't intimidate Jenny. She'd dealt with imperious custodians before. But if there were doubts about her job, that was another story. What would she do? All she had was the hundred-dollar cleaning deposit refund from her apartment to last until her first paycheck. She felt shaken as she started the car and headed up the road to the Douglas mill, which was a mile beyond the school, according to her directions. Steve Douglas was the president of the board. She would confront him at once with the Coates woman's statements.

She drove past a post office, Flint's General Store and a bar and grill with the quaint name He's Not Here. After cresting a hill, she saw the mill set in a half-moon clearing. Adjacent was a large pond filled with logs. Hovering around the mill, like a hen and chicks, were two dozen rustic cabins. She turned off onto a washboard driveway that ran by a shed that appeared to be the office. She sat for a moment and watched a man pole a log into a device that lifted it onto a carriage that fed it into the whining saws.

She got out of the car and inhaled the astringent aroma of freshly sawed lumber. Sawdust spattered her like a fall of paprika as she climbed the steps to the office. The door was open, a common custom in the area, apparently, and she stood for a moment before going inside.

The office appeared orderly and functional with shelves of unfinished lumber holding ledgers and files. A man sat at the desk, studying a sheet of figures, one hand fingering an adding machine. She caught her breath at the head of brown wavy hair. *Cut it out. Do you have to see Luke in every man you meet?* Besides, the hair was lighter than Luke's, with a touch of gray at the temples. Late thirties, she judged. He looked up and rose as she approached.

"I'm Jenny Valentine," she said, and held out her hand.

He enveloped hers in a firm clasp. He was almost as tall as Luke, and the warmth of his smile reassured her. "Miss Valentine! Jenny, is it? I've been expecting you." He set out a chair for her and gestured grandly. "Welcome to Woodhaven, heart of the redwoods, population two hundred souls, altitude fifteen hundred feet, rainfall eighty-four inches a year." His eyes twinkled.

She laughed. "A regular walking atlas. Perhaps you should join my class—that is, if I'm to remain here. I understand my contract is under question."

"What are you talking about?"

"Well, I stopped by the school where I met Mrs. Coates and..."

He grimaced and gave an exasperated shake of his head. "Don't tell me Etta Mae's been at it again. I thought we quashed all that. She's been carrying on a one-woman campaign to get the job for her granddaughter, Corrie, who hasn't the education much less the inclination for the job. Etta Mae makes a lot of noise and has a small following, but don't worry."

"But she said—"

"Yes, I know what she said. I know it by heart. Just because the county office sometimes has to issue emergency credentials in order to get a teacher up here, she thinks she can twist the board's arm to do the same for her granddaughter. Etta Mae is pushing for the job, not Corrie."

"But, Mr. Douglas, I haven't earned my credential, either."

"I know, and don't be surprised if the old girl makes a ruckus. We'll handle it."

Jenny felt uneasy. Steve Douglas didn't seem all that reassuring. "Arriving in the middle of such a dispute isn't the most ideal way to start," she said.

He shrugged. "Oh, these battles are par for the course in Woodhaven. Coffee?"

"Please!" Woodhaven was growing less and less like the idyllic village she had envisioned.

He poured two cups from the urn on the counter, handed her one and sat down again. "Well, Miss Valentine, I'm delighted our little school lucked out for a change."

"Oh?"

"Both brains and beauty this time. We seem to get one or the other, mostly the other, what with a long line of elderly spinsters and a slightly deaf, retired army officer."

"Well, thank you, Mr. Douglas, I think," she said. "Actually I am a pretty good teacher."

"So the county superintendent informed me. We're impressed with your background, and you certainly are pretty. I hope you don't mind my telling you, but you see, when you came in just now, I was absorbed in a time sheet, then I looked up and saw you standing there with the trees and sky against your hair. You cut quite a picture." He grinned, but she sensed a certain reserve as though he salted away whimsy or joy to bring out only on special occasions.

"You don't sound like what I expected from a lumber man, Mr. Douglas."

"And you don't look like any teacher we've had around here." His eyes held a friendly gleam, but something else, too. Sadness? Resignation? She couldn't put her finger on it.

"I hope the other members are as amenable, but I can't help worrying about the faction led by Mrs. Coates. I can understand why a small community would prefer one of its own."

"Etta Mae is high-handed, conveniently blind to Corrie's shortcomings and the best damn custodian in the business. She's a rebel who needs a cause. Any cause. Forget her. Let's go have a look at the cottage. It hasn't been used for a couple of years, so I can't say what what condition it's in. Corrie offered to clean and get it ready a while back, but I'm afraid I've never checked. If it's not fit, there are a couple of families you can room with."

He took a ring of keys off a hook, and they walked outside. Jenny liked this man. She believed that in him she'd have at least one ally in this unexpectedly hostile situation.

She pointed to the large pond just below. "On the way up here I noticed that a couple of mills had their logs stacked in huge piles instead of in ponds. Is there a reason?"

"It depends on the mill's location. It just so happens that a river edges our site, which made flooding this area to form a pond feasible. And a pond is the ideal storage place for logs. In water they're protected against insects, fungi and fire. As well, the dirt and grime are cleaned off, which helps to protect the saws, and also the floating logs are easier to handle."

A Jeep skidded onto the driveway, spraying dust at their feet. The man at the wheel called out something, and Steve ran to meet him, then quickly returned. "Sorry. Problems in the woods. A loader overturned." He handed her the keys. "Turn left on the road next to the school. It ends in a cul de sac a quarter of a mile off the main road. And, Miss Valentine, I can't tell you how glad I am that you've accepted this position. Woodhaven deserves someone like you. I only wish my own son could have you for a teacher." He stepped into the Jeep and raised a hand. "See you tonight," he called as he sped away.

His son? For no reason at all she'd imagined Steve Douglas was a bachelor. Thoughtfully she climbed back into the pickup and drove back toward the school. There were dozens of questions she'd wanted to ask before tonight's meeting.

For example, the superintendent had mentioned the bountiful tax money, so why was there no playground equipment, and why was the schoolroom so devoid of learning aids? She'd seen no movie or slide projector, no tools for science, such as a microscope. There had been no sign of easels or art materials, no phonograph or piano. Not even the standard bookcases full of books. Was this the kind of bare-bones environment the community preferred for its school? Even though Steve dismissed Etta Mae's campaign for her granddaughter, Jenny still felt apprehensive. Would the woman appear tonight at the board meeting to cause a stir?

She came upon the cottage, situated at the end of the tree-shaded lane. Set in a small clearing, it had an alpine flavor, with its A-frame roof and window boxes bright with impatiens. Honeysuckle crept against the porch, and the deep blue-green forest hovered at the very edge of the premises. Surprisingly, the windows glistened as if they'd recently been washed. The place looked anything but neglected, more like a stage set for Hansel and Gretel.

She got out of the car, and Fat Cat's basket sprang to life, rolling and pitching and finally falling off the seat and onto the ground as he screeched feline profanities. Jenny opened the latch and the cat, fur ruffled, tail switching, stalked off into the forest like a lion returning at last to his habitat. Not to worry, she thought. He'll come home. In spite of his macho pose, he wasn't likely to find his favorite canned kitty flavors in the jungle.

Suddenly the sound of a childish voice in song interrupted the silence. Jenny saw a towheaded urchin of perhaps seven or eight straddling the low fence alongside her cottage. Barefoot, in jeans and faded blue sweatshirt, he sat with eyes closed, face turned up to the sun, singing,

"Down in the valley, valley so low. Hang your head over, hear the wind blow."

Jenny was startled at the beauty of the child's voice. She knew the folk song, and as it ended, she walked over and raised a hand in greeting. "Hello," she said. The boy grimaced as if panic-stricken, jumped from his perch and scampered away, his hand flapping against the fence rails, a beautiful golden retriever on a leash scampering ahead.

She felt rebuffed. Surely the boy knew this was the teacher's cottage. She hoped his attitude wasn't shared by the other children, but knew quite well the resentment some classes felt for substitutes. She could work that out in time, but the incident lent one more sour note to her arrival.

She'd wanted to say to him, "Hey, come sit on the porch with me. I'll get my guitar and we'll harmonize some songs. Maybe some other kids will join us."

She picked up her suitcase, walked up onto the porch, slipped her key into the lock and was amazed when it turned readily. Inside, she caught her breath. Someone had been busy. Her impression was one of shining floors, warm color and a very large window framing a woodsy mural. There was a fireplace at one end of the tiny living room. A pine rocker, a lamp and a sofa were grouped on a multicolored rug. She loved it! The room had a classic simplicity. Someone in Woodhaven knew how to create charm and beauty out of practically nothing. She looked forward to meeting that person.

Eager to put away her belongings, she changed into a T-shirt and jeans and went to unload the pickup. As she was carrying her second armful toward the house, she fell back, disconcerted to see a husky young fellow standing in her doorway, one arm barring the entrance. A woodsman? He had a deeply tanned face and hair like dusty straw with the sun on it. Heavy boots were laced to the knees of his skin-tight jeans, and his flannel shirt was open halfway down his chest, showing an abundance of curly golden hair. She recognized his arrogant pose and the cynical set of his mouth as those of young toughs one could see anywhere.

Her first feeling was one of annoyance. He couldn't be over nineteen. Then she considered the isolated location of the cottage without a neighbor in sight and suddenly felt self-conscious in her snug T-shirt.

"Hello," she said carefully.

"Mornin'," he drawled. "If I'd known it was you on the road, I'd have pulled over and made your acquaintance on the spot." It seemed to Jenny that he'd pitched his voice unnaturally low, as if he were trying to make it suit his image.

A shaft of sunlight caught his fair head. Of course. It was the truck driver who had almost run her down earlier. "Sorry. I didn't catch your name," she said.

He grinned lazily. "Didn't say it."

"It's time we introduced ourselves then. I'm Jenny Valentine."

His eyes wandered over her boldly as if to compute her measurements. "Oh, everybody knows your name, all right. What they don't know is that the new schoolmarm is one sexy lady."

"I believe the subject is introductions," she said stiffly, and hoped she didn't show the unease she was beginning to feel.

A wide, winning smile—no doubt reserved especially for devastating females—spread across his face. "Dirk McCleod. If you haven't already heard it, you will."

"Well, I've only just arrived."

"Sure, I know that. I also know you had a little chat with Etta Mae and made a big impression on old Steve."

He picked up a pinecone and aimed it accurately at a fence post.

"My, you do get around."

"Don't have to. We got a top-notch grapevine goin' most of the time."

"I'll keep that in mind. I gather you work nearby."

"I haul for the Douglas mill. There's a breakdown in the woods, so just thought I'd mosey over and get acquainted. I'll give you a hand with your gear," he said, taking a carton from her and allowing his hand to cover hers in the exchange.

She drew it away quickly. "Please don't bother. Actually, you've reported a little early. School doesn't start until Monday."

He threw back his head in a hearty guffaw, reminding her of an unruly colt. "Hot damn! A schoolteacher who's a barrel of laughs. That's a switch from prune-faced old Ballard." He set the carton on the porch and went back for another load.

"Thanks very much, Dirk. I'll take care of the rest." She hoped to dismiss him with her tone, but instead he moved in so close that she felt the warmth of his breath brush her cheek.

"Oh, I've time to spare. Anyway, I haven't got around to what I really came for. Just thought you'd like to meet the folks around here, so I'll be glad to take you to the weekly dance tomorrow night. We hold them in the old CCC hall. Lots of food—live music, too."

She set a stack of books between them, wondering how he always managed to maneuver himself next to her. "Well, that's nice of you, but I'd like to get settled in first, and I have a lot to do to get ready for the first day of school."

"So what's the big deal? You have the weekend."

"Thanks, but I'm not accepting any invitations until I meet with the board and find what's expected of me. I haven't even signed a contract yet. It's even possible I won't be staying."

"Hey, don't let old Etta Mae get under your skin. She's up to her usual tricks. No one minds. We even look forward to it. Keeps the pot boilin'. Up here we have to make our own excitement. So how about it? Dance starts at eight."

"Sorry. How about a rain check?"

His expression turned sullen. "Bet you'd go if Steve Douglas asked you."

She hid a smile as she realized his adolescent insecurity had just gotten the better of his macho facade. "Anyway," she teased, "I don't really know you. How do I know you aren't one of those Mafia godfathers?"

"So get to know me," he said with a grin as he followed her up the steps with her armload of books. She missed the last step and briefly stumbled. He caught her unnecessarily and held her firmly. She forced down her anger at his unrelenting strength and was able to jerk away.

"I have a lot to do, so I'm afraid I'll have to end our little visit," she said.

"I've got plenty of time. I'll stick around and fill you in on your new neighborhood." He lit a cigarette.

"Well, Dirk, you're confronting me with quite a problem. Either I must give up my reputation for hospitality and ask you to leave or else go along with your fun and games. Neither option is attractive."

"What's the matter? Afraid your high and mighty ancestors might turn over in their graves if you entertain a truck driver?"

"Oh, I don't think they mind changing position once in a while. As a matter of fact, I'm not averse to stretching or shrinking a bit now and then. The thing that bothers me in our short acquaintance is that you seem to have no interest at all in its quality."

He flicked an ash on the rug, and Jenny cringed when he ground it out with his heel. A deep flush suffused his cheeks. "Don't play any schoolteacher games with me, Miss Jenny Valentine. I'm not interested in that jazz."

"Not schoolteacher talk, Dirk. At the moment I feel old enough to be your parent, so let's just call it a bit of motherly advice."

He grinned as he rose. "Well, mother dear, you can save all that crap for your school kids, that is if you can stick it out long enough to spiel it." He reached for her chin, holding it so firmly it pained her. "Me and schoolteachers never did get along, but this time it's going to be different," he said, not smiling. He turned and sauntered down the steps toward the woods with an exaggerated swagger.

Jenny sat down on the front steps and rubbed her bruised chin. Threat or merely bluster? She wondered. *Valentine, you've really blown it today. You no more than arrive than you send the world's best custodian into a tizzy, you scare the first pupil you meet right off the map, and now you get into a hassle with some junior Don Juan. Disaster seems to be your middle name.* "A teacher should always conduct herself with decorum and discretion," she said aloud. She must have read that somewhere.

If this is an example of how she was going to make friends and influence people, there would have to be some changes made and mighty soon, like in the next five minutes.

CHAPTER SIX

A ROBUST LAUGH BROKE the silence, and a girl darted around the porch, startling Jenny out of her reverie. A gypsy fall of dark hair fell over one bare shoulder, and the girl's low-cut peasant blouse revealed a generous eyeful of voluptuous figure. She stood, hands on hips, feet planted sturdily apart as if she were about to break into an aria from *Carmen*, except the effect was ruined by an oversize pair of purple sunglasses.

"Hi, Jenny Valentine. I'm Corrie Coates. It's about time someone told off that small-time Romeo."

This was the girl who vied for Jenny's job? Etta Mae must eye her granddaughter with the same perplexity an old hen might show if it hatched a peacock. Jenny indicated a place on the porch beside her. "Nice of you to stop by. So you overheard our conversation?"

"Didn't have to. Just took one look at his face. Let me clue you in. He doesn't discourage easy." She plunked herself down in a flurry of tangerine skirts, and Jenny caught a whiff of perfume that probably had a name like Passion's Flame. "He's all mouth though," Corrie concluded.

"Not altogether. I noticed a couple of hands."

"Yeah, he's convinced he's irresistible. Unfortunately, most of the teen population in these parts thinks so, too. All except me. I refuse to be another notch on his belt, and it's driving him crazy. He dates every new thing with skirts and makes certain I see them together. If he thinks it'll make me jealous, he's way off his rocker.''

Jenny hid a smile. So that was why the fellow was so insistent she go to the dance with him. It figured. "I understand you and I are rivals for the teaching position here,'' she said.

Corrie rolled her eyes. "Are you kidding? Even if I had a credential, I wouldn't take that position if they tripled the salary. Granny Etta Mae won't give up trying to run my life.'' She pursed her lips and adroitly aped her grandmother's nasal twang. "You hear, Corrie, I don't want any on-again, off-again cocktail waitress in my family. Get off your duff and amount to something.''

"And do you intend to?'' Jenny asked, amused.

She stretched a shapely foot to examine her magenta toenails, and Jenny tried to picture her in a classroom—without success.

"Haven't lost any sleep over it,'' Corrie said. "Anyway, I'm doing all right. I work at the Otter Bay Inn, a real classy place. Caters to folks who like to 'discover' a quaint fishing town. I'll bet I make more than you do, what with tips and all,'' she added. "And I only have to work weekends. Now honestly, wouldn't you rather trade places with me than hold down a roomful of bratty kids five days a week?''

"No, I wouldn't, Corrie. I've wanted to be a teacher for as long as I can remember.''

The girl gave an unladylike whistle. "That long?''

"That long. Actually the idea occurred to me around the time of Lincoln's inauguration.''

"Oh, sure. I'll bet you're not much older than I am. I'll be nineteen this month. You sure picked a helluva place to teach.''

"What do you mean?''

"Until Captain Ballard arrived no one lasted a year, if that long."

"Care to fill me in?" Jenny asked.

"Oh, you'll find out soon enough. Actually, the nosy school board causes most of the problems, along with our location. City teachers come down with cabin fever. Can't adjust to living in the boondocks. Of course Steve Douglas is president this year, and he keeps things in line a lot better. A real neat guy, right?" Corrie grinned, bursting with innuendo.

"A very neat guy," Jenny said briskly. She wished she could tactfully end the conversation. It wasn't doing anything for her morale, and she had a million things to do before the meeting tonight. "I appreciate the preview, Corrie. It looks as if I'll need all the help I can get."

"You can depend on me. Steve, too. Too bad about his wife." She grinned slyly. "You were wondering, weren't you?"

Jenny rolled her eyes. "Corrie Coates, you're not only the village newspaper but the Woodhaven town crier, too."

"Right on!" Corrie agreed heartily. "I'm a gold mine of information. Ask me anything—past history, family skeletons, who's not speaking to who and who's sleeping with who, too. What I don't know I'm willing to second-guess in favor of the listener if I happen to like him. Or her. Gossip is people's meat and potatoes up here—their TV, their movies and every other entertainment. If you have any secrets, better hide 'em real good."

Jenny's eyes glazed for a few seconds. "Thanks for the tip."

Corrie looked at her through narrowed eyelids. "So don't you want to know about Steve's wife?"

"Go ahead. I can see you're going to explode if you don't tell me."

Corrie stuck her nose in the air and hunched her shoulders in elegant disdain. "Well, she was a commercial artist and us hillbillies weren't couth enough for her. She lasted for a couple of years, then took off for the big city last June. Left the kid with Steve. He took it real hard. No one knows the state of the divorce—if any—and boy, is that a problem to unattached females for miles around, not to mention a few attached ones."

So that was it. Jenny had sensed pain in that sensitive face. "I would offer you a cold drink, but I'm afraid my cupboards are bare at the moment."

Corrie leaped up. "There are some Cokes in the fridge. I'll get them."

Jenny followed the girl into the kitchen. "In this fridge? Here?"

Corrie tossed her thick dark hair. Her eyes sparkled. "Oh, I always keep a few mixes handy."

Jenny stared blankly. "You do?"

"Sure. And some dishes and silver. Just enough for two, though. The Corrie Coates method for fun entertaining without Granny." She laughed at Jenny's startled expression. "Hey, for a flatlander you're a babe in the woods. No pun intended."

"Well, I'm sorry I'm spoiling your, uh, your entertainment center."

Corrie tossed her head and gave Jenny a knowing smile. "Not to worry. I have the promise of a snazzy apartment in San Francisco—all free and clear, mind you. How do you like them apples, schoolteacher lady?"

"If you're saying what I think you're saying, I wouldn't trade this cottage for a dozen San Francisco apartments."

"So we differ. No big deal. I left a few things in the closet. That's what I came for. I thought I'd get here before you did."

Jenny tried to digest everything Corrie was implying. "You have a key then?"

"Who do you think fixed up this place? Not the ladies' sewing club, I can tell you."

"You did all this?" Jenny made an encompassing gesture.

"Sure did, and I spent nary a nickel except for a little paint. I picked up the furnishings from rummage sale leftovers. Loved every minute of it."

"Well, it's charming. You have real talent, Corrie. You ought to make a career of interior decorating."

Corrie struck an expansive pose. "Yeah, I can see my shingle now, tacked on that big sugar pine over there. Corrine Coates, Interior Decorator, Specializing in Cookshacks, Sheep Pens and Outhouses."

Jenny laughed. "Well, think about it. In the long run it might be more satisfying than—" she hesitated "—a ritzy apartment in San Francisco. You know, exploring your abilities and all that good stuff."

"You can mellow out concerning this kid. Little Corrie knows what's good for little Corrie."

"Just so it's right for little Corrie."

"Same difference."

"Not in my book, but I have too much to do to get into any philosophical discussions. I'm taking my gear down to school now. Come along and help me arrange some flowers for tonight's meeting if you like."

Together they cut some ferns and pink lilies—naked ladies, Corrie called them, because they had no leaves. Then they drove down the bumpy dirt road in the pickup. The tree-shaded lane would be much more pleasant to walk than to ride, and she'd do that in the future, Jenny decided.

She glanced at Corrie. Someone ought to paint her, she thought, someone like Gauguin. Corrie's dark hair shone with blue highlights against her armful of pink flowers, and her eyes had momentarily lost their brash gleam, leaving a lethal mixture of hoyden and innocent.

"What do you think of our little schoolroom?" Corrie asked when they arrived.

"Very nice."

"Oh, yeah? You don't say *nice* if you can think of a better word."

"Arrange your flowers," Jenny ordered, and filled her homemade bookcases with volumes she'd checked out from the county library.

Corrie added one last stem to her bouquet and stepped back to survey the effect. "Don't get carried away," she said, pointing to the bookcases. "Number one on the top ten up here is the Sears Roebuck catalog."

It took the rest of the afternoon to unload the cartons and set up the equipment for music, art, science and math centers on the generous counters along one side of the room.

"Boy! You sure know how to sugarcoat schoolwork."

Jenny made a face. "The word is *motivate*, and look at the time! I've barely an hour to grab a bite and get ready for the meeting." But Corrie's appraisal set her to thinking. Maybe she'd allowed her eagerness for this job to get out of hand. The duty of a substitute was to carry out the plans of the regular teacher, she belatedly reminded herself. But Captain Ballard had left no lesson plans nor a single direction. Anyway, she admitted, even if he had, she was pretty sure she wouldn't have followed them.

They locked up with a set of keys Mrs. Coates had left in the desk for her, and Corrie ran down the path to the main road, turning once to give Jenny a saucy wave. A car slowed and picked her up before she'd gone a dozen steps. No wonder. Her provocative walk could have been set to music.

Jenny took a deep breath of the clean, sweet air. Life didn't flow in a placid stream here in Woodhaven, but at least there were no facades. People knew who they were and declared it as distinctly as pieces set out on a chessboard.

She was going to like living and working here. The tranquil beauty of the tall trees seemed to offer a healing quality. The ache of Luke might last forever, but in her little cottage, embraced by the majestic trees and the scent of honeysuckle, perhaps the extremes of hurt and frustration might disappear.

BARELY AN HOUR LATER Jenny drove back to the school, nourished with a cup of soup, showered and wearing her blue suit pinned with a sprig of oxalis, which she wore for luck since it looked a lot like clover. She'd brought along her coffeepot, paper cups and a batch of brownies she'd made a couple of days ago. Maybe a little hospitality would help smooth any ripples she made.

No other cars were parked at the school yet. Good. She needed a few minutes to cool her jitters. Shadows from an ancient madrone reached the school's bell tower, and the blue-green forest made a muted backdrop in the early twilight. The school's sturdiness reassured her, and she ran up the steps with a rush of pride. Jenny Valentine, schoolteacher! Shouldn't there be fireworks spraying the sky?

Inside, she reviewed her arrangements and wondered if she had time to scoop up some of the displays and equipment, then decided against it. Being one's self was almost a behavior code here. In the coatroom she filled and plugged in the coffeepot but left the brownies in the cupboard. It was better to wait and see how the evening progressed before overstepping any more boundaries.

Steve Douglas entered and gave a low whistle as he surveyed the room. He looked as much at home in his immaculate white shirt and blue blazer as in the work clothes he'd worn that morning. His admiration seemed genuine. "Would you accept any adult pupils?" he asked.

"I hope I'm not jumping the gun," Jenny said.

"On the contrary. Such preparation is downright refreshing."

A measure of relief washed over her at his hearty tone. If only the others were as agreeable.

Three more board members walked in then, and Steve introduced them. First there was Alice Mallory, a shy-acting woman who had four children enrolled in the school. "How do you do?" was all she said. Her pale green eyes roamed the room in a probing assessment, but her expression gave no clues to her thoughts.

Simon Flint, owner of the general store, looked wispy and nervous, thirty-two going on seventy, she guessed. He'd missed his calling. He should have been a mendicant toiling in some ancient monastery. Amos Botts, the postman, a heavy, sandy-haired, jolly fellow, pumped her hand and said it was a pleasure to meet the pretty new schoolmarm. He'd been a member of the board forever and was looked upon as Woodhaven's unofficial mayor, Steve had told her earlier.

Jenny pretended to busy herself at her desk, meanwhile watching the board members check out the room. The arrangements caught their interest, all right, as was the purpose, but what were these people thinking? Alice Mallory glanced through the titles on the bookshelves, then joined Steve to share the microscope at the science center. Amos Botts noisily rattled and pounded all the percussion instruments Jenny had made when she'd taught at the school for the blind. Then he strummed the autoharp. But Simon Flint stood in the center of the room nervously opening and closing his fists as if he suffered from claustrophobia.

In a few minutes Steve called the meeting to order, and everyone sat around the oblong table that Etta Mae Coates had set up at the front of the room for the occasion.

"I think we should get started. Fred called from Eureka and said he might be late. Fred Burkheimer is president of Sierra Savings and Loan in Otter Bay," Steve added in an aside to Jenny. "We're included in their district since our children attend their high school."

Otter Bay, the place where Luke now lived, a place she didn't want to think about.

"I've already briefed all of you on Miss Valentine's qualifications," he continued. "You're aware she comes highly recommended, but while we wait for Fred, if you have any questions, now's the time to ask them."

Simon Flint stirred. "What about all this play-party stuff clutterin' up the place? Distractin', ain't it? Captain Ballard kept this room as slick as a whistle. We go for the three R's up here, Miss Valentine."

Jenny winced at the sudden attack and wondered if there was any way to communicate with this diverse group. Steve gave her an encouraging nod. "I assure you my whole approach is based on the three R's, Mr. Flint. But I believe children's minds should be stimulated to think, to be creative and to find it enjoyable. If a schoolroom is dull, children may decide they want learning, like medicine, in very small doses."

Alice Mallory looked up with interest, but she said nothing. "Wait and see" seemed to be her watchwords.

Simon's lips moved silently as he struggled in vain to form a statement.

Amos Botts spoke up. "You can't get around the fact that Cap'n Ballard got results without all this folderol. He saw to it the kids wrote their spelling words a hundred times every week. Plain old drill did the trick, which works with most subjects."

"I teach spelling in another way, but I think you'll find that the class will learn to spell and will remember what the words mean, as well. I don't think we should confuse repetition with reasoning, Mr. Botts."

"Reasoning? What's that got to do with it?" Simon asked, his tone clearly belligerent.

"Put it this way," Jenny said, trying to argue her point without sounding pedantic. "If boys and girls learn to solve problems, they'll gain confidence in themselves. They'll learn they can handle almost anything that comes along. That's important in life, Mr. Botts."

"I couldn't agree more," Steve said.

Simon jumped up angrily. "There's a lot of fancy talk goin' on here, and you all know I'm no good at that kind of palaver. I sure wish Cap'n Ballard could have been here tonight. He'd set you all straight in no time. Things are different up here, Miss Valentine. Gotta keep that in mind. Kids get married right out of high school. Boys go into the mills and girls have babies. All they need to know is how to read and write and do a little figurin'. Like I say, up here you gotta stress the plain old three R's."

Up here! Already Jenny felt as if she'd been assigned to write those words a hundred times on the blackboard. She wished she hadn't worn her suit. She was too warm. Her face felt as if it were glistening with perspiration, and her voice had begun to tremble with the desperation she felt. With all her heart she longed to communicate with these people, but she was getting nowhere. "I like to think in terms of individuals," she said, and remembered to smile. "Who knows? We might have a Rembrandt, an Einstein or an astronaut right here in Woodhaven."

At that point, everyone started to talk at once. Steve rapped the gavel and suggested they get on with the agenda, but Jenny only half listened. Two board members against her, one iffy and one ally. Why did she always jump in with two left feet? She would have been much smarter to have left the room as it was and ease in gradually, proving herself as she went along.

Listen to me! I love kids, she felt like saying. *I'm going to do everything in my power to help them learn.* Couldn't they tell that?

A stir in the group and a nod from Steve indicated the other board member had finally arrived.

"Mr. Burkheimer was unable to return tonight in time for the meeting. In any case, he's transferring to Eureka soon, and I've been appointed to fill out his term," the fellow said from the back of the room.

Steve beckoned. "Come join us. You're here just in time to sign Miss Valentine's contract." He rose and held out his hand. Jenny looked up and felt as if she'd just been pushed over a cliff.

She was painfully aware that she had been in the habit of seeing and hearing Luke in every man she met, but this time there was no denying the truth. She stiffened as Steve carried on the introductions, his voice fading in and out like a TV dissolve. Jenny stared straight ahead in a kind of hopeless desperation, praying that she could carry off the next few minutes without falling apart.

"Mr. Beaumont is the manager of the new Beaumont Business Services in Otter Bay," Steve concluded. Steve must have just introduced Luke to her, judging from the way everyone was looking at her so expectantly, but her tongue refused to function.

She noted that Luke's forehead also shone with perspiration, but he cleared his throat, allowing only a few seconds of awkward silence. "Ah, yes, well, this is a surprise!" Luke said, his voice taut and unnatural. "You see, Miss Valentine and I met last year where we attended the University of California at Berkeley."

Jenny would always marvel at how she got through the next few minutes. Surely everyone must have noticed her queer, dazed reactions. Fortunately Luke rose to the occasion with a savoir faire she hadn't realized he owned. His hand was firm as he shook hers, but the familiar feel of it continued to render her speechless.

Luke carried on until her cheeks grew rosy with embarrassment. Her sterling qualities rolled off his tongue as though he were presenting them to a jury. He spoke of her excellent scholarship, her way with children, her creativity, her dedication, ad nauseam—all of which he had somehow managed to observe as a mere casual acquaintance.

Shut up! she wanted to scream at him. *Stop before you tell them about my terrific crab cioppino, how talented I am at mending your socks, and how good I am in bed!* What a master! She hadn't known how well the ordinarily quiet-spoken Luke could handle words.

The contract was signed without further argument, but she wondered if she imagined a certain hesitation and reticence in all but Steve and Luke as they affixed their signatures. By the time she wrote her own name, she'd recovered enough to thank everyone. In fact, she felt certain she'd made quite a speech, even though five minutes later she couldn't remember a single thing she'd said. Actually, she didn't calm down until Alice Mallory asked if

Jenny would be willing to lead a girl's 4-H group in sewing and cooking. After that everything snapped back into focus.

"I'd love to, and what about woodworking for the boys? I'm handy with tools, at least for simple projects." She pointed out the bookcases she'd made for her apartment, and glared at Luke to forestall him from extoling her talent as a cabinetmaker.

"Sounds more like it," Amos Botts said, and even Simon Flint grudgingly nodded.

Jenny suddenly remembered the refreshments she'd prepared and hurried to serve the coffee and pass around the cookies. Everyone chatted amiably, enjoying the unexpected treat, the earlier strife set aside at least for the time being.

She finally offered the plate to Luke. "Do have a fudge bar, Mr. Beaumont. It's my own recipe. I wonder if you've ever tasted any quite like them?"

Luke looked uncomfortable, which didn't prevent him from taking two. He popped one into his mouth, apparently swallowed too quickly and found himself seized by a fit of coughing.

Good. I hope you choke on them, she thought, and passed fudge bars around again.

A little later Luke came to join her as she explained one of the math puzzles to Amos Botts. Amos moved on, and Luke fingered a piece of the puzzle.

"How are you, Jenny?"

"Great. Odd that you should ask."

He shifted uncomfortably and examined a set of directions, which he held upside down. "Why did you take a job in Woodhaven of all places?"

She bristled. "Oh, are your territorial rights being violated?"

"God, no! Didn't anyone inform you this area is no woodland Shangri-la?"

"I'm a big girl now, Luke. I grew up in a hurry these past few weeks." She glanced over her shoulder and supposed she looked like any person at a social occasion renewing a former acquaintance. She prayed she'd be able to maintain her outward composure, telling herself she probably had any number of gritty Irish ancestors.

Luke examined a trapezoid block as if it were the Hope Diamond. "Listen, Jenny a lot of crooks hide out in the woods from the police. There are shady characters all over the place. And for heaven's sakes, stay out of the woods when hunting season opens." He lowered his voice and leaned closer as Simon Flint started to come their way, but the fellow struck up a conversation with Steve instead.

Jenny put her hands into her pockets when she saw they were trembling. Luke's nearness terrified her. It was so intoxicating, so hopeless. "Your concern really moves me, but I like everything about this place, and the pay is excellent."

"You know you don't have to work, Jenny. I'm going to support you."

"Yes, I have to work, and no, you are *not* going to support me. Didn't I make that clear?"

He threw up his hands. "And I suppose you're going to stay in that godforsaken cottage?"

"Oh, you've been there?"

"No, I haven't, but Mr. Botts informed me. Out in the forest, not a neighbor in sight. I don't like it!"

"That's a real laugh, Beaumont. I lived alone in Berkeley. Every day the papers were full of robberies, murders and rapes. If that's what you're concerned about, what's the difference?''

Luke seemed to keep his voice low with effort. "Jenny, be serious! Do you have locks on all your doors?''

She shrugged. "I suppose. So far it seems folks around here leave their doors open.''

"I'll see to it then.''

"Please don't bother.''

"You weren't always so stubborn.''

"Oh, there's plenty you don't know about me. How I hate liver and onions and never part my hair in the middle, for example.'' And how she had loved him with all her being, but it hadn't been enough.

He sighed. "You're a challenge, Jenny.''

"Diminishing returns here, Luke. You'd better split. Folks won't believe we're all that enthused about trapezoids. It's inevitable that we'll run into each other now and then, so let's make it a quick hello and goodbye. I'll even be pleasant about it.''

Luke looked taken aback, as if she had slapped him. "Believe me, Jenny, I'm trying to believe all this makes sense.''

Jenny stiffened. "Don't abuse any words, Luke. I'm not interested in how you need space to find yourself, how you crave freedom from emotional involvement, or how we met and parted in this vale of tears and are richer for knowing each other. Listen, my boy, I don't have to add two and two to figure there's some snappy little number in Otter Bay and that you dumped me for her about five minutes after you took off.''

Her tirade silenced him, and his expression turned inscrutable. Only his eyes looked bleak. He gazed at her face as if he were trying to memorize it. "I see," he said in a kind of quiet desperation. "Well, I guess that's a natural conclusion, isn't it?"

CHAPTER SEVEN

As HE DROVE HOME, Luke clenched the steering wheel so tightly that his fingers ached. So Jenny thought he had something going with Stacy? Maybe that belief would solve things. He hardly knew the young woman, but he needed a wedge, a no-man's-land, something between him and Jenny that neither dared cross over.

Tonight when he'd waited for a while in the coatroom, watching Jenny stand up to that Simon fellow, he'd wanted to hug her, to tell her how proud he was of her. The need for physical contact had been like an ache. It had come as a surprise that his conviction that they had to break up didn't automatically wipe out awareness and feelings.

Wrought up and tense, instead of going home and despite the late hour, he drove to the office. Bury himself in work. Finish up the Johansen estimate. Blot out the thoughts that ravaged his mind. He parked and locked the new BMW Charles had insisted Luke drive.

For a few minutes Luke weighed the pain that had a name all its own: Jenny. For a week or two he'd cherished a wistful hope that when he settled into his work he'd find it wasn't so restrictive, that with judicious planning he'd be able to manage marriage and family, after all. Instead, matters were far worse than he'd expected. He'd been working twelve- to fifteen-hour days, and last week Charles had asked him to spend some time assisting the new manager of the San Diego branch, which was losing out to a competitor. So he'd been flying down in the company plane once a week, trying to help the San Diego office get back on its feet—all of which snatched valuable time away from his own work. Charles was right. This job was all-consuming.

For an hour he checked every item in the estimate. It was important to get this contract. Johansen owned the largest planing mill on the coast. To win the account would be a feather in his cap. To put it more accurately, Charles would expect it.

Doggedly he juggled figures until he was bleary-eyed. Anything to avoid going back to the empty apartment. No matter how he fought the image, he would see Jenny sitting on the sofa poring over a book, Jenny in the kitchen whipping up a cake, Jenny lying in bed, the soft lines of her body sweet and flowing.

A sharp knock startled him. He flung open the door to find Stacy Adams holding two cups of steaming coffee.

"Hi," she said. "I saw your light still on and thought you could use a break. I've been working, too."

They'd spent no time together since the first hectic weeks when she'd introduced him to the town. Now they sometimes ran into each other and paused briefly to chat as they arrived or left their offices across the street from each other.

He beckoned her inside. She was as thin and tall as a model and walked with a model's practiced assurance as she set the coffee on his desk and arranged a chair to sit across from him. She looked at him with a frankly provocative smile. *Oh, my. Isn't this interesting? Just the two of us in the middle of the night,* her look said.

He couldn't help comparing her to Jenny. Jenny with her summer-golden hair and steady blue eyes completely devoid of guile. Jenny with her perfectly proportioned body that he wanted to touch as much in appreciation as in desire.

Stacy was all lines and angles, straight black hair cut short, perfect teeth showing in the requisite smile she used in her profession. She was very attractive if you liked smartly dressed women who talked a lot. He didn't mind the chatter. Her information about the area was informative and useful, although he could see a time when it might become redundant.

They sat down and sipped the strong coffee. "Thanks," he said. "I needed that."

"You're working too hard. All work and no play, you know. How are things going?"

"Better than expected. I've lined up ten new accounts this week. At the moment I'm working on a bid for the Johansen planing mill."

She whistled softly. "The big one! You don't fool around with peanuts, do you? Maybe I can give you a hand. I know some of the staff over there. I'll make a call. Tell them you're the best."

"And how do you know that?"

She slowly lifted an eyebrow, which had the effect of conveying something secretive and delicious. "Oh, I keep my feelers out."

He considered the offer, certain the young woman's call would make no difference, maybe even turn off Eric Johansen, the crusty old timber baron who seemed to own almost everything in this town. Luke suspected the fellow trusted no opinion but his own. Stacy's business was promotion. Superlatives were her stock-in-trade. Her brand of help might even prove a detriment.

"Thanks, but I'm turning in the bid first thing in the morning. What keeps you working at this hour?" he asked, hoping to change the subject.

"Boning up on my lecture for a tour group visiting a lumber mill tomorrow. Got to keep my facts and figures straight."

"Such as?"

"Such as—" she struck a tour leader's pose and lectured "—redwood trees are the world's largest living things. California is the home of two kinds of giant trees, the coast redwoods, which are the *tallest* in the world and the big trees of the Sierra Nevada range, which are the *largest* in the world. Some of our coast redwoods have reached heights of 365 feet, a diameter of twenty feet and have lived for twenty-two hundred years. Their thick, coarse bark is remarkably resistent to fire and disease, giving the trees self-healing powers that have fascinated people for years." She relaxed. "That sort of thing."

"Very informative. I could go for a tour like that."

She beamed. "Really? You mean it?"

He looked away. Something in her eyes was at odds with her questions.

She put her hands on her knees and leaned forward with a beguiling smile. "Tell me something, Luke, are you engaged or otherwise attached?"

He stiffened but managed to keep his expression impassive. "No attachments."

"You're certain."

"Very certain," he said, accenting the words a little too hard.

"Good heavens, I would have thought—"

He held up a hand to stop her. "Yes, I know. How come a nice guy like me isn't married?"

"Exactly."

"Well, Stacy, you've seen only one facet of my personality. Normally I kick cats, scare babies and steal olives out of martinis."

"Oh, my. The subject is off-limits, is it? Well, seeing as how you're free and clear, how about taking me to the benefit dance at the Cabrillo Yacht Club a week from Saturday night?"

"Benefiting what?" he said, stalling and wondering how he could gracefully refuse. On the other hand, he could hear Charles saying that keeping on good terms with the Chamber of Commerce's popular city hostess was part of his job.

"Does it matter? Here we use any excuse for a party."

"I'm not much of a dancer. Haven't been to a dance in ages."

She jumped up and circled the date with a black marker she found on his desk. "Then it's time to rejoin the human race." She marked a heavier line under the number. "So you won't forget."

Distractions. Maybe that's what he needed. "Thanks, I'll look forward to it."

"Good. This is what I really came for, you know, to snag you for my date before the rest of the predators get their greedy little hands on you." She swept her eyes slowly over him, lingering on his shoulders and waistline as if to store his physical attributes in order to review them later.

"What should I wear?" he asked, uncomfortable under her scrutiny. "Black tie and all that?"

"No big deal. Dressing up around here means clean jeans and no hobnailed boots." She glanced at the office clock. "Hey, I'd better get going. Would you believe it's after one?" She picked up the empty cups and headed for the door.

He followed. "Thanks for the coffee," he said.

"My pleasure." Suddenly she turned, set down the cups, took his face in her hands and kissed him with an impatient gesture. "I see. Beware when a man protests too much. You're still very much involved, aren't you? Well, count on me not to ask questions. And if I do say so myself, I can be indispensable when it comes to providing diversion." She started to pick up the cups, then ignored them, flashed her brilliant smile and left.

THE NEXT FRIDAY Luke told his secretary he would be out of town for the afternoon. He went to the telephone company, explained that he was a member of the county school board and requested that a telephone be installed in the schoolteacher's cottage in Woodhaven. He asked that the bill be mailed to him. Then he went to the hardware store and bought two deadbolt locks. He would slip into Jenny's cabin, install them and leave before she returned home from school. At this point he wasn't up to another confrontation, especially after last week's board meeting.

The thought of Jenny in that remote cabin drove him up the wall. How could she be so naive? Didn't she realize how isolated she was? Apparently all she could see was the beauty of the place. Didn't she realize the woods were also a haven for rascals? An attractive woman in a lonely cabin in an area swarming with woodsmen was downright hazardous. He couldn't believe how the other members of the school board could ignore the situation.

He drove the twenty-five miles down the coast highway in his old Volkswagen, which he still kept. He wasn't on company business, so to hell with the company BMW. Anyway, a BMW would be conspicuous in Woodhaven, and he didn't want his errand to attract any attention.

Today the cloudless sky dazzled the eyes, and the ocean was a blue miracle splashing foam on the thrust of cliffs along the rocky shoreline. Luke knew this area received the eighty to one hundred inches of annual rainfall required for the survival of the redwood forest, but today held no hint of rain.

At Cabrillo Cove he left the highway and turned onto the narrow dirt road that wound ten miles uphill through the big trees to Woodhaven. Protocol demanded that he check in with the president of the school board, so he headed first to the Douglas mill, where he found Steve in his office.

"Hope I'm not overstepping any boundaries," Luke said when he finished explaining what he planned to do.

"On the contrary, we appreciate your interest. It's refreshing to find a board member who's concerned about the teacher's welfare. Mostly the members concentrate only on seeing that school procedure doesn't deviate from the good old days—whenever and whatever they were. Jenny and I hope to change that this year."

"You can also count on me," Luke said stiffly, resenting the implication that Steve and Jenny represented a team.

Steve gave Luke a duplicate key to the cottage and found some tools for him. "We've never had to take such precautions before, but then we've never had a beautiful young schoolteacher, either. These woods have always attracted a lot of fine folk, but they've been home to some tough characters, too. The rough terrain and thick stands of trees offer perfect protection for a man who doesn't want the authorities looking over his shoulder. Years ago the place was full of stills, which furnished liquor for San Francisco speakeasies during prohibition. Under cover of darkness boats slipped into Cabrillo Cove to pick up the stuff."

Luke could believe that easily enough. He thanked Steve for his help, and ten minutes later he arrived at the cottage. He was dismayed to find that it was even more remote than he'd expected. Not another house in sight.

To his disgust he found the door unlocked. What was the matter with the girl? If she hadn't been so damn stubborn, she could be enrolled at the university safely completing her degree instead of living in this godforsaken place.

It was no surprise to Luke to find the cottage neat and attractive inside. Pots of various ferns and a vase of pink lilies brought the outside indoors, and there was the lingering cinnamony fragrance of pastry, the wonderful scent of home cooking that helped turn a house into a home.

He walked slowly through the cottage, feeling as if he knew every step of it. His throat constricted when he saw the bowl of apples on the kitchen table. There had always been a bowl of apples on their kitchen table in Berkeley.

Resolutely he laid out the tools and began to work. He installed the front lock with no problem, but two hours later he was still struggling with the back door. It hung crookedly, and he simply couldn't make the lock fit. He looked at his watch. He knew he should leave and come back another time. But it was too late: he heard Jenny singing, and a moment later, her step on the porch. Her voice sounded clear and sweet in a vaguely familiar tune. He grabbed his tools and had one foot out the back door as she entered the kitchen.

She stood, eyes widening, a load of books in one arm and a spray of colored leaves in the other. "Luke! What on earth?"

"School board business. Installing some much-needed locks. Did you know you left your door open?" he asked, all business.

She grimaced. "I see what you mean. Who knows who might walk in!"

He felt his face flush and pointed to her armful of leaves. "What have you got there?"

"These? Lovely fall colors, aren't they? I couldn't resist. I intend making an arrangement for my schoolroom."

"Better not, not unless you want to be called a jimhead flatlander, the local vernacular for ignoramus, in case you haven't heard it yet. That's poison oak you're hugging so tenderly."

She stared at the colorful leaves. "Surely not these!"

"Yes, surely those. I hate to tell you, but by tomorrow you're going to be scratching like crazy."

"Oh, no!" She dropped the branches on the counter.

"And unless you wash down with soap right away, you'll be a patchwork quilt of red blisters."

"But I thought they were maple leaves."

"On the other hand, your disposition being what it is, you may be one of the few lucky ones resistant to the stuff."

She stiffened. "Meaning?"

"Well, let's just say you're intractable. Also stubborn, perverse and mule-headed. If anyone can be immune, you'll be the one."

"You forgot short-fused. And now if you're finished..."

"Not quite, but I'll come back another time." He turned to leave, then stopped as he noticed the huckleberry cobbler on the counter. "I suppose you made that?"

"No one else does the baking around here."

He sniffed. "Smells delicious."

"It is. Picked the berries myself."

"Naturally. I don't suppose you'd care to share a small sample with me?"

"You're right. I wouldn't."

He leaned closer and inhaled deeply. "You used to make terrific cobbler."

"Still do. But I'm having company tonight, so if you'll excuse me..."

"Okay, okay, you don't have to hit me over the head. So long. But please keep in mind that you're all alone out here and lock your doors. I've ordered you a phone, but since the lines will have to be run from the schoolhouse, it might not be installed for several weeks."

She put her hands on her hips and glared at him. "What's with you, Luke Beaumont? You're acting like some overprotective parent."

"Well, damn it, I'm concerned about you." He paused, and even though his throat ached, he had to grin. "Listen, Jenny, girls who can't tell poison oak from maple leaves need all the help they can get." He walked out the door and quietly closed it behind him.

Jenny pounded her fists on the counter. Why couldn't he butt out of her life? It was over between them, so for heaven's sakes, let it be over! She was no wounded mouse to be toyed with. If he didn't shape up, he'd find he was dealing with a tiger. She'd lock her doors all right. In fact, she would change and install a few locks herself.

Fat Cat leaped up on the counter and pushed his head against her hand, purring loudly. She set him back down on the floor none too gently. "Get lost!" she cried. "Smooth talk doesn't even meet minimum requirements around here."

While she scrubbed her hands and arms with soap, the sweet soprano voice she'd heard her first day in Woodhaven sounded suddenly under her window. Now she knew it must be Steve's young son, Robbie. The possibility banished her anger. She'd tried to get acquainted with the shy youngster, but thus far, the moment she spoke, he would dart off along the fence, his hand grazing each picket, his ever-present golden retriever galloping along beside him.

The boy looked to be about eight or nine, but his name wasn't on the school roll nor had he attended yet. When she'd questioned Steve, his sudden hurt expression had made her sorry she'd asked.

"He's blind, Jenny, one of those unfortunate premature babies who was given too much oxygen at birth. My wife thought it best if he remained with me until next fall when he'll be eligible for a special school for the blind in San Francisco. I'd hoped Captain Ballard would allow him in the classroom, at least part-time."

"You're not saying he prevented Robbie from attending school?"

"I'm afraid so. 'You can't expect me to baby-sit a blind kid with everything else I have to do.' Those were his exact words."

Jenny felt her eyes fill as she recalled the small, lonely figure leaning against the gate near her cabin. "That's unforgivable," she murmured.

"I know parents can't be objective about their kids, but Robbie's bright. We'd had him tutored, and he was reading braille primers before...before he came to stay with me. It took him and Rosie, his dog, only a few times to learn that path through the woods between the mill and the school yard."

"Bring him tomorrow. I've had experience teaching in a school for the visually impaired in Berkeley. Oh, Steve, this is tragic. He needs to be with other children." Her mind raced. There were braille transcribers guilds whose members transcribed texts and other necessary material for blind children. She would contact them immediately. Then Steve could get the boy a braille typewriter as well as a standard one, and she would teach him how to use them.

But Steve hadn't promised to bring Robbie to school. He'd been certain the boy would be terrified to go. And thus far, Steve had been right. Robbie had refused to come to school. Captain Ballard's attitude plus the cruel taunts of the children had shoved Robbie into a shell of solitude.

Now, Jenny picked up her guitar and slipped noiselessly onto the porch. Robbie straddled the fence a few feet away, singing softly. His face was turned up to the sky as if to feel its blueness. Just below, his dog, Rosie, cocked an attentive ear.

Please don't run away! she begged silently while she added a few quiet chords to his song. He smiled, and for a while he kept singing, as if he'd been hearing an accompaniment all along. Suddenly he became aware of her presence, and he stopped in midverse, his body tense.

Jenny continued the song where he'd left off. "I know that song, too," she said when she concluded. "If you like, I'll show you where to put your fingers on the strings of my guitar so that you can play it."

He acted as if he were a frightened forest creature, leaning first one way, then the other, unsure of which way to turn.

"Just follow the fence to the next post, then reach across for my porch railing. I'm Miss Jenny, your father's friend."

"I know," he said finally. "You're the new teacher. I don't like school."

"Well, never mind that," Jenny said. "Right now I'd like to show you my guitar. You need only two chords for that song."

He hesitated and then, as if Jenny's words offered some magic, walked slowly but surely toward the porch. Rosie followed and curled up beside him, meanwhile eyeing Jenny as if to determine her intent. Steve had said that

Robbie had a limited capacity to distinguish light and dark and could see objects as blurs. Even so, she guessed Robbie knew the way very well, had no doubt used the porch of the empty cottage as a refuge during his past lonely months.

He sat beside her on the step, and she put the guitar in his lap. His face shone as his hands roamed over the instrument, feeling the shape of it, noting the frets, plucking the strings softly. After a while she placed his fingers on the strings to form a chord. He caught on at once, and she sang the first phrase of the song as he strummed.

"Now another," he cried impatiently. In no time at all he was able to play the two chords with ease. Together they sang the song, and his keen musical sense told him where to change chords without a cue. A rosy tinge touched his cheeks, and his fingers trembled as Jenny and he sang the song again and again. She would remember forever the elation she saw on that small face.

The five o'clock mill whistle abruptly blasted their duet. Robbie handed her the guitar as carefully as if it were glass. "I have to go. My dad expects me."

"Come on Monday and I'll teach you some more chords. If you like, you may borrow my guitar and practice the ones you learned over the weekend."

But he turned into the forest creature again, snapping his head first one way, then another, as if to sniff out danger. "I'd better not. Something might happen to it, but I'll come again next week," he said, and backed away.

"Well, Robbie, I'd be pleased if you'd come to school. There are lots of things I'd like to share with you besides music."

He put a few more steps between them. "I can't do what the other kids do. They don't like me," he said in a stout voice, and she wondered how hard it was for him to say that.

"But you can. You see I've taught kids like you, and I know some special ways to help. I can get you some books in braille, and with a typewriter you can do your school-work."

He was silent for so long that she wondered if he'd understood. He started down the path adjacent to the fence, then stopped. "Thanks a lot for the music, Miss Jenny, but I can't come to school." He picked up Rosie's leash and the dog bounded ahead. Robbie ran so swiftly and with such assurance that no one would have guessed he was blind.

She watched until he disappeared into the forest, wisps of his song floating back to her. She resolved not to feel discouraged. Trust was the issue here, and trust was a gold necklace whose beads had to be strung one at a time.

CHAPTER EIGHT

JENNY PUT AWAY her guitar and went to the kitchen to make a green salad. She was expecting Steve and Corrie to arrive by six. She'd wanted Robbie to come, too, but he usually spent weekends with his mother. Steve or one of his crew members took him to Steve's wife's apartment in Sausalito just north of San Francisco on Friday evenings and picked him up late Sunday afternoons.

Both Corrie and Steve liked Mexican food, so Jenny had made a chili relleno casserole the night before. Now she put it in the oven to heat, finished the salad and then set the table. For some time Jenny had wanted to have her two friends over for a social evening. Their loyalty and friendship meant a lot to her in this place, which thus far hadn't shown much warmth.

Woodhaven was a typical remote village; outsiders were suspect until they proved themselves. Steve was only now being accepted as a real member of the community, and he'd been there three years.

But Jenny was still treated as a stranger. When she went to Simon Flint's store or to the post office, people nodded politely and returned her greeting, but there was always a wall of reserve. It was as if she were a different breed, and folks needed to study and examine the specimen before they dared get too close to it. How long did it take? she wondered.

What puzzled her about the local folks was the way some of the older ones would sometimes throw in odd-sounding words along with their ordinary patter. If the words were from some foreign language, she couldn't identify it.

Just a few days ago when she'd bought a money order at the little two-by-four post office, a couple of women who'd been chatting with the postmistress had lapsed into a strange vernacular.

Deliberately Jenny had taken her time at the counter so that she could catch some of the words. "It must have been some ruckus," one had said. "Highpockets gonna land on featherleg at the airtight or I'm no codgyhead."

Jenny had asked Steve about the strange talk a day or two later when he'd come to repair the school's contrary water pump. He'd explained that during the early part of the century, the natives of the area were so suspicious of outsiders that they'd developed their own jargon in order to converse in public without outsiders being able to understand.

"Universities and linguists have studied it and consider it a bona fide American lingo, but it's rarely spoken anymore, except a word now and then among some of the oldsters.

"Of course a number of colorful expressions have survived. My wife was fascinated with them and collected quite a list. As to the meaning, *airtight* indicates the sawmill, and *Highpockets* undoubtedly refers to me. I believe *featherleg* is used for a cocky or belligerent person." He grimaced. "Dirk McCleod fits the bill. You probably overheard a conversation about some fracas at the mill," Steve had concluded.

Now she thought about the episode. She earnestly hoped people here wouldn't always shut her out, and only yesterday she had been rewarded when she'd run into one of the local women at Simon Flint's store and asked her how she made the delicious oatmeal cookies her daughter had shared with her at school. The woman had acted surprised and pleased and had insisted on writing out the recipe on the spot. If that was what it took to thaw Woodhaven, she was willing to collect enough recipes to fill an entire cookbook.

Steve arrived a short time later and handed her a bottle of wine as he came in the door. He inhaled the fragrance of the Mexican spices with an ecstatic expression on his face. "Wow! I've looked forward to this all day," he said. "There's always more than enough food at the mill's cookshack, but the cook doesn't go for variety. One can count on beef stew about seventy-five percent of the time."

"Shall we have a glass of wine while we wait for Corrie?" Jenny asked.

"She called from Otter Bay just as I left. It seems there was some mix-up in the work schedule, and her relief didn't show. Her boss was trying to get a replacement, but she said not to wait dinner."

"How long do you think?"

"Depends on her replacement. You know Corrie. She was fit to be tied, really disappointed."

Jenny was disappointed, too. Likely the girl would come very late if she arrived at all. Jenny put the meal on the table, and Steve poured the wine. He reached over and touched her glass with his. "To us! Woodhaven's two prize flatlanders—even if you and I are the only ones who think we're any sort of prize specimens!"

She laughed. "Right! They don't realize it, but we're their most valuable citizens. You provide the town's most important source of livelihood and I provide the education."

She told him of her afternoon session with Robbie and how quickly he'd caught on to fingering the guitar.

"I'll buy him one right away," Steve said. "Maybe I should make it a reward for attending school?"

"Oh, never! Please, give him the guitar. He's exceptionally talented, and right now he needs something to build his self-esteem. I wish he could have been here tonight so that we could have gotten better acquainted."

Steve's expression turned desolate. "It's tough for a little guy to bounce back and forth between his parents. Robbie already has too much to cope with. I still don't know if Leah is coming back to me. I worry continually that she's considering divorce. I'm not sure I can handle that."

For a few moments he put his head in his hands. "My life has been hell, Jenny. I love my wife—God, how I love her!—but she left me anyway."

Pain seared Jenny like a burn. "How well I know," she said.

He looked up sharply. "You were divorced?"

"Engaged. We were to be married last June, and then he found someone else."

"You're still in love with him, too?"

"I'm still in love with the man he used to be. Not with the man he is now. Tell me about your wife, Steve," she said, knowing she wasn't ready to share her own heartbreak yet.

He peered into the distance as if to get a clear picture. "Leah is beautiful and tremendously talented. Folks here thought she was snobbish, but really she was shy and was deeply hurt that people weren't friendly.

"When we took over this mill two years ago, I was a real greenhorn. I'd been a biologist with the state before that. The mill had been shut down for almost a year and was in bad shape. I had to work day and night to get things running again. You can't believe all the things that went wrong. Workmen's cottages had been vandalized during their vacancy. Machinery had broken down. A winter flood washed out the water system. Our forklift was stolen. Someone pulled the cap on our thousand-gallon gas tank, and we lost every drop. Then just as we were ready to start up, our sawyer ran off with one of the local belles, leaving his wife and kids behind. You name it, it happened to us! I worked night and day. My wife and I hardly saw each other."

"So she couldn't cope with the loneliness?"

"That and a lot of other things. I put it up to her as a kind of pioneer situation, thinking she'd be willing to stick it out up here for nine or ten years until we'd cut all the timber we owned. Then we could turn the place over to tree farming, take our profits and move back to town. But she wasn't willing to wait. Said any talent she had would atrophy by that time. She's a commercial artist and doing well."

"I guess I can sympathize with her on that score. I think I'd die if I had to wait ten more years before I could be a teacher. Women need a creative outlet as much as men, you know."

"I used to think homemaking and raising children fulfilled a woman's need on that score."

"To a great extent, but most of us need something more, something that expresses our unique selves. I guess we think it makes us a more worthwhile person or at least it increases our self-confidence."

"I don't know, Jenny. Seems to me that if you love someone, you can forget about personal needs."

"Why? One doesn't necessarily preclude the other."

"Well, I'm not convinced. What about you? Did your man expect you to stay home and raise a family?"

"On the contrary, he supported my career. He didn't want a family," she said, and knew her bitterness showed.

"And you did?"

"Passionately. I wanted both—children and a career."

"And you're just the one who could handle them. Any chance for a reconciliation?"

"Positively not. His values have changed. He's going in for the big time, the fast track and upward mobility, and besides..." It was too hard to say it.

"There's another woman," Steve finished for her. "Where is he now, or shouldn't I ask?"

"He works for a San Francisco firm."

"You have grit, Jenny. You'll manage. Maybe start dating again. How about our new board member, Luke Beaumont?"

"Good heavens! He's not my type," she said far too quickly, and heard her voice break.

"At the board meeting he mentioned that you two knew each other in college."

"Not well." That was no lie. "Oh, I guess you could say we had more than a nodding acquaintance."

"He seems to be a nice guy, shows a lot of interest in our school, and I think he has his eye on you. He certainly was anxious about those locks on your doors."

"A real fussbudget, isn't he? Thanks but no thanks."

For a while they talked about school business, and she asked if it would be possible to get some much-needed playground equipment. Steve said he'd take it up at the next board meeting.

"Are you saying it's going to be a problem?"

"Could be. The general idea seems to be that marbles and hopscotch are sufficient playground activities. Present your arguments, and I'll back you up."

It occurred to Jenny that it was too bad the two of them hadn't met a few years earlier. In many ways they were right for each other, but their hearts still clung to someone else.

When Steve got ready to leave, he pulled some tickets out of his pocket and stared at them a second as if to recall what they were doing there, then seemed to remember. "I capitulated to a hard-sell artist and bought these tickets to some benefit dance a week from tomorrow. Care to go?"

"Why don't you ask your wife?"

"Believe me, I'd like to. I'm working up to it, but she's not quite ready. At times I think there's hope, though."

"I'd like to meet her."

"I'll see if I can arrange it. I know you'd like each other. So will you go with me to the dance?"

"I'll go. After all, we two abandoned babes in the woods had better stick together."

"Ha! You act about as much like an abandoned babe as a mother tiger."

"Thanks, friend. You're not doing so badly yourself," she said.

They chuckled, but Jenny's eyes stung and Steve's laugh was far from hearty.

THE FOLLOWING WEDNESDAY Luke arrived in Woodhaven at noon. He was anxious to install a deadbolt lock on the back door and leave without another painful confrontation with Jenny. When he stopped at the Douglas mill to pick up the key, Steve filled him in on Jenny's request for playground equipment.

"We're going to have to push hard, as far as the other board members are concerned. You know what Simon Skinflint will say, 'Kids around here got along without all that nonsense for the past seventy-five years. What's so different about kids today?' So we'd better be ready with some persuasive arguments."

Luke said he'd try to get some figures together from the Otter Bay schools, then drove to Jenny's cottage. He hoped to accomplish the job quickly. Being around her shook him up more than he liked to admit. He needed time to lay some kind of buffer between them before he saw her again.

At her cottage he turned the lock, but the door remained fast. He tried again and realized some other kind of fastening had been applied, probably one of those sliding devices easy to install and easy to break, easy for anyone but Luke. He knew she had probably installed it herself, specifically against him. Apparently Jenny owned the only back door key. There was none on the ring Steve had given him. He considered forcing the door open. The flimsy upper device wouldn't hold, but he didn't care to deal with the fury the broken lock would generate. Either he would have to admit cowardice, give up and go home, or go ask her for her key.

Slowly he drove by the school. Music blared in gusty decibels from a phonograph, and a circle of children whirled in a frenzy of energy on the playground. He stopped the car and watched. It was a round dance, and every child, from the smallest to the largest, stamped, clapped and turned in jubilant time to the music. Jenny's eyes sparkled, and the sun highlighted her expressive face as she called out the directions.

He tried to dismiss the pang he felt, got out of the car and walked to the playground. The moment the music stopped he approached her. "Sorry to interrupt," he said in a low voice, "but I'd like to finish installing the lock, and I need your key."

"Hello, Mr. Beaumont," she said. "Boys and girls, Mr. Beaumont, a member of the school board, is visiting us today. Let's show him how well you can dance." She adjusted the needle on the phonograph, and the children performed with even more vigor.

"You could turn it down a little. I'll bet people can hear it clear over to Flint's store."

"You're certain?" she seemed to ask hopefully. "Well, what do you know, here comes Mr. Flint now." She gestured toward Simon who was hotfooting it onto the playground as if he were going to a fire.

Damn! Luke didn't want to get into any long-winded arguments with the fellow now.

"The key!" he said impatiently to Jenny's deaf ears.

The children finished their dance, and a red-faced Simon, looking as if he were about to explode, demanded, "What's going on here, Miss Valentine? I could hear the commotion clear down to the store. Where did that phonograph come from?"

"It's mine, Mr. Flint. It's old, but it serves the purpose."

"The key, Jenny, and I'll scram," Luke interrupted.

"A fine how-do-you-do! Teachin' dancin' on school time!" Simon roared.

"I remind you this is the lunch hour, Mr. Flint. Actually the older children wanted to play baseball, but our only bat is cracked. Of course we have a volleyball, but there doesn't seem to be any net. A jungle gym would be nice for the young children, but I understand they're very expensive. Children need exercise, so we're dancing."

He sneered. "Dancin'! Teaching dancin' to boys!"

"Oh, I don't know," she said sweetly. "Big boys around here go to dances every Saturday night. Dancing is good exercise, Mr. Flint. Join us and you'll see. Earl, take your father as your partner and help him with the steps."

Earl Flint, the heaviest and tallest boy in the school, as well as one of the most enthusiastic dancers, eagerly grasped his father's hand and dragged him into the circle. Jenny put on the music and Simon protesting and complaining was gleefully shoved, pushed and dragged through the dance. Luke hid a smile at the spectacle, then sighed, knowing he would fare little better with this wily woman.

When the dance ended, Jenny dismissed the children, saying she would ring the bell in ten minutes. "Do come in, gentlemen, and look around," Jenny said. "We're always pleased to have visitors."

Apparently the children were identifying and studying the local plants and trees. Leaves with their names inscribed underneath were individually mounted on construction paper and hung around the room.

"Good idea," Luke said. "I don't see any poison oak, though. You'd be surprised how many people can't identify it."

Jenny gave him a fierce scowl and pointed to the spelling papers on the bulletin board. "Mr. Flint, I know you'll be relieved to see every child got a passing grade on his spelling test this week."

Simon Flint, still panting and breathless from the exertion, looked around the room. "Place sure is cluttered up. What's that screen and projector doing here? Wastin' time with movies, are you?"

"We're learning to identify the trees and plants of the area. The visual aids department of the county office is loaning us the equipment and a set of excellent slides."

"I don't go for the county buttin' into things up here."

"Oh, the county is anxious to improve education, Mr. Flint, especially schools that are needy and have little or no resources."

Simon's face turned a deep red. "We're no charity case, Miss Valentine. In fact, we've got more money in the bank than a lot of school districts."

"Really! I never would have guessed it. I mean, we've barely got enough pencils."

"Watch it, the guy's going to explode," Luke said sotto voce. "And if you'll hand over the key, I'll get out of your way, too," he added as Simon Flint strode out of the classroom.

"I hid the key under the porch. You'll never find it. Anyway, I've taken care of the locks."

"So I've noticed, but it'll never hold."

"You're paranoid, Beaumont. At least it'll hold long enough for me to get to the phone. It was installed yesterday. Thanks very much."

"Maybe I ought to resign from the school board."

"Good idea. It would save us both a lot of friction."

"On the other hand, another Simon Flint might replace me. After today's display, you're going to need all the help you can get."

"You keep saying that. Believe me, I'm doing just fine." She suddenly turned and waved to the postman, who had just stuck his head inside the door.

"Brought you some fresh corn, Miss Valentine. The missus just picked it. I'll set it in the storeroom out back."

"You're a dear, Amos. It'll be a real treat!" She blew him a kiss, and he grinned, his face turning into a series of concentric circles. "He really likes me, you know," she said after Amos left. "He just can't get the hang of this modern education."

"You'll convince him," Luke said wearily.

"Stop worrying, Luke. Anyone who gets through my back door will find little worth taking." She picked up a large brass bell, walked outside and rang it. The children lined up quickly outside the door, looking at him expectantly.

"Would you care to join our class, Mr. Beaumont?" Jenny asked, and the children giggled. "The subject is math. It might interest you. Today it's possible that we may study how to travel the shortest distance between two points. Like between the schoolhouse and your car, for example. Draw up a chair. We'll find you a book."

A thin-edged answer was on Luke's lips when he saw Steve walking toward them carrying a carton. Luke said a brisk goodbye to Jenny and thanked the children for allowing him to see their dancing. When he met Steve, he handed him the keys.

"All finished?" Steve asked heartily.

"Guess everything is taken care of," Luke said, and headed for the car, cursing under his breath. A parade, no less! What were all these guys trying to do? Make an impression? Moths around a flame! A wonder the woman found time to teach. He walked to the car, deliberately taking a circuitous route.

CHAPTER NINE

JENNY LOOKED at the few dresses hanging in her closet and wondered what to wear to the dance that night. She really needed to do something about her wardrobe. Maybe next week she'd drive to San Francisco, visit Joel and Beth and go shopping.

At least she'd done something about her hair. Corrie had come by that morning and had cut and styled it for her. Soft bangs swept her forehead. Her old-fashioned knot was gone. Now her hair fell in waves, barely brushing her shoulders. She had to admit the effect was more becoming than her old coiffure.

"I like it," she'd said when Corrie had completed the shearing.

"Now you're really with it. I have to say that you looked like something out of the last century with that crazy bun."

"So I've been told," Jenny said dryly. "I agree. It's time for new beginnings."

"So there was a reason for your coming to this backwoods place after all. I thought as much. Who was he?"

"That crystal ball of yours again!" Jenny debated whether to share the past dark months with her friend. Then, in a burst of confidence, she gave a sketchy account of her recent past, omitting names and places.

"You're something else," Corrie said. "Why didn't you take the money he offered? Man, you really deserve it!"

"You mean you would?"

"Positively. Make 'em pay. That's my motto."

"I don't want any guilt money. I think I like myself better, making it on my own."

Corrie seemed to consider that remark for a few moments, then brightened. "Well, you all, have a good time with Steve tonight. Now there's a guy you should go for."

"Don't get any foolish ideas. Steve is still in love with his wife, and I'm going to do all I can to help him."

"O-ho, aren't you generous! First step—get all gussied up and go to a dance with him."

Jenny frowned. "On the surface it doesn't sound sensible, does it? But honestly, I consider him a good friend, and I'm sure he considers me the same. We have quite a lot in common, you know."

Corrie rolled her eyes. "Boy, are you the one!"

"I'm the one who would *not* add to the breakup of a marriage. Are you going to the dance tonight?"

Corrie's eyes narrowed. "Depends."

"Well, Dirk is still hanging around with bated breath."

"Squirrel bacon! I wouldn't go with that guy to a cat fight!"

"Squirrel bacon?"

Corrie grinned. "Yeah, one of Granny's favorite expressions. Suits him, right?" She gave Jenny's hair a final pat. "I'm the world's best stylist if I do say so myself. You'll knock 'em dead, kid!" Corrie had said, and left.

Jenny hadn't been to a dance since she and Luke had gone to one of his honorary fraternity affairs. It seemed aeons ago. She still had the dress she'd worn—a sleeveless white cotton sprigged with tiny pink roses, a scooped neckline and a full skirt.

She pushed the hangers aside in her closet one at a time, reviewing the possibilities. Unless she wore a blouse and skirt, the white dress appeared to be the only appropriate choice. Could she wear it without recalling that Luke had given her a pink camellia that night, which she'd tucked in her hair? He'd told her how beautiful she was and how much he loved her. Some fairy tale!

The dress deserved happier associations. She'd make sure that would happen.

Jenny was ready when Steve came by at eight. He gave a low whistle. "Wow! Whatever you've done to your hair, I like it. You look lovely, Jenny."

"Thank you, kind sir. Now tell me where we're going," she asked as they got into his ten-year-old blue Buick—polished for the occasion, she noticed.

"It's at the Cabrillo Bay Yacht Club, a high falutin' name for anyone who owns any kind of boat from a dinghy to a fishing trawler. Nice place. Right on the ocean."

"And the benefit?"

"For a high school, I think. So they can buy new band uniforms."

"School benefit, eh? Great idea."

"Do I see wheels turning?"

"You just might, if Simon Legree won't loosen the purse strings."

He grinned. "I can hardly wait!"

Cabrillo Bay was only a few miles south on the highway. The parking lot was already almost full. She knew dances were popular events up here, since there was little else for entertainment. *Up here!* She was getting the habit.

Inside the building a band was playing a fifties tune. The room was finished in log-cabin style, and helium-filled balloons, like multicolored flowers, floated from every table. They located a table for two near the dance floor and were about to sit down when Dirk McCleod lumbered up. By the looks of his stance as well as his ruddy complexion, he'd had too much to drink.

"Where's Corrie?" he bellowed. He put a hand on a chair to steady himself.

"She didn't come with us. I don't know her plans," Jenny said quietly, and hoped the fellow wasn't going to make a scene. Her first public appearance highlighted by a fracas with a drunk!

"The hell you don't. You were with her all morning."

Steve took his arm. "Listen, fellow, you're drunk and you'd better go sleep it off in your car before you're booted out. Come on, I'll get you a cup of coffee."

Dirk jerked away. "Not before your snooty schoolteacher tells me the truth." He lunged forward, almost losing his footing as he shook his finger at Jenny. "You stay away from Corrie, see. I don't want her hanging around you all the time getting crazy ideas. Me and her were doing just fine before you came along." Dirk waved his arms and continued his diatribe. People at nearby tables stared at them now.

"Yes, Dirk, tell me all about it," Steve said, and taking a firm grasp of one of Dirk's arms, forcibly walked him out of the hall.

Steve returned a few minutes later. "Fortunately the sheriff just drove up. They'll see to it Dirk stays out of trouble tonight. Don't take his gibes seriously. He's never been able to get to first base with Corrie. He has to blame someone, anyone but himself. Let's dance."

With relief Jenny slipped into Steve's arms as the band started a polka. "Good, that's one step I know well," Jenny said.

"Haven't done it in years," Steve told her.

"Don't worry. I'll cue you," Jenny replied, and they were soon going through the pattern with abandon. "I haven't had this much fun in ages," she said, laughing breathlessly.

"Good. It's about time," he said wistfully.

She squeezed his hand. "I know. I wish she were here, too."

When the music stopped, the audience clapped with enthusiasm, and along with the other couples, Jenny and Steve acknowledged the applause with a wave and left the floor. They'd barely reached their place when Jenny spotted the couple at the adjoining table and felt ice surge through her veins. There sat Luke and a striking dark-haired young woman.

Oh, no! It had never entered her mind that Luke would be here. He'd never cared for dancing and, in fact, did the same two-step to any music that was played. What a way to spoil an evening!

"Hey, look who's here!" Steve said heartily, and shook hands with Luke, who looked stunned. The young woman unwound her arm from Luke's and managed the kind of remote smile that let it be known they were invading her space. Jenny did her best to compose her own expression and wondered if Steve realized he was the only pleased member of the group.

Luke introduced Stacy Adams. Steve as always spoke in gallantries. Jenny said, "How do you do?" and wondered how the young woman got her spiked pompadour to remain so startlingly rigid. So this woman with the clever face was the one who in a few short weeks had made mincemeat of her and Luke's commitment!

She was certainly attractive in a dramatic kind of way. Her red gown looked as if it were from a designer house, or else it was the assured way she wore it.

Now that Stacy had managed to control her initial disappointment at the intrusion, her smile turned cordial and brilliant. However, the way her eyes shone when she looked at Luke, the manner in which her hand caressed his arm when her hand slid into his, left no doubt where she'd staked out her territory.

"Let's push our tables together," Steve said, and at once the men shuffled chairs and tables around.

"Good idea," Stacy said. "Let's get cozy. I hate shouting over the music. You two are great dancers, a regular Ginger Rogers and Fred Astaire!" Her eyes swept approvingly over Steve, as if to note for the first time that there were two attractive men in this foursome.

"I doubt they went in much for polkas," Jenny said.

"So you're the new schoolteacher in Woodhaven. Pardon my saying so, but you hardly look old enough," Stacy said, taking in Jenny's girlish dress and the flowers in her hair.

"Oh, I'm old enough and then some," Jenny said, suddenly aware of the contrast between her simple gown and Stacy's sophisticated one—not that she would ever have chosen the red dress for herself.

Matters were becoming a lot clearer. There was no doubt that Luke would realize his dream of becoming head of the Beaumont chain some day. He'd been propelled headlong into upward mobility. A country schoolteacher didn't move on that track. But Stacy was obviously hungry for status. Yes, she would be the kind of woman Luke wanted for his changed circumstances.

It seemed apparent that Luke now viewed women as products, measuring them in terms of timeliness and suitability. Any use he'd had for one hard-working, supportive student and devoted lover was past.

Goals. That was something else that split them apart. Why hadn't she seen this disparity? Oh, she'd seen it, all right, but had deliberately ignored it. Jenny wanted no part of that kind of life. Well, it was good to get second sight.

It would make the situation easier to deal with. Right. Positively.

The other three had been conversing, but she hadn't been listening, other than to realize the subject was dancing. At that moment the band broke into a rock number. "Come on, Luke, we've got a good one," Stacy said, rising and dancing in place.

Luke swept a glance over the frantically gyrating couples and looked apprehensive. "Maybe we ought to trade this one," he said. "Steve here is the guy who's got rhythm. You ought to know by now I own two left feet." The understatement of the evening, Jenny thought, and nodded in spite of herself. "Maybe Miss Valentine wouldn't mind sitting this one out with me?"

Miss Valentine would mind very much. "Okay with me. I'm still breathless from the polka," she managed without enthusiasm. She watched while Steve and Stacy got lost on the crowded floor and tried to ignore the way Luke had begun to stare at her. She finally pointed to the balloons and made a comment on the decorations.

"What did you say? I can't hear you over this blasted music. Why don't we go out on the deck? The volume is getting to me!"

"Good idea," she said, and preceded him out of the glass doors to a series of decks cantilevered down the cliff hanging over the water. Anything was preferable to sitting across from him at the table trying to make conversation.

They followed the stairway down to the bottom deck, which hung so close to the water that mist from the breakers sometimes soared over them. Leaning against the railing, Luke pointed out how the path of the three-quarter moon on the water lead directly to them. "Nice place," he said after an awkward pause. "You get the feeling you're on a ship's deck."

"Yes, very attractive."

"Lucked out in the weather, too. No fog or wind."

She frowned. "Considering our special circumstances, Luke, we can wait out this dance without feeling we have to make conversation."

"If you wish, but first, tell me what you did to your hair?"

"Had it cut."

"I liked it better the other way."

"Really? I seem to recall numerous gibes to the contrary."

"Oh, I don't mean it's unattractive. It's just that you look so different."

"Believe me, I am different."

"Not the dress, though. I remember it well, even the last time you wore it. It was at that dance just before I graduated."

"My goodness, what a memory!"

"And I gave you a white gardenia which you pinned in your hair."

"You do have a mind for details. It was a pink camellia, Luke."

He sighed. "Sometimes I wonder..."

"Yes, I've done a lot of that recently, too."

"I'm trying to do the right thing. In spite of what you may think, I want what's best for you." He reached for her hand, gave it a squeeze as if to emphasize his meaning, then tipped up her chin. "I mean that, Jenny." His fingers moved to her cheek, then slowly outlined her jaw.

Jenny stood as if paralyzed as old sensations burst like a Roman candle inside her. She closed her eyes and let remembered feelings pulse through her. She could allow that for a split second or two, couldn't she, without anyone knowing?

She opened her eyes, looked into his and caught her breath at what she saw there. Suddenly she was in his arms. Her lips parted beneath his, and her pulse thundered in her ears. They locked themselves against each other, seemingly unable to get enough of being close. It was always the same. The minute he touched her, reason fled. Time meant nothing. Only the present was real.

Stop, you idiot! some distant voice told her, but like an addict, she needed, wanted more. She slipped her hands under his jacket to feel the familiar muscular back and shoulders, then freed her arms and wrapped them around his neck. They rocked together. Some dreaming spirit within them awakened and seized possession of their bodies, setting them afire. The pounding surf shut out the world as well as his whispered words, leaving them unheard. How she's missed this tenderness! Dear God, how she wanted to love, to be loved.

Suddenly she heard her inner voice crying out at her weakness, and she jerked away from him with such force that she had to steady herself against the railing. "Stop!" she cried. "What do you think you're doing?" She pressed her fists against her eyes, fiercely determined not to cry.

"My God, Jenny! I'm sorry. You're so lovely, that dress, the memories...! What can I say?" He held out his arms in a helpless gesture.

Humiliation at her own actions almost overwhelmed her. It took every bit of strength she could summon to plod up the stairway. Gasping and mortified, she struggled to dredge up some remnant of poise. "You'd better hurry," she called down to him. "The music is ending. You don't want to disillusion Stacy so early in the game, do you? You're quite a womanizer, Luke. I'd never have believed it."

He took two steps at a time to catch up with her. "That's not true and you know it. I'm sorry this happened, and I promise it won't happen again. Your happiness is my real concern," he said, his voice breaking.

She had no answer. Her blame was as great as his. They marched stiffly to their table, Luke several feet behind her. Steve and Stacy were already seated and looked at them oddly as they took in Luke's flushed face and Jenny's pained expression.

Conversation proved awkward for a while, but Luke soon recovered and even told a couple of his Irish jokes, which seemed to restore everyone's equilibrium. Except Jenny's.

"Quiet little thing," she heard Stacy remark to Luke as Steve walked her onto the dance floor again.

"You feeling okay?" Steve asked as he guided her expertly around the crowded floor.

"Yes, I'm fine."

"I thought you seemed a little upset."

She laughed and hoped it didn't sound too strained. "Mr. Beaumont and I got into a little argument, and I let it annoy me. Like I told you, we just don't seem to hit it off."

"Strange. I sized you two up right away as being downright compatible. School problems, I suppose? You both ought to forget about them for a while. Well, give yourself a little time. Who knows what may happen?"

"Don't hold your breath. It isn't possible. Now if you're taking bets on Luke Beaumont and Stacy Adams, I'll go along with you."

"You may be right. But if I were you, I'd give the guy a chance. I don't think his sole purpose in trekking to Woodhaven is to install a bunch of locks, if you know what I mean."

"You're a lousy matchmaker, Steve Douglas, but you're a terrific dancer. Let's have another whirl at those fancy steps you just tried, and this time I'll try not to step on your toes."

As they danced, Steve's mind seemed to be off somewhere else, and she could tell he was indulging in happier memories. At times she knew he wasn't even dancing with her. It was his wife he was holding in his arms.

She was glad if she could do that for him. Their friendship held special meaning. "Two of a kind," he'd called them, and she knew they'd silently pledged to support each other, to counsel and help each other in any way they could.

CHAPTER TEN

BY SUNDAY MORNING after the dance, Jenny was exhausted from lack of sleep and suffering from an aching head, and she was still unable to make sense of what had happened between her and Luke. She'd spent half the night berating herself. How could she have succumbed to his embrace, to his kisses? Worst of all was her own response. For a few brief moments she'd been totally vulnerable to his touch, to his words.

She felt hollow and alone, and it was all she could do to keep from crying. But she wasn't alone, not really. She had good friends here. But they weren't enough. *I want someone who will come home to me every night, someone who will share the scars of the day and make them seem negligible. I want someone who will put his arms around me and listen to me and tell me he loves me.* She wanted someone like the Luke she'd known and loved.

Wearily she decided there was nothing else to do but to attribute her lapse to human weakness. Maybe she was going to have to accept that Luke would always remain somewhere at the back of her mind. Everyone had a lapse once in a while. Maybe she'd had one coming. At least she'd make certain there would be no others as far as Luke Beaumont was concerned.

After forcing herself to drink a cup of coffee and eat a bowl of cereal, she baked a batch of huckleberry muffins and decided to take them to Steve. She took the shortcut through the woods and paused midway to examine a clump of young redwoods known as a family circle.

Steve had told her that most redwoods died, not from disease or lack of water, but because they eventually toppled over. Around an injured parent tree or stump, a circle of new young trees would sprout, feeding on the root system of the parent, the only conifer that could form such a family.

In subdued sunlight Jenny walked along the spongy path. In spots it was almost overgrown with sword fern and oxalis. The branchless, rough-barked redwood trunks stretched high above the trail, like columns in a cathedral, their crowns intermeshed in a dense canopy, above which the sky was more surmised than viewed.

She'd come to think of this stretch of woods as her own private sanctuary. The majesty of these cloud sweepers that surrounded her, their enduring strength, always helped to set her own life in perspective. She had failed with Luke, but she needn't fail at being a real person, they seemed to tell her.

The creek was reduced to a mere trickle since the rains of last spring, and she easily crossed it by stepping on rocks that now jutted above the surface. Fat Cat appeared from nowhere, sat on a log and watched her with single-minded concentration, as if he'd never witnessed such an electrifying spectacle. She sat down beside him, and he purred loudly. "Good gracious," she said. "This place must be getting to you, too."

A while later Jenny tracked Steve down in his office, a smile on his face as he pored over his books.

"Hi," she said. "You look mighty chipper for a guy who has to work on a Sunday morning."

"Well, it's good to learn that the Douglas mill is finally alive and well. I'm knocking on wood, but for the past three months not a single cable has broken, the blasted bearing on the upper shaft of the band saw hasn't gone out, no flu epidemic has gutted my crew, the log pond has a good backup of logs, and I've finally got a reliable contract with a company to haul off my slash.''

"I thought sawmills burned their slash and sawdust in those huge wigwamlike burners. I've seen pictures of them. They're rather picturesque.''

"Maybe so, but it's highly wasteful and pollutes the environment, as well. They were outlawed a few years ago. I've got a contract with a nursery that picks up all my sawdust, and another with a paper company that takes every bit of the slash. Even the bark is used for insulation. Not one thing is wasted from the redwood tree.''

"I can't imagine how much lumber comes from one of those giants.''

"A lot of board feet, all right. There's a large church located in a Santa Rosa park that was built completely from one tree.''

"Amazing! But doesn't it hurt you to cut down these big, old giants?''

"Most of my tract was logged over years ago, so we saw mainly second growth. We're designated as a commercial tree farm. Growth and harvesting are controlled. This guarantees the perpetuation of the lumber industry and saves the few remaining giants that have taken over two thousand years to mature.''

"I can imagine tree farms were a long time coming.''

"Yes, almost too late. A continual battle has raged between conservationists and the lumber industry, but the Save the Redwood League has managed to promote a few national parks and preserves where the public can still view them. And what's that in your basket, lady? Smells wonderful!''

"Muffins. Just baked. And I'm not going to interrupt you, so I'll just leave them on the counter and take off."

"Oh, no, you don't. Sit down. I have a lot of good news to share."

"I'm all ears."

He pulled out a chair for her, reached for a muffin and bit into it. "Mmm, ambrosia! First of all, the braille type-writer for Robbie arrived yesterday, and I have an extra standard one he can use. As it happens, he'd begun to use both of them at the special school he attended before moving here, so he's not going to take a long time to learn."

"And I just heard from the Sonoma County Braille Transcribers Guild," Jenny said. "One of their former members now lives in Otter Bay and will volunteer her services translating school texts into braille. I plan to meet her tomorrow after school and show her the material Robbie needs. The county library also has some children's books in braille and will be sending them soon."

"We still have a problem. Robbie acts terrified every time I mention school."

"With good reason. Don't force it. Perhaps music will be the key."

"But all that extra time you spend?"

"I'm doing it because I want to."

"How can I ever thank you, Jenny?"

She gave a mischievous smile. "Well, my school kids could use a basketball hoop and a couple of balls, a volleyball net, a baseball bat and a few swings. Then there's—"

"Hey, I'm on your side, remember? I've talked my head off to get the majority vote to spend the money. So far a stone wall. Maybe you should have taken these muffins to the other board members."

"No bribes. I just want them to come to their senses. So what's your other good news?"

"Well, the struggling Douglas mill has just received a giant shot in the arm. This past week I signed a three-year contract with—hold on to your hat—the Richter Corporation!"

"Oh, Steve, that's wonderful!"

"You'd better believe it! The Douglas mill is finally on the road to success! I'll be furnishing lumber for several condominium complexes being built on the peninsula south of San Francisco. I still can't believe I won that contract!"

"And with a large and established company! When do you start?"

"We begin lumber deliveries the first of the year. That gives us enough time for the survey crew to locate old boundary stakes and for the foresters to complete selective tree markings for harvesting in my tract of timber."

"Sounds as if you've got a smooth road ahead."

"I can't foresee any obstacles—knock on wood. Of course, if the deadline isn't met, there's a considerable daily penalty, with the contract canceled two weeks later if still unfulfilled. No problem, though. The survey will start next week."

"It's about time everything came up roses for you."

He was silent for a moment. "Not everything, Jenny."

"Are you making any headway with Leah?"

He gave a helpless gesture. "That's the hell of it. I don't know. Sometimes I think she's on the verge of giving us another try. But she's so damn determined to go on with her artwork."

"And you're so damn determined to make a success of this mill."

"It's not the same."

"Why isn't it? Creating something, reaching your individual potential is what life is all about. It's no different for a woman than for a man, Steve."

He gave a sheepish grin. "Well, I must admit I gave it some thought after you raked me over the coals the last time we talked."

"The idea is to clothe the thought with action, Steve."

"One of my problems is that I can't talk commercial art with her. How can I show support for her career when I don't know a damn thing about it?"

"Well, for starters you could build her a studio of her own near your house so that she doesn't have to crowd her work into your living quarters."

He looked at her as if she'd just discovered a new galaxy. "You're right. She always had to work on the kitchen table, and had no real storage place for her materials. And I could arrange a private phone for her with special long-distance rates," he said with growing excitement. "When she was here, she was continually frustrated trying to make calls on our busy office phone." He made a hurried rough sketch and showed it to her. "I know just the place for it," he said. "Come along and see if you agree."

They walked up to the rise toward his house. On a knoll to one side a huge oak spread generous shade. They walked under the tree and took in the view of the mill below and the forested hills that rolled toward the horizon.

"It's perfect," Jenny said. They chatted for a while longer about the plan and even stepped out the approximate dimensions. Neither mentioned the unspoken possibility that the gift might come too late.

"You've really opened my eyes, Jenny. I can't believe how imperceptive I've been." He gave her a brotherly hug. "Damn it, I wish I could do something to help you. Any chance of a reconciliation with your guy?"

"None at all. Your situation and mine are entirely different. Anyway, I'm past wanting it, and he's very much involved with someone else. Thanks, Steve, it's good to know I have a shoulder when I need it," she said. Then Jenny took the typewriters for Robbie and bid Steve goodbye.

As she headed for the shortcut to her cottage, she passed a couple of Steve's mill hands, and she could tell from their gestures and the few words she caught that they were speculating on the state of a romance between her and Steve. She was well aware such gossip was going around and decided to be more careful in the future. She didn't want to do anything that would injure the delicate state of Steve's relationship with his wife. Friendship was all she and Steve wanted or needed from each other. People eventually would figure out the truth. Hopefully Steve would get his act together and win back his Leah soon.

Later that afternoon Corrie drove up in a brand-new sports car and honked until Jenny came running. "My goodness, look what just popped out of the woods. Is it yours?" Jenny asked.

Corrie tossed back her dark hair, and her huge loop earrings swayed and sparkled like twin neon lights. "You bet it's mine. Hop in. I'll take you for a spin."

Jenny got in and sank into the black leather seat. "Mmm, gorgeous. Did you win the lottery?" The car certainly didn't come with a waitress's salary.

Corrie turned the car around and gunned down the road in a cloud of dust. "Hell, no. I've got a far more reliable source, with more to come. Aren't you envious? Like I told you, schoolteachers don't get perks like this."

"I see. And what creative enterprise earned you this little beauty?" As if she didn't know. It was common knowledge that a certain affluent businessman whom

Corrie had met at work had fallen hard for her. The dreary cliché seemed to be that he had a wife and family, which thus far hadn't strained the progress of the relationship.

"And have you furnished the new apartment? The one in San Francisco?" Jenny added.

"Haven't found one yet. Still looking."

"And what will you do there? I mean, besides the usual fee required. Sit on a cushion and sew a fine seam?"

"You bet. This little Corrie knows a good thing when she sees it. I can hardly wait."

"And what about your future?"

Corrie tossed her an unfocused look. "Rosy, right?"

"I mean that talent you try so hard to hide. You could be a real success, Corrie."

"Hey, I have other talents besides decorating."

"And what if your...special friend suddenly finds someone else or has a heart attack?"

"What's with you today? I don't need any more Granny lectures."

"Just asking. We missed you at the dance the other night. Dirk did, too. He thinks I'm a bad influence on you."

Her laugh rang out, peeling up and down an octave. "Now that makes my day. Jenny Valentine, a bad influence on Corrie Coates! Just remind him that by now he ought to be able to figure that nobody influences this kid."

"Oh, you mean little red racers and fancy apartments wield no clout?"

"Oh, shut up and stop acting like a school teacher. You and your lofty ideas! How does it feel to be so pure?"

Jenny thought about their conversation for a few moments. "Sorry. Didn't mean to lecture. I guess the only criterion is whether you still like yourself after making these important decisions, and Lord, how I hate myself when I try to be profound! Not another word on the subject. That's a promise."

"Good. Let's stop by old sourpuss Simon's and see if he's got in the six-pack of Perrier water I ordered. Gotta get classy, you know, now that I'll be moving to San Francisco."

MONDAY MORNING Jenny brought the braille typewriter to school and showed the class how it worked. She allowed some of the children to feel the raised dots that were made on the paper, explaining that the typewriter belonged to Robbie and that he could do a lot of his lessons on it.

"Robbie! That dummy can't come to our school. He can't see," Earl Flint said with his usual authority. After all, his father was on the school board.

"You're wrong, Earl. It's true he can't see with his eyes, but he has another kind of sight with his fingers."

"Yah, yah!" Earl cried, and danced around the room, bumping into everything. "What good are fingers when you're blind?"

She held up a paper with the configurations. "He can read this with his fingers. Can you?"

"Those pinpricks! You're fooling, Miss Valentine!" the children cried.

"I'm telling the truth. Robbie can do the same work as you, except he'll be reading with his fingers, and he can write his answers on two different typewriters. He might even do it a lot better, because he wouldn't be distracted by Earl over there making like a clown."

The children buzzed excitedly, crowding around to run their fingers over the raised dots the braille typewriter made. "Why doesn't he come to school then?" a small girl asked.

It was the question she'd been waiting for, and for a while she talked about how lonely it felt always to be in the dark, how one never knew what green was or red or purple or even what a person looked like.

The children grew very quiet, and the rest of the day at noon or recess she saw them taking turns blindfolding one another and walking about, usually with help. Jenny felt confident she'd laid the right foundations. At least one thing was going well in her life, she thought.

CHAPTER ELEVEN

LUKE GROANED and turned off his alarm. Just because Charles could get along on five hours of sleep a night didn't mean he could. It had been a hellish four days. Charles had arrived on Monday night with a Texas cousin, Sue Anne, in tow, and the week had started with her damn birthday dinner. What a waste of time.

Several times lately Charles had brought up one of his "suitable" young women. Luke had discouraged them quickly enough. He'd give them a whirlwind tour of the city, which had nary a Neiman-Marcus, a Geary theater or a symphony hall. Then he'd stop for a drink at the town's picturesque but rowdy lumbermen's bar. By then the girl's eyes would be glazed over, assuring him he'd never see her again. Thank God for that. Not one of them held a candle to Jenny.

Earlier, Charles had emphasized there would be little time for socializing outside of business requirements, and that was only too true. He still put in seventy-hour weeks, and every minute allotted to anything else put him that much behind. Talk about being married to one's job! Surely no wife ever demanded such devotion!

Charles's behavior in producing all these available young women didn't make sense. If his purpose was to erase Luke's thoughts of Jenny, he was failing completely. As far as Luke was concerned, Charles could stop parading his San Francisco socialites. It was all he could do to keep

Stacy at arm's length. She was the ultimate manager—which was okay until she concentrated her skills on him. Last week she'd even wanted to choose his toothpaste, for God's sake!

"I don't get it, Charles," he said after lunching with the latest young woman Charles had arranged for him to meet. "You know how busy I am. In fact, you're the one who pointed out that I wouldn't have time for a family, much less any social life."

"My dear boy, you exaggerate. Who said you had to be a monk? Now is the time to play the field. Forget about commitment. That's what takes up time."

Luke gave his uncle a level look. "Isn't that pretty self-serving?"

"Hell, no. It's organizing your life. What's wrong with that?"

Luke felt an icy quiver pass through him.

The meeting yesterday took the cake. Thank God, Charles had left for San Francisco right afterward—taking Sue Anne with him—or there would have been fireworks.

Luke had won the Johansen Forest Products account, one of many of Eric Johansen's vast holdings. Luke liked the crusty old timberman, who by his own hard work and ingenuity had risen from a lowly redwood peeler to the owner of vast stands of valuable timberland.

Johansen had called and asked for a conference concerning a boundary problem in a new tract of timber he wished to log. The first thing that had teed off Luke was that Charles, uninvited, joined the meeting.

Johansen got straight to the problem. To get to his new tract he needed to cut an access road through an adjoining piece of property. But the owner of the property wouldn't cooperate.

"Did you consult your attorney? This appears to be more of a legal problem," Luke said.

"No, and it's not entirely. Tax-wise, because of my projected income, it's best for me to log the property immediately. That's why I wanted your opinion first."

"Very wise of you," Charles chimed in.

"Because I've spread myself thin opening two new businesses this year, profits will be down, meaning my income will fall into a lower tax bracket."

"Why won't the fellow give you a right of way? Not because you wouldn't give him a fair price for it, surely?" Luke asked.

"Well, from his perspective, this O'Neil has a point. He's operating a stud mill on a shoestring. Has himself in hock for machinery, and up until recently has had a problem keeping up with his payments. The right of way would cut his property square in two and cause all kinds of inconvenience."

"Buy him out, man!" Charles cried impatiently.

"I tried, but he refuses. I have to admire his guts. He's determined to make a go of his little mill. Actually, Luke, you're getting a reputation for mediation around here. Yes, I've done some checking, so I wondered if you would talk to the guy and see if you can work out something. I seem to be the heavy in this case."

Charles had been looking at the tract map and piped up before Luke could answer. "Doesn't this guy also need a right of way to the highway to get his studs out? Who owns that small piece that blocks his entry? I assume he's been using it."

"I checked on that. He has a verbal agreement."

Charles waved a hand impatiently. "Simple. We'll threaten to buy the piece and block his passage. Then we'll buy it if we have to. Don't tell me the owner won't sell. I'll be glad to take care of the negotiations myself. Right down my alley."

"Oh?" Johansen said. "Just for argument's sake, what if that doesn't work?"

"Hey!" Charles said with a wide grin. "We'll buy up his machinery loan, and the first time he fails to make a payment, we'll foreclose."

Johansen scratched his chin. "Hmm, you *are* an expert."

"Hold on," Luke interrupted. "Is this fellow's name *James* O'Neil?"

"Right," Johansen said.

"He was one of my first clients," Luke said. "He's had hard luck that won't end. His mill burned down a couple of years ago. Then some of his machinery was vandalized. On top of all that he lost his oldest son in a logging accident. He asked me to go over his finances to see if he had a reasonable expectations for success. We worked out a financial plan, and after a lot of hard work, he's on his way. We can't put a man like that out of business."

Charles banged his fist on the table. "My God, Luke, whose side are you on?"

"Ours!" Luke snapped angrily. "I refuse to have our name connected with dirty tricks." He ran this office, didn't he? He ought to tell Charles to get the hell out and stop meddling, and if Johansen didn't like his advice, let him go elsewhere.

Charles glowered. "Nothing illegitimate about my proposals!"

"But downright unethical. There are other alternatives we can explore."

Johansen's sharp blue eyes narrowed. "Now you're talkin'."

"According to this map, a narrow segment of your property edges the highway," Luke pointed out. "Why can't you cut your access through there?"

"A deep gully runs along the entire strip," Johansen replied.

"How much would it cost to build a bridge?"

"At least a hundred thousand."

"Well, it's a temporary bridge, so you can use it as a tax write-off. You're going to make millions on the timber. You can use a tax benefit."

A brief discussion followed, with Johansen accepting the solution, although Charles argued against it to the end.

When they'd finished, Johansen was wearing a wry smile but said nothing. His lack of comment had left Luke bewildered. Who knew what went through his mind? Maybe Johansen would take his future business elsewhere or deal directly with Charles in San Francisco. So be it, Luke had decided. It was time to stop letting Charles walk all over him.

Now Luke drank a cup of bitter coffee left over from yesterday, which added nothing to his well-being, then took off for the office. As soon as he arrived, Steve Douglas called.

"Hi, Steve, what can I do for you?"

"A little school board business. I want us to be prepared for the meeting Friday night. There's something going on here, and I don't like the smell of it. I have the feeling Simon is stirring up something. No one has said anything, but I overheard some talk about a letter he's going to circulate. He almost blew his stack when I mentioned the cost of new playground equipment. No doubt it has something to do with that."

"You're sure? I don't trust that guy."

"Neither do I. Stirring up trouble is his forte. I tried to feel him out on the subject but got nowhere. There's no way he'll go along with the equipment. The meeting is next Friday. I'm appointing you and Jenny as a committee of two to get together a report to present at the meeting regarding her request for the playground equipment."

"Uh, have you asked her yet?"

"No, but she'll serve, all right. She's the one who's plugging to improve the playground."

"Well, Steve, I'm terribly busy this week—a lot of work to catch up on. I'll make the meeting, of course but—"

"Listen, Luke, you and I are the only board members who support this. The others are Simon's yes-men. That's a three to two vote in their favor. Jenny has no vote, you know."

"Well, frankly, Steve, I got the feeling that Jenny would prefer not to work with me."

"Nonsense. Jenny's the most fair-minded person around. You just need to get to know her better. She's the best teacher we've ever had up here, and I'm really anxious to get a decent playground for her—and for the kids of course."

"Of course." It wasn't hard to figure out whose welfare came first in Steve's mind. The guy had fallen for her, all right.

"You know, Luke, in order to get the go-ahead, it really comes down to us winning over one person, so it's up to you guys to prepare a persuasive report. In the meantime, a little arm bending of the adamant three might not hurt, either. I'll see what I can do on that score."

Reluctantly Luke greed. What more could he say? Well, it was time for him and Jenny to start behaving like adults instead of emotional adolescents. Right. Keep remembering that. Still, he wouldn't like to see Jenny's face when she learned she'd been appointed to the small committee, Luke and Jenny. Just the two of them.

JENNY CHECKED to see that the papers on her classroom bulletin board were neatly arranged and wiped the blackboards once more. The school board meeting was scheduled here tonight, and Mrs. Coates would have apoplexy if she left any clutter.

Only twenty minutes remained before school was dismissed. She looked down at her pupils' heads, noting the wide range of hair colors, the uneven partings, the bows, cowlicks and barrettes. Each child was bent in earnest concentration, writing invitations to parents for an upcoming school program.

She felt a pang of regret as she walked up and down the aisles. Her months with these children would be too few and were going too fast. She'd spent extra hours before and after school helping the Jacob twins who were having trouble with arithmetic, and working with Tommy who was at last beginning to read with comprehension. She'd sent to the county library for some science books for Earl Flint, who had a passion for dinosaurs, and for some books on sketching for shy Annie Leigh, who had extraordinary talent for drawing. It had been a banner day when she'd found that every child had improved over last year's county test scores.

Still, she felt success as a teacher would elude her until she could motivate Robbie to come to school. Steve had purchased a guitar for him, and he already knew the fingering for enough chords to accompany the folk songs she'd taught him. He was an avid reader, consuming the braille primers faster than the library could send them. Progress on his typewriters had been slower, probably because he preferred spending time with his guitar. She considered his refusal to come to school a personal failure.

The class now finished their final task for the day and cleared their desks. "Let's sing a song or two while we wait for the bus to arrive," she said, and gave the starting tone on her pitch pipe for "Old Smoky," one of their favorites. Suddenly from under the open windows came a faint guitar accompaniment. Puzzled, the children stopped singing in order to listen to the clear, sweet voice that carried into the room.

She'd suspected for some time that Robbie had monitored classroom activities from a bush under the windows. On occasion, she'd caught a glimpse of the small figure scurrying around the building.

"It's Robbie," she said quietly.

"Wow, he really can sing," Earl said.

"And play the guitar!" the children cried, and clamored to have him come inside and sing for them. Two of the boys slipped outside. Jenny strained in vain at the open window to hear their conversation, then held her breath as all three came back into the room, trailed by Rosie, Robbie's golden retriever. The atmosphere grew thick with suspense as they walked to the front of the class.

"Robbie's going to show us how to read with his fingers," Earl announced importantly, as if he were the one who'd taught him.

Jenny took one of the library's primers and handed it to him. His hand shook. As his fingers trailed across the raised configurations, his voice grew firm and his shoulders straightened, a boy emerging from his concept of himself as a person to be shunned to see himself as an equal among peers.

The children sat as if stricken dumb. At the end of the story there was only silence, and after a few moments,

Robbie turned his head back and forth as if in a desperate attempt to sniff out an escape hatch.

All at once the children began to clap and shout, crowding around Robbie, all talking at once, asking him to show them over and over the magic of reading with one's fingers.

Jenny busied herself at her desk and didn't enter into the conversation. Her pupils would accomplish what she had been unable to do. A few minutes later the school bus arrived and the children reluctantly left.

In the quiet of the classroom, Robbie still stood by her desk, shuffling his feet and putting one hand in and out of his pocket. Jenny looked at the brave little boy, and a pang of tenderness filled her. "Thanks for reading the story, Robbie. The class has wanted you to join us for a long time," she said.

"Yeah, okay," he said, dismissing his action, "but I really came to bring a song I made up for you."

"A song? Oh, Robbie, what a wonderful present!"

"It's for helping me with the guitar. It has a name. I call it 'I See with Music'." He stood motionless for a moment as if to make certain no one else was in the room, strummed a few chords, then sang in his clear, flutelike voice:

"I cannot know what red is,
Or yellow, green or blue.
The stars and sun and moonlight
Are all a mystery, too.

But my world is not all darkness,
The lonely times are gone
Because you've opened windows
And filled my life with song."

He sang the words in a poignant minor melody. Her throat contracted so that she could hardly speak. "That's a beautiful song, Robbie," she said when he finished. "Did you make up the tune?"

"Yes, and most of the words, but I had to ask my dad to help me make them rhyme. I made you a copy to show you that I've been practicing my typing. It's for you to keep. Promise not to show it to anyone," he added anxiously, and thrust a folded paper into her hand. She understood. Too many fingerprints ruined the shine. He scampered out of the room, his guitar hugged against him, one hand gripping Rosie's leash as she strained against it.

Jenny opened the paper and read the words he'd just sung. There were several typos, but they didn't hinder the meaning. Tears stung her eyes. Robbie's gift assuaged any feeling of failure.

It had been a long week, and now she would much rather have gone for a walk in the woods than get ready for the school board meeting tonight. She was in no mood for dissension, and there would be plenty of that. Regardless of the presentation Luke would make, she felt certain the expenditures wouldn't be approved.

She'd had an odd feeling the past few days. When she'd gone into Simon's store, he'd ducked out and let his wife wait on her. Then when some women came in together, talking intently among themselves, they'd stopped abruptly when they spotted her and moved to the dairy section of the store in order to avoid speaking to her—so Jenny had felt certain she'd been the subject of their discussion. Jenny was puzzled and hurt. The townsfolk had grown much friendlier, and she'd come to believe that, if not yet totally accepted, at least she was no longer an object of suspicion.

In addition to that depressing state of affairs, Steve had asked her to work with Luke on the presentation for the school board meeting. She supposed she'd been irrationally irritated. It seemed Steve was determined to throw them together, as if he were doing her a favor, for heaven's sake. If he only knew.

Luke had arrived after school on Wednesday as they'd previously arranged in a stiff little phone conversation. She'd been correcting papers when he'd knocked at the doorway.

She'd tried to swallow the sudden tightness in her throat before she spoke.

"Come on in," she said at last. "You'd better take my desk. I'm afraid you won't fit into the others." She handed him a tablet and moved to Earl's desk nearby. He pulled out a pen and sat quietly—a model pupil. She wished he didn't look so clean-cut and wholesome. Such contradictions were annoying.

They said nothing for a minute or two as they settled themselves, and the silence started to grow obtrusive. She imagined that without being too obvious they were gauging each other's mood.

"Have you talked with anyone on the board, besides Steve, I mean?" she finally asked.

"I stopped by Simon's store on the way over. He seems to think you're deliberately trying to overturn the entire school system. I think he's mislaid half his brain. The other two members huddle so tightly under Simon's umbrella that they don't even know the sun is shining."

"A teacher, of all people, doesn't go out of her way to disrupt education much less offend the school board. Rule number one, two and also three," she said crossly. "Simon probably would like nothing better than to have me climb a tall tree and stay there."

He grinned. "An uncreative solution. Hey, we need you. You're a whole battalion with banners. Better that we clobber him with your sterling arguments. Name 'em off and I'll take notes." Here he was acting responsibly and sensibly, which only made her feel childish. She gathered her wits and for the next hour enumerated dozens of reasons for a safe and adequate playground, quoting physical education experts to back up her statements.

Throughout the session, Luke remained so doggedly businesslike that she was tempted to try to muffle him. She was glad she resisted and complimented herself. She was coping. The hurt was receding. Disillusionment remained, but that wasn't nearly as hard to deal with as her reactions every time she saw him.

The only personal reference he made was when he got ready to leave. He kept putting his pen in his vest pocket and taking it out again. "I still can't get used to your hairstyle," he said finally. "I look at you and wonder if you can be Jenny." He tore off his notes and handed back the tablet. His fingers touched hers in the exchange, and it was as if some disturbing emotion brushed off into her mind. But then he'd left quickly before she could make a response.

And a good thing he did, Jenny thought.

Just then Etta Mae Coates entered the classroom and started spraying furniture oil and flipping a dust cloth with all the vigor of an invading army. Jenny had engaged in little conversation with Corrie's grandmother, feeling that a smile, a pleasant greeting and asking after her health were the safest communications. But Jenny had the feeling that the sharp-eyed woman could have given a day-by-day commentary on everything that went on in the classroom if asked—which didn't make Jenny feel very comfortable.

With Etta Mae bustling about, Jenny left quickly, but by the time she got home it was too late for dinner. She changed into the new green wool dress she'd purchased on a recent shopping spree in San Francisco with her old friend, Beth Spencer. She'd splurged and bought a malachite necklace and matching earrings. Her usual uniform was a blouse and skirt. Maybe the new outfit would pick up her spirits.

Jenny got her first clue that there was something different about tonight's meeting as soon as she arrived at the school. There were ten cars parked out front, in addition to those belonging to the board members. The meetings were open to the public, of course, but to her knowledge no one ever attended.

Good heavens! Had her request for playground equipment, the first in the seventy-five-year-old life of the school, caused that much commotion? Inside, she paused at the back of the room and looked at the gathering, feeling as if a forty-foot wave were washing over her. Something told her this assemblage had to do with her.

People sat erect and silent in folding chairs or at the desks if they could squeeze into them. Tight-mouthed and grim, they could have stepped right out of a Grant Wood painting. The board members sat at a table facing the audience.

A worried-looking Steve was still setting up extra chairs. Luke hadn't arrived yet. Steve paused at her side for a moment as he got another chair from the storeroom.

"Haven't a notion what this is all about," he whispered. "Simon sent out letters a few days ago asking the community to attend tonight's meeting. Who can predict what he has up his sleeve?" He gave her arm a squeeze, which lent small comfort.

She nodded and found a seat. There was a stir at her entrance, and people averted their eyes or seemed to stare right through her. Etta Mae arrived then, her wide, mannish shoes squeaking shrilly in militant rhythm as she marched down an aisle and plunked herself into a front row seat, directly facing Simon. Luke hurried in, along with one more couple, and looked around, obviously amazed at the unusual attendance. For a split second their eyes met and at once turned away as if they'd poked by mistake into forbidden territory. Jenny focused on the jagged haircut of the man in front of her and tried to ignore her racing pulse.

At exactly seven-thirty Steve called the meeting to order. Jenny saw her knuckles turn white as she gripped her hands together. The minutes were read by wispy little Mrs. Mallory in a monotone that hardly reached half the listeners. Old business was brought up and quickly dispatched.

Jenny took a deep breath. Next would come the request for the playground equipment. She rather looked forward to the excitement. She'd accumulated some surefire arguments, and Luke could be a convincing speaker.

Steve now said something about a lot of new business on the agenda tonight and that Mr. Flint had asked to be allowed to speak first about a topic "of imminent concern to him and the community."

Simon rose, a tic in his cheek twitching erratically. "Everyone knows that no one takes the welfare of Woodhaven school any more seriously than I do." Several people nodded, and Simon went on for several minutes about how he didn't mind the time and effort he spent as watchdog for the community interest, since it was for everyone's benefit. The tic increased its frequency, pacing his rising passion.

"I wouldn't be standing here if Captain Ballard hadn't been put out of commission with that accident. I knew right from the night we signed the substitute's contract that the county had snookered us, but I figured the fair thing to do was to give that substitute a chance. Well, friends and neighbors, we gave that chance and the substitute has come up wanting."

Jenny felt as if someone had punched her in the stomach. A personal attack was the last thing she expected. There was an ominous-sounding murmur from the crowd.

Simon shook his finger at them. "Does this so-called substitute teach the basic concepts that our fathers and grandfathers thrived on?"

Substitute! Can't he say my name? Both fear and anger roiled inside her.

Simon's high-pitched voice cracked in its intensity. "Look around, folks, and you can imagine what happens to your hard-earned tax money." Wound up now, he waved his arms, gesturing grandly. "Look at these games, drums and other fiddle-faddle that waste our kids' time. And would you believe that ant colony over there in the see-through plastic contraption?"

Luke stood up and pounded a fist on the table. "Just a minute, Simon!"

But Simon outshouted him. "And if this play-party stuff isn't enough, now she wants to shoot our budget for a lot of unnecessary contrivances for the playground. Next thing you know, she'll want to outfit the place with a lot of those fancy dan computers." His voice had risen to fill the room, but now it dropped to a stage whisper.

He paused to let the effect of his words sink in. He's missed his calling, Jenny thought, entranced in spite of the apprehension she felt. He should have been one of those hellfire-spouting evangelists instead of a grocer. But he wasn't through yet. She didn't want to guess what he was leading up to.

"I realize this is the young woman's first job, but I have to wonder if she can find five minutes a day to teach arithmetic. A while back I visited here myself and she had the whole school a dancin', the phonograph blastin' clear down to my store, and this happened not only once but *five different times*!" He pounded a fist to underline each word.

"Maybe this stuff is okay for city kids, but up here we take education seriously. And one more thing, whoever heard of allowing a dog in the classroom? Can't help but distract the pupils. Blind kids ought to be in a special school, beggin' your pardon, Mr. Douglas, since it's your son, but you know it's true."

Steve held up a hand and Luke leaped up simultaneously. "Damn it, Simon, sit down!" Luke shouted. "Everything you've said is rubbish!"

"You've made a lot of serious accusations here, Simon," Steve said, his own temper scarcely concealed. "I think it's time for me to clear up your misunderstandings. Miss Valentine would probably like to say a few words, too."

Simon frantically waved a hand to stall off interruption. "Now you just wait a dang minute. I'm not through. Let me tell you, folks, I got such a crawful I hied myself down to the county office all on my own last week, and wait till you hear what I found out." He paused for several seconds to allow the suspense to balloon. "This here so-called teacher we hired doesn't even have a credential!" He turned to Steve. "Sir, as an elected member of the Woodhaven school board, I hereby move that Jenny Valentine, Woodhaven's substitute teacher, be asked to resign."

CHAPTER TWELVE

JENNY'S NAILS DUG into her palms so hard that they marked her skin. She sat straight and unmoving as the meaning of Simon's words beat at her. For a few seconds there was a dead silence. Then everyone talked at once. Luke rose, his face flushed, the set of his jaw showing barely controlled anger. Steve said something to him, and Luke scowled and sat down. Steve pounded the gavel in a succession of rapid bangs until everyone grew quiet, but before he could speak, Etta Mae Coates jumped up and shook her finger scarcely an inch from Simon's nose.

"You featherleggy codgy! You're blind, teebowed and plum crazy! You haven't a notion what goes on in this schoolroom. Now I admit at first I had more doubts than anyone, and I don't change my mind easy, either, but workin' here every day like I do, you find out plenty. This substitute might be shortchanged on some things, and I admit she has some pretty far-out ways of doin' her job, but results don't lie. I'm tellin' you one thing, Simon Flint, credential or no credential this schoolch knows how to teach kids!"

Jenny couldn't believe her ears. Etta Mae Coates was the last person in the world she would have expected to support her. She sat dumbfounded as the woman described her teaching techniques precisely and mentioned the kids by name as she told how well they responded. Etta Mae must have planted herself in the coatroom for hours, considering the number of details she mentioned.

Jenny watched in fascination as Etta Mae's voice rang out. Her gestures were large and decisive as she hammered out each point, winding up her speech with the announcement that for the first time in history, Woodhaven school had tested above average in the county tests. "And there's no hokum about it. I checked each score myself."

Simon leaped up. "Goldarn it, Etta Mae, I never thought you'd be taken in by all that frippery. How much time did you see these kids spend on the three R's while you did all that spyin'?"

"Sit down you serowlsh!" Etta Mae thundered, and Simon sat. "We don't want any more of your blather about the good old days. You ride to town in your new Ford pickup, I've noticed, and you got some flu shots from old Doc Painter recently—pretty modern medicine, ain't it? You bought some mighty fine refrigerators for your store, not to mention that fancy coffee grinder. So enough of this nonsense about keepin' kids back in the Dark Ages."

The moment she sat down there was a burst of applause. Steve, grinning like the legendary cat who'd swallowed the canary, shot a glance at a steaming Simon and pounded the gavel. "Mrs. Coates has clarified this situation far better than I could. However, if anyone has any questions, I'm sure Miss Valentine will be happy to answer."

Everyone left then, opting not to stay for questions, much less the balance of the board meeting. Most merely nodded at Jenny or smiled shyly as they went out, but the smiles and nods told her as much as any words they might have spoken that they approved of her and respected her.

Jenny decided to leave now, too. In spite of the positive turn of the evening, she still felt bruised from Simon having asked for her resignation. She'd had enough excitement. Let Luke and Steve hassle over the playground equipment. Simon would probably act more hardheaded than ever, now that he'd come out on the short end tonight.

But before she left, she wanted to thank Etta Mae, who was busy stacking the folding chairs in the storeroom with efficient slams and bangs.

"I want you to know how much I appreciate your support, Mrs. Coates," Jenny said. "I can't tell you how much it meant to me."

Etta Mae continued her chore as if there were no one in sight. Jenny waited patiently. Finally Etta Mae turned, her familiar scowl rigidly in place. She dusted her hands on her apron with a few brisk swipes.

"Now you listen here, young woman. Just because I gave Simon Flint what for, don't let it go to your head. I keep my eyes peeled around here, and don't you forget it." She slammed the closet doors shut and stalked back into the schoolroom.

Jenny hid a smile. She was discovering that other things stood tall around here besides the trees.

As she walked home, a thin fog gathered secretly over the forest. A crescent moon sliced the sky, its light softened by the gauze veil. She looked up at the redwood tops piercing the mist. "The first to touch the rosy beams of morning...the last to bid the sun good-night," the great naturalist, John Muir, had said about the trees. What a lovely night, Jenny thought.

When she reached her cottage, she was surprised to see a car parked in the shadows.

"Hi," a familiar voice called. The girl sat so quietly on the front steps that Jenny had to look twice to verify that Corrie Coates was her visitor.

"Come on in and I'll make some tea. You look as if you could use some," Jenny said, puzzled at the girl's subdued manner.

Corrie rose and stretched. "I could use something stronger, if you want the truth, but I know I won't get it in this house of virtue."

"Oh, my, aren't we caustic tonight! You wouldn't be wanting to unload something, would you?" They went into the kitchen. Jenny put a teakettle on the stove and set out two mugs. "Don't tell me Dirk has been giving you problems?"

Corrie's frown deepened. "Hell, no. I can handle that yo-yo."

Jenny studied the frowning girl. "Would you believe that your grandmother just rescued me from a hatchet job by Simon Flint at the school board meeting?"

"No foolin'! Yeah, I got his invitation in the mail. What else is new? Old skinflint is always stirring up something."

"Etta Mae was fabulous, Corrie. Too bad you weren't there," Jenny said, and gave a quick account of the meeting.

Corrie grinned. "Good for her. I guess Granny takes after me after all. But Steve must have come to your rescue, too, and how about Mr. Wonderful from Otter Bay? Didn't he put in a word or two?"

"Didn't have to. Your grandmother said it all."

"And speaking of Mr. Beaumont, he's a guy you should go for, since you're so noble and won't go after Steve."

"Not interested. Besides, he's already attached."

"Who said? He's brought several different women to the bar where I work at the Inn."

"That's what I mean. Don't fancy becoming a member of the pack," Jenny snapped, and poured the tea.

"Hey, look who's on a high horse! I didn't mean he had a stable. I see him with that toothy city hostess once in a while, and one day he was in Jake's Bar with a real nifty dame. Not exactly the place where you'd take Miss Society Page if you ask me."

"Drink your tea. It's probably turned to battery acid by this time. And how's the apartment hunting coming?"

"Null and void if you have to know."

"Oh?"

"And you can save your five-minute lectures for someone else. My 'special friend' did *not* die, much less find a lady more fascinating than me. The offer still holds. In fact, the ante has been upped."

"What happened to the little red racer? Isn't that your old Chevy I saw parked outside?"

Corrie stared at the tea leaves in the bottom of her cup. "Hmm. Weird. The leaves say money. That's a laugh, considering."

"Considering you no longer have the red car?"

She shrugged. "Oh, that. I just decided the dues were getting a little high."

"Hmm. Wisdom from the mouth of babes."

"Oh, shut up," she said. "Listen, I've been chewing on something, and I want a straight answer, no strokes, no sweet talk."

"I think I can handle that."

Corrie toyed with her cup as an uncharacteristic shyness seemed to come over her. "Okay, I'll say it plain out. Were you kidding when you said I had a knack for, well, you know, interior decorating?" A momentary anxiety touched her expression, and for once her wide blue eyes were devoid of artifice.

"Corrie, believe me, I was never more serious. You have a natural gift. With some training, you can become a professional."

Corrie poured herself another cup of tea, and sipped it. It looked so strong that Jenny's tongue curled. "Mmm, perfect," Corrie said, and held the cup, her little finger curled out in an exaggerated pose, again the old Corrie. "Think of that. Corrine Coates, professional. Classy sound, don't you think?"

"Very classy."

"Well, see, recently one of my co-workers in Otter Bay asked me to help her fix up her bedroom, and the place turned out really nifty, if I do say. So I got to thinking. I found out that the Otter Bay city college offers some classes in interior decorating. But before I get into anything, I want to make certain I'm not off on a wild-goose chase."

"Heavens, no! I'll bet my eye teeth on it!" Jenny cried.

"Now wouldn't you look pretty without 'em. Don't go overboard. Maybe I'm just kidding myself."

"No way."

A wicked gleam shone in her eye. "Anyway, I always have an ace in the hole."

Jenny merely raised an eyebrow, refusing to comment.

Corrie's laugh rippled up an octave. "Hey, what happened? No lecture for little Corrie?"

"Little Corrie doesn't need one."

"Think you're smart, don't you? Okay, I confess. I've got no aces. I dumped that pack of cards."

"Good to hear it. Now tell me about your classes."

They chatted for a while longer, then Corrie drove home. Jenny washed the few dishes and put them away. She noticed that the tuna salad she'd made for dinner was still untouched in the refrigerator. She hadn't even missed the meal. The nourishment she'd received from both Etta Mae and Corrie tonight would last for a long time.

IT WAS THE FIRST Saturday in November. Jenny stepped out on her porch and felt the crispness of autumn. Gone were the Indian summer days of October, but the skies were still a brilliant blue, and the sun lay like honey on her face.

The big-leaf maple on the far side of the meadow had exchanged its summer uniform for a riot of red, orange and yellow, and a chipmunk gave her a saucy stare before it raced up a tree. Fat Cat wove circles around her feet, sniffing her ankles as if they exuded rich and exotic scents from mysterious places. Autumn was her favorite season. It always seemed so in tune with itself, so at one with the world in contrast to frenetic spring and blatant summer.

This afternoon there would be a community potluck dinner at the community center to celebrate Amos Bott's retirement. Amos had been the postman here for thirty years. Jenny had written a humorous skit and had worked with some teenagers to present it. She'd also made up some words to the tune of "For He's a Jolly Good Fellow" for a musical toast in which everyone would participate.

She adored Amos, with his shock of thick white hair and leprechaun grin. He kept her in fruits and vegetables from his garden and let her know that he thought she was "some punkins." She knew she would never win him over to this "modern educashun," but concerning that subject he always acted more bewildered than critical.

Jenny was going early today to help Amos's daughter, Mrs. Duncan, set the tables and decorate the hall. Her contribution was four pies—two each of pumpkin and lemon—which was a lot more than was expected for her share, but then a flatlander needed to go the second mile in Woodhaven, didn't she? Jenny stowed the pies in the pickup along with some orange and yellow gourds and the costumes she'd put together for members of the skit.

She's chosen a full-skirted yellow-checked cotton for herself, and decided to wear ballerina slippers, since there would be dancing later. Her newly washed hair refused to behave, so in exasperation she pulled it up into a ponytail and tied a yellow ribbon around it.

She parked at the school to use the copy machine to run off the words to the song for Amos, so everyone could join in the singing. As she went back to the truck, she stopped in dismay. A tire was flat. She knew how to change it, but she'd left the spare for repair at the local garage yesterday. She'd never be able to walk the two miles, juggling the pies and all her other paraphernalia. She raced back to use the school phone. Maybe she could reach Mrs. Duncan if she hadn't left yet. As she started to dial, she heard a car drive up. Maybe she was in luck after all. She glanced out the window. Luke! What was he doing here? She felt the familiar twinge at the sight of his dark head and wondered if she'd ever overcome it.

He carried a baseball bat in one hand and a large carton in the other. Good heavens! Had old Simon finally capitulated? Luke stopped in his tracks as he noticed the flat tire. He looked around as if to see where she was, then peered into the truck bed and saw the pies. Noting the eager way he leaned over to inhale their aroma, she wouldn't be surprised if he absconded with the lot of them.

For a moment Jenny considered remaining inside the school until he deposited the equipment in the adjacent storeroom, but promptly chided herself for the childish cop-out and met him as he came up the path. "Hello, Luke," she said, making the simple greeting courteous but not cordial.

"Hello, you look about sixteen," he said, giving her an avid inspection.

She shrugged, dismissing his appraisal. "Don't tell me that equipment is for us? Did Simon actually relent?" Steve had told her that Simon had walked out of the fracas at the meeting several weeks ago, vowing to turn in his resignation. Unfortunately he hadn't.

"Actually the board won't meet again until next week. But I don't think there'll be any problem. However, by the time we process all the damn red tape, the semester will be almost over."

"So who's the fairy godfather, as if I didn't know?"

He gave a deprecating gesture. "Just a soccer ball, a volleyball net and a replacement for your broken bat. I'm on my way to some friends in Mendocino, so I thought I'd drop off the stuff when—" He stopped abruptly.

"When I wasn't around," she filled in.

He flushed. "Well, Jenny, you do make it clear that I'm persona non grata. Did you know that you have a flat? I'll change it for you."

"Thanks, but I left the spare to be repaired yesterday at the gas station and forgot about it. The station's closed, but if you want to do your good deed for the day, you can drive me and my pies down to the clubhouse—that is, if you have the time."

"No problem," he said, and put her pies into the trunk of his car, inhaling their aroma with such a look of yearning that in other circumstances she would have given him one on the spot. They drove in silence over the rough, curving road. The constraint between them still fed the awkwardness. No matter what degree of surface naturalness she achieved, something always rubbed a raw place or evoked a memory she wanted to forget.

The huge log community center was situated in a meadow at the bottom of a canyon. Amos Botts had told her the building had been constructed by the conservation corps during the thirties. As it came into view, Jenny thought it could have been a scene for a picture postcard. Smoke curled from its chimney against the blue-green pines in the background. A river curved around one side, where a wide spot had been dammed for a swimming hole. Redwoods offered ample shade for the picnic area, although with today's brisk temperature, they would eat inside.

No other car had arrived, and the building was locked. "I guess I showed up too early," Jenny said. "I need to gather some greenery, so I'll tend to that until Mrs. Duncan arrives with the key."

They set her things on a bench on the porch. "Thanks again for the playground equipment, Luke. Very generous of you. The children will be delighted," she said, sounding more stiff and formal than she intended.

"I'll help you gather the greenery," he offered.

"You needn't bother. It won't take long."

"I'm not on any rigid schedule."

She shrugged. It had come down to being stuffy and rude or accepting his help. They started down the path leading from the back of the building. For a while they were like two people moving in pantomime. She pointed out the length of sword fern and bracken she wanted, and he silently broke the stems. Along the way they gathered colored leaves and cones.

Once their eyes met briefly as they paused to admire a flaming clump of poison oak, and they couldn't quite hide their recollection of her earlier mistake. His slow grin made him look so young that she felt tears stinging her eyes and she quickly glanced away.

She sped along the path, putting distance between them. But a minute later he called to her. "Hey, you up there ahead of me, what's your name?"

"I don't tell my name to strangers, sir," she replied in the same spirit, relieved that the silence between them had ended.

"There's a spot of sunlight on this mossy log. We could sit for a while and ponder the wonders of the forest."

They sat on the log and for a while fell easily into the familiar banter that had once been so much a part of their relationship. It fit like an old shoe and felt as comfortable.

He asked her if teaching was all she'd dreamed. She described some of her pupils, painting their individual pictures with swift brush marks of words, her enthusiasm bubbling over with the telling.

"Foolish question. I should have known," he said, and described his own excitement at his thriving business.

A little later they gathered their armloads of greenery and walked back to the clubhouse. This was the first civilized conversation they'd had since their breakup. It would have saved a lot of pain if they'd behaved like this all along, Jenny thought. So why wasn't she feeling relieved that they'd at last reached this state, instead of feeling this poignant emptiness?

Mrs. Duncan still hadn't arrived, and Jenny and Luke piled their greenery on the porch and sat down on a log overlooking the river. It flowed briskly through the rock dam that formed the swimming hole, then plunged down a gully and, laced in white, rushed down the canyon.

"You needn't wait any longer, Luke. Something must have happened to delay Mrs. Duncan."

"I know."

"So?"

"So why don't I get going? I don't know, Jenny. Maybe it's this persistent need I have to explain things to you, but nothing ever comes out right."

"I've pretty well figured things out for myself, so you needn't bother," she said. *Leave, Luke. We've finally reached a decent plateau, so don't spoil things.*

"But I'm certain you've never understood. Probably because we never talked it over, the way it all happened."

"True. I always thought it was odd that you didn't want my input. But don't worry about it."

"It was do damn hard to explain. My main concern was for you, for the family you always wanted."

"Sure, Luke, sure. I'll bet dear old Uncle Charles convinced you of that."

Luke stiffened. "He merely pointed out the scope of my job for the next ten years. It didn't take much figuring to see that I'd be a prize, A-1 absentee father. That's what I had as a boy, and I vowed I'd never do that to any kid, much less ask it of you."

She shook her head. "Oh, Luke. How you do delude yourself."

He picked up a pinecone and heaved it hard against a stump. "You're wrong, I tell you!"

"I don't think so. You have a passion for success, and I can go along with that as long as it isn't exclusive. I had a passion, too. All I wanted was a family of my own, the assurance that there would be lives adjoined to mine. I didn't think that was too much to ask."

"And that's what I want for you, too, Jenny, darling. Can't you see?" The endearment slipped out without his noticing. It hung like a chord over the rushing water.

"My, now noble and unselfish."

He winced as if she'd slapped him. "Well, whether you believe it or not, it's the truth. That's the reason I broke things off. Damn it, how could I decently ask you to wait ten years to start a family?''

Jenny couldn't believe his job was so all-consuming. People could manage their lives if they put their minds to it. He had time to squire around all those women, didn't he? "Maybe we each have tunnel vision, Luke, but I've never figured you for a coward. Somewhere along the line, you lost your nerve to live life on more than one plane."

Mrs. Duncan's pickup rattled down the grade and pulled up to the building. She hopped out of the car and hurried to unlock the door, nodding at the two of them. "Sorry I'm late. My husband went fishing early this morning and just got back with the car."

"I had problems too, a flat, but luckily Mr. Beaumont came along and gave me a ride."

They all carried the greenery and pies inside. Luke stood about awkwardly, and Jenny felt a glimmer of sympathy in spite of herself, seeing his miserable expression.

In a minute Mrs. Duncan went to her car for another load, and Luke said, "I wish we could have talked longer, Jenny. We barely got started."

"Barely started? True. That about sums us up from the very beginning. Maybe we're lucky. Anyway, we're sailing on different ships now, headed into different waters, so it's time to stop rehashing our feelings."

"Well, goodbye, then," he said, and his expression was filled with such longing that she wanted to put her hand on his forehead and smooth out the lines. Instead, she picked up one of her pies and handed it to him. "A small thanks for the equipment and the lift," she said, then turned to join Mrs. Duncan in setting the tables.

When she glanced up a few minutes later, he was gone. She chided herself for giving him the pie, then chided herself again for the grudging thought. She vowed she

wouldn't allow the past hour to get to her, and even though
she felt light-headed, she plunged into a frenzy of activi-
ty. She and Mrs. Duncan set and decorated the tables with
the ferns and cones, and Jenny filled a basket with pome-
granates, dried corn and gourds, creating a centerpiece on
the buffet table.

An hour later families began to arrive, and the air was
filled with the fragrance of fried chicken, mingled with
other smells from the bountiful assortment of food for the
potluck dinner. Jenny worked along with the other
women, slicing homemade bread, setting out jellies, jams
and butter and filling pitchers with milk and juice. As the
women worked together, gossip proliferated like the food
on the table and was as savory. Considering the openness
with which they aired Dirk's latest conquest, an Otter Bay
nurse, as well as the latest affairs of other local stallions,
Jenny figured they were beginning to accept her.

The men sat and talked or pitched horseshoes. Then a
baseball game with the teenage boys and girls got started,
and immediately the rest of the crowd formed a rooting
section. The young fry chased one another around the
clubhouse, and some skipped rocks in the swimming hole,
but the water was too cold for swimming.

Just as everyone lined up to fill his plate at the buffet,
Simon Flint and his family arrived. Earl and his two
younger sisters carried small platters of corn bread and a
bowl of pickled beets. They added their offerings to the
buffet table and fell in line.

Jenny took in Simon's cold gray eyes and tight-lipped
mouth, then watched his colorless wife who followed doc-
ilely several paces behind and couldn't help the irreverent
thought that the Flint children must have arrived via immaculate conception. She greeted them. He merely nod-

ded, without changing his expression, and his wife followed suit like a shadow.

The bounty and variety of the food surpassed anything Jenny had ever experienced. Later when desserts were served, folks were so extravagant in their praise of her pies that she wondered if they thought it was some kind of miracle that a teacher could wield a rolling pin.

The affair took on a jolly mood as the focus turned to Amos's retirement. The skit had everyone howling with laughter, and Amos beamed as Jenny directed everyone in the song she'd written. They were on the last verse when Earl Flint burst into the room. "Mama," he cried, "Mattie Lou fell into the swimming hole and we can't find her!"

CHAPTER THIRTEEN

PANDEMONIUM EXPLODED as people shoved their chairs back and pushed through the double doors. Jenny scooted out the exit through the kitchen and reached the swimming hole ahead of the crowd. There was no sign of the child in the water, which was now clouded and calm in the deep shadows.

Without hesitation she tore off her dress, kicked off her shoes and dived in. The shock of the cold water almost paralyzed her, but she was a strong swimmer and had acted as a lifeguard one summer at a public pool. Kicking hard at the confining folds of her clothing, she circled the bottom. Then in the inky green depth she saw Mattie Lou floating faceup, like a tiny mermaid, a long strand of her pale blond hair tangled in the branch of a fallen tree. It was only seconds, but it seemed like minutes as she loosened the four-year-old's hair and brought her to the surface, ashen and unconscious.

She laid the child on the grass, checked her mouth for foreign matter, and at once started mouth-to-mouth resuscitation, praying that it wasn't too late. Mattie Lou's mother screamed and was quickly hushed as the crowd moved in around them.

Jenny had taken a course in the technique several years ago, but she'd never had occasion to use it. Now she probed her memory for the procedure. Miraculously it came: with a child, blow shallow breaths every three seconds. Keep one hand under the neck, partially tilt the head back and pinch the nostrils shut.

Nearby, the child's mother moaned like a wounded animal. Relentlessly counting and blowing, counting and blowing, Jenny turned into a machine. She felt for a neck pulse between breaths and was almost certain there was a faint flutter. Now if only the child would start breathing. Although the crowd was completely silent, she felt their apprehension tighten around her like a tourniquet. She kept the pace until she felt her own lungs would burst, but still the child showed no life. Murmurs rose and people became restless. "Too late, too late." The words drifted like a poison cloud. The child's mother whimpered continually.

Suddenly Jenny felt a spasm in Mattie Lou's chest, then a gasp and the child's eyes flickered open. "Mama!" she cried weakly, and Mrs. Flint rushed to gather the little girl in her arms. Simon reached for his daughter's foot and massaged it with vigor as if frantic to do something to make up for his lack of action in the tense drama. The crowd broke into cheers, embarrassing Jenny with their praise, while the Flints took Mattie Lou inside the hall.

Jenny rose and swayed dizzily. Soaked and suddenly aware of her clinging, wet clothing, she asked Mrs. Duncan to drive her home to change. By the time they reached her cottage, she felt so ill that all she wanted to do was take a hot shower and crawl into bed. There would be dancing until late night, but the day had wrung out any desire for levity. "Don't wait," she said to Mrs. Duncan. "I won't be going back. I think I'm having a delayed reaction."

"Small wonder," Mrs. Duncan said, and insisted on making some hot tea and bringing a cup to Jenny. "You were wonderful the way you rescued little Mattie Lou, but

I can't believe those Flints! Not one word of recognition that you saved their child's life!''

Jenny hadn't noticed. She slid gratefully into bed. "What difference does it make? Mattie Lou is safe."

By morning Jenny knew her light-headedness had been more than just a reaction to the stress of the previous day. She'd caught some bug that kept her down with a fever and a cough during the rest of the weekend. Somehow the word must have gotten around because, to her amazement, people called and brought things from their gardens and so many baked goods that her refrigerator was filled to bursting.

When she arrived at school on Monday, pale and pounds lighter, Earl Flint set a canned ham on her desk.

"Mama said to tell you it's from the Flint family," he said expansively, clearly impressed with the magnificence of the gift. Jenny thanked him and said she would save it for some special occasion such as Christmas dinner.

That evening as Etta Mae swept the room, she noted the ham on a shelf in the coatroom. "Where'd that come from? Not one of the kids?"

"It's from the Flints."

"Well, don't that beat all!" Etta Mae exclaimed. "A historic event if I ever saw one. Simon 'Pinchy' Flint never donated nothin' to nobody. Maybe we ought to write it up and get it in the congressional record."

But Jenny knew the gift was every bit as exceptional as Earl had believed it to be. A ten-pound ham made up for a lot of talk, didn't it? Especially from a "pinchy" man who found kind words so hard to come by.

THE NOVEMBER SCHOOL board meeting had been changed to a Saturday that month in order to accommodate Steve and another member who couldn't make the usual Friday evening. Jenny decided that she would invite the members to her house for dinner, since she would have plenty of time to prepare it. All had accepted. Except for Simon, she believed the group was now one hundred percent behind her, and they'd been so solicitous after the near-drowning that she wanted to do something to show her appreciation.

She planned the meal with attention to the likes and dislikes of everyone she knew about in the group, giving no consideration to Luke. He liked everything. In abundance. Lemon pie for certain would be the dessert, considering the raves she'd had at Amos Botts's party.

Saturday evening arrived at last, and everything was ready. A fire crackled in the fireplace and the fragrance from the beef rouladen filled the cottage. She had wanted to use yellow candles to match her centerpiece of dahlias, but didn't want to risk any suspicion that she was putting on airs. Candles in these parts were stubby, utilitarian objects reserved for when the electricity failed.

It had rained hard all week, and even now it was still pouring. School had gone on as usual, despite the difficulty in maneuvering along the muddy roads. There hadn't been a single absence. And trucks carrying lumber from Steve's mill still rolled down the hill on their way to the city as usual. She observed that it would be a rare day in Woodhaven for life to be curtailed by anything as incidental as the weather.

Jenny had set the dinner for six o'clock, which should give ample time to eat before the meeting. By six-thirty, when not a single guest had arrived, she felt more than a little apprehensive and went through endless excuses from the unlikely prospect that the group had decided to boycott her, to the possibility that there had been an accident. It was dark now, and thunder rolled only seconds after the jagged streaks of lightning pierced the sky. Ordinarily lightning was a forest's most dangerous pyromaniac, starting rogue fires indiscriminately. But with all the rain, there was no danger now.

She stood at the window, peering through the dark, willing the lights from a car to show. The lane to her cottage was muddy, but not any more so than the main road. The group wouldn't be put off on that account. She went to telephone Steve, but her phone was out of order. She hadn't thought of that possibility. Maybe the line to the school was still intact. She would try from there.

She put on her raincoat and boots, grabbed a flashlight and got into her pickup. She hadn't been outside all day, and saw that the storm was far worse than she'd realized. The wind wailed off the sea. Landbound at last with its burden of moisture, the gale eddied around her cottage and whipped the treetops in drunken salvos.

The condition of the lane had deteriorated so much that she wondered if the car would bog down before she reached the school. The headlights' thin yellow beams penetrated the driving rain for scarcely a foot so that she had to creep along, praying she wouldn't stray off the edge of the road. Too often she had to cling hard to the steering wheel when she felt the wheels skid out of control. As she crossed the narrow bridge, her alarm escalated even more when she saw the water roaring fiercely below almost overlapping the bank.

At last she pulled into the gravel parking area by the school. If she hadn't known the way so well, she doubted she could have found it. She leaned her head on the steering wheel to relieve the tension, realizing she'd tightened every muscle.

Battling the wind, she followed the beam of her flashlight up the path to the school. Moments later she unlocked the door and flicked the light switch. Nothing. In a storm such as this, the electricity could be off for hours, even days. She reached for the telephone, certain before she lifted the receiver that it, too, would be dead. Obviously there would be no meeting tonight, much less a dinner.

Now all she could think about was getting back inside her warm cottage. Staggering back to her car, she held her balance with difficulty against the angry wind. Again she steered the car with infinite caution and suddenly braked hard, skidding within inches of the creek bank. The bridge was gone. A part of it lay upended in the swirling current. Her heart pounded at the narrow escape.

There was no way to get back to her cottage except on the old logging road from Steve's mill, which wound through the forest to her cottage. After spending endless minutes trying to turn around on the narrow lane, she at last got to the main road and headed toward the Douglas mill.

Not another car braved this night. She felt as if she no longer controlled the pickup as wind and rain relentlessly whipped her all over the road. At times she stopped, completely blinded. Never had she experienced such darkness. Even though bitter cold penetrated her old pickup, her hands were slippery with perspiration. The mile drive to the mill took almost an hour.

At last she dipped down the hill that overlooked the mill site. She parked by the mill office and slogged through the mud toward the spillway, where she saw a swarm of lanterns moving slowly, like indolent fireflies. Men were piling sandbags to prevent the dam from breaking, working in a frenzied contest against the elements. If Steve's dam broke, every log in the pond would plunge into the river and be washed out to sea.

A few minutes later Steve, his raincoat flipping like some great night bird, walked over to her. "My God, Jenny! What are you doing here?"

She explained her predicament. "I'll have to use the old logging road."

"Well, have a care. The wind is getting worse, so watch out for widow makers. Sorry about your dinner." He gestured toward the hard-working crew. "I shanghaied most of your guests to help me out. The poor guys have been at it since late afternoon without a bite of food."

"I could make some coffee. You have a gas stove, right?"

"That would be a godsend. Take my lantern. There are plenty here." He handed her the light and hiked back to join the workers.

Jenny scanned the group, trying to see if Luke were among them, but even though the rain had let up, it was too dark to distinguish anyone. He'd probably heeded the weather report and stayed sensibly in Otter Bay. He might have called, but she had no idea how long her phone had been out of order. She hadn't used it all day.

In Steve's kitchen she started the coffee and found two thermos bottles to hold it. In a cupboard she selected several tins of corned beef and took bread from the freezer. While the coffee perked, she made a couple of dozen sandwiches, wrapped them in paper napkins and set everything in a carton along with paper cups and carried it all to an upturned cable spool not far from the workers.

Steve joined her and scanned the sky, his face haggard in the lamplight. "It's nip and tuck. If the rain continues to let up, we have a chance. Otherwise . . ." he shrugged in a gesture of despair. The unspoken reality was that to lose his log harvest at this point would be too great a loss to recover from. He poked inside the carton. "You're a wonder!"

Jenny went from man to man, passing out the sandwiches and coffee. She almost missed the last fellow, who was working below the dam shoring up a weak spot. He paused to accept the coffee and kept his fingers around the cup for a few moments to glean warmth for his hands. "Thanks," he muttered in a voice husky with exhaustion. She glanced up sharply at the unexpected amenity. The other man had been too weary to do more than nod.

She was positive the hooded figure was Luke, but the heavy raincoats provided by the mill had the effect of making the men look like a dozen clones. As she handed him the sandwiches, his icy hand brushed hers. She wanted to take it between hers and rub some warmth into it, but she refrained.

He wolfed down the sandwiches, then picked up another sandbag and threw it into the levy. Jenny went on with her task. It was Luke all right. She couldn't mistake the determined way he threw that sandbag, as if the entire operation depended on his accuracy. *Oh, Luke. Always so serious.* She drew an arm across her eyes to wipe away a sudden blur.

After tidying Steve's kitchen, Jenny got into her pickup. Cautious now, she crawled past Steve's office. The turnoff to the abandoned logging road that cut through the forest wasn't more than a hundred yards. The rain had stopped, but the wind had risen to gale proportions. She'd barely passed the cookshack when she felt the car sink into the mud, at least to the hubcaps. She got out to check. It only took a glance to see that the situation was hopeless.

Wind buffeted her back and forth, as if she were a blade of grass. Suddenly fear ballooned. She'd forgotten all about the open fire she'd left in her fireplace, thinking she'd return in a few minutes. Reverse drafts could fling the fire into the room, couldn't they? Alarm tore at her lungs as she tried to run, sinking ankle-deep into ooze with each step.

Once she entered the forest, she sped along the mud-free, spongy path. It was the route Robbie took when he visited her or walked to the school. She knew the shortcut well, had walked it many times.

But now the familiar path seemed strange. Wind whistled through the trees in eerie moans and high-pitched wails, almost human in their sounds. Her eyes swept the ceiling of trees continually, particularly around the sugar pine stumps that had been logged out years ago. Branches, called widow makers, often got hung up on other trees during the logging, to be swept down on unsuspecting persons much later. It was a common cause of accidents in the woods.

In a few minutes the hiss of rushing water filled her ears, and she came upon the creek she ordinarily crossed with ease, merely stepping from rock to rock. Now she stared, appalled at the raging torrent. It was hard to believe that this little creek that meandered so casually through the woods could turn into this savage monster. But, of course, it was this very creek, joined with another tributary, that had torn out the bridge earlier tonight.

It looked as if she would have to go back and beg shelter from Steve. The thought tempted her. Windblown and wet in her inadequate rainwear, she turned to start back, then remembered the fire in the fireplace. She'd laid it with a long-lasting madrone log from the pile Amos had delivered.

She swept the flashlight along the creek and estimated that it was almost thigh-high. The depth ordinarily would pose no problem, but the swiftness of the water would prove hazardous. She walked a little way into the woods, searching for something to use as a walking stick, and found a moss-covered picket that had once been part of the fence that bordered these woods.

As she tested the depth with one foot, water poured into her boot. She removed both of them, and tossed them with her purse to the other side of the creek. Again she carefully planted a foot and stabilized herself with the picket, praying she could keep her balance in the turbulent water. She estimated that three or four strides would get her across.

With each step she sought a firm foothold before she put any weight on it. Two steps, three, she was going to make it. Suddenly a swirling back current caused her to stumble. She dropped her flashlight but planted her feet just in time to keep from falling. At once she winced as her right foot sank into a tangle of roots. She tried to pull her foot back, but couldn't budge it. Captive in the sudden dark, Jenny knew the terror little Mattie Lou must have experienced in the swimming hole.

Don't lose your head! A foot can wriggle and twist out of a clump of roots. But it wasn't going to be easy. Bracing herself against the strong current, trying to pull her foot free and still keeping her balance, proved impossible. A feeling of panic stole into every bone in her body. Even if she could stand anchored in the creek all night, which was next to impossible, how long would it take before someone missed her and started a search?

Oh, for a pocketknife! All she had was a nail file, but it was in the purse she'd thrown across the creek with her boots. How long had she been in the creek? Minutes, hours? She no longer had any sense of time. She moved her foot in every position that she could manage, but it seemed to be lodged in a slipknot, which tightened every time she lifted it.

Who would hear if she called out? Both the distance and the wind would defeat her. Her feet and legs grew numb. She seemed to float. Eventually fatigue and fear gave way to a kind of euphoria. Everything would be all right. Why hadn't she figured it out before? The creek passed her cottage, didn't it? All she had to do was to lie back in the water and allow it to carry her home.

CHAPTER FOURTEEN

IT WAS MIDNIGHT when Steve finally called a halt to the sandbagging. Luke joined the remaining half-dozen men who had stuck it out to this point. "The river crested an hour ago. The storm is over," Steve said, relief weighting his tone more than his exhaustion. "You guys come up to the cabin, and I'll rustle up some bacon and eggs."

"Thanks," Luke said, "but I'd better head back to Otter Bay if I can get through. It's pretty late."

"Well, okay, but if any trees are down across the road, come back. You're welcome to bunk here."

Luke thanked him and hiked over to the cookshack, which had the only gravel parking area, and started to get into his car. Then he spotted Jenny's pickup on the road below. She was still here? He knew that it was she who had brought him the sandwiches and coffee. It was exactly the kind of thing Jenny would do. He'd wanted to hear her voice, to exchange a few words, but exhaustion had kept him silent. Where was she now?

He looked up the hill to Steve's cabin, but refused to examine the possibility that she was asleep in his bed. He walked down to the pickup and examined it. It would take some doing to get it out of that muck. He dug his flashlight out of his pocket and flashed it down the road. Boot prints still left murky depressions, and he saw that Jenny must have taken a road through the forest.

Crazy girl. Someone would have driven her home. Why hadn't she asked for help? As if he didn't know. Misgivings attacked him like a swarm of mosquitoes. He didn't like the thought of her going through this pitch-black forest alone. Did she even have a flashlight? He plowed along the muddy road, his back and arms aching after the long hours of swinging the sandbags. Anxiety reached a fever pitch by the time he reached the forest path, and so many *what ifs* beat at him that he knew he wouldn't rest until he determined that she was safe in her cottage.

Miraculously he got his second wind and sped along the path through the trees. Now he understood Jenny's reasoning. This was a far easier way to walk or ride than the main road. He slowed his pace and willed the knot in his chest to go away.

Then he stopped short at the creek. It rushed swiftly, boiling and swirling over half-submerged rocks and tree stumps. By the look of flattened ferns at its edge, it must have crested much higher not too long ago. There was no way Jenny could have crossed it. Surely she'd turned back.

He swung his flashlight around, and then he saw the still figure lying facedown on the far side of the bank, one foot still in the water. Jenny? Drowned!

He plunged into the turbulence, crossing at an angle with the current, battling to hold his balance with every step. Gaining a foothold at last, he reached the far side and sloshed through the fern and underbrush to the prone form.

"Jenny!" he cried with a sob. His hand shook as he felt for the pulse at the base of her throat. Nothing. He held her wrist, trying not to push too hard, saying her name over and over. Was that a faint flutter? He was certain of it. Then he saw her ankle, raw and bleeding and guessed what had happened.

She was ice-cold, and who knew how much blood she'd lost! He threw off his raincoat and took off his heavy jacket, wrapping her in it, then put on his raincoat again, picked her up and carried her. "Live, Jenny, live!" he said with each step until it became a litany. A hundred yards more and he came to the meadow with her cottage near the edge, now a dark clump in the forest shadows.

For once he gave thanks that she'd left her door open as he elbowed his way in. The cabin was warm; several embers still flickered in the fireplace. He set Jenny down on the rug nearby and threw on some kindling and another log. It flamed at once.

In a closet he found a blanket. Looking at her soaked clothing, he hesitated only a moment, then pulled off her sweater, her dress and her torn, ragged stockings.

He wrapped her in the blanket and placed her on the throw rug in front of the fire. He searched the cupboards hoping, but not expecting, to find some brandy. Finally he spotted an unopened bottle of wine on the festive table. Jenny's dinner party! He hadn't thought of it once during the frantic hours at the dam. How disappointed she must have been!

He opened the wine, poured himself a glass and one for Jenny when she awakened, then sat down on the rug beside her, holding her icy hands in both of his, praying that she'd soon regain consciousness. Relentlessly he blocked out the knowledge that people could die of shock.

He didn't know how much later it was when she began to shiver in violent spasms. He picked her up and cradled her in his arms, rocking her back and forth. "It's okay," he said. "You're okay."

She opened her eyes and looked at him without recognition, then pulled the blanket to her chin. "I'm so cold," she said.

"No wonder. If you have to romp in the creek, the least you could do is wear a wet suit."

She sat up with a start. "The creek! Luke, what are you doing here?" Awareness returned with a rush, and she felt for her foot and winced as she touched the wound. "What happened? The last I remember I was caught fast by some roots when I tried to wade across the rushing water."

"Well, you obviously managed to extricate yourself." He explained how he happened to look for her. "I found you unconscious on the bank. Now we'd better take care of your ankle," he said, his voice husky at the thought of what could have happened if he hadn't gone after her.

He handed her the glass of wine and found some first-aid cream and bandages in the medicine cabinet. He wondered what she was thinking as she silently noted her state of undress. As Luke carefully bandaged her foot, something so powerful willed him to take her in his arms and toss his vows to the winds that he knew he had to leave as soon as it was decently possible. "I'm going to put you to bed now. If you think you'll be all right, I'd better leave. I left my car at the mill."

"The roads may be impassable. Sleep on the sofa if you like."

"And give Woodhaven more fodder for scandal? Before I got halfway down the hill, it would be all over town that I spent the night in the schoolteacher's cottage."

"I suppose you're right, but can you get back?"

"I made it across the creek, didn't I? It'll be easier now that the storm's over."

He picked her up, carried her into the small bedroom and tucked her in. She pulled the blanket up around her shoulders and stiffened as if to still the shivering. He found an afghan and gathered it around her, but the spasms persisted.

"Sorry," she murmured. "I don't know what's the matter with me. I feel as if I'm going to be cold forever." She closed her eyes, and he grew apprehensive at her pallor.

He kicked off his shoes and crawled in beside her, pulling her against him, assuring himself that his intent was solely to warm her. For a moment her body went rigid, then abruptly relaxed. She nestled close as if to dismiss all restraint. Gradually she seemed to absorb his warmth and finally stopped shaking.

"Oh, my darling," he whispered. "I was afraid I'd lost you." He kissed her deeply, reveling in her response as she opened her lips to him. He knew he should leave, but could find no exit. Too late. She had to be the strong one. God knows he couldn't be. "My dearest Jenny, how could I let you go when I love you so?"

"Oh, Luke, what happened to us?" she asked, and kept her arms around his neck even as he shed his clothes and slipped off the few that remained of hers. They wrapped their limbs around each other, and he relished the wonderful feel of flesh against silken flesh, remembering.

He saw them in their Berkeley apartment. He could even see the outline of the picture of the sailboat above their bed. Memories surged around him, the recollection of fulfillment given and received, the sense of joy, of love, of completeness.

He gathered her into his arms and pulled her close, her cool softness melting against him. Their bodies met in an embrace so exquisite that it seemed as if they were the only two people alive in the world. "My dearest love, how I've missed you, how I've wanted you! My life has been hell without you," he said.

She studied his shadowed face. Had she heard him correctly, or did she hear only the words she was desperate to hear? "What do you mean?"

"That I love you. I've never stopped loving you."

"Again. Say that again," she said, and he repeated it. The words held truth, didn't they? And there was no mistaking the tenderness in the way he held her, comforted her, sheltered her. This was the Luke she knew, the Luke she loved. Her eyes glistened with tears and her mouth trembled as she tried to form an answer. He touched her cheek.

"What are you trying to say, my darling?"

That I need you, Luke, that I want you as you were before. "That I love you," she said.

"Oh, Jenny." He pulled her to him again, covering her hair with kisses, her face and then her mouth. Their lips moved softly against each other, saying tender things, making wordless love sounds. He felt both invitation and acceptance in her kiss. Happiness filled him to bursting.

He moved his hands over her soft curves and she responded, moving hers over the hard outlines of his body. Now his lips relentlessly followed the paths his fingers had prepared, reverently exploring her shoulders, her back, the crescent of her hip and all the tender, secret places, then with infinite delicacy, her breasts. She clung to him, seeming to hover in breathless expectancy. "Yes," she whispered. "Oh, yes." The past savage months dwindled and died, and they returned to each other again.

AFTERWARD THEY LAY with limbs entwined, allowing their hearts time to beat normally again. "Oh, Jenny, the months we've lost," Luke said finally. "What happened to us?"

"Not *us*, Luke. I never changed."

"Neither did I. I love you more than ever."

She pulled out of his arms and leaned on an elbow in order to scan his expression. "How can that be?"

"Look, I know how much having a family life meant to you, especially since you never had one. When I took this job, it was made very plain to me that I would have to give my whole life to it for at least ten years, which would preclude any hopes for the large family you longed for."

"Lots of men have demanding jobs and a wife and children."

"Yes, and I was a child of that kind of family. My dad was never home. I can't begin to tell you the hurt he caused my mother and us kids."

"I still say that if people love each other enough, they can manage. Anyway, if that's the way you feel, there are alternatives."

"What alternatives? There's no other job I could have gotten right out of college that would enable me to pay off my father's debts as well as my education expenses so soon, plus offering me a fantastic future."

"I see. So you're willing to give up all of that now?"

His eyes widened in apparent incredulity, and he moved away from her. "Do what?"

"You heard me."

"How can I? I have financial commitments as well as an obligation to my uncle. I want us to get back together more than anything in this world. But, Jenny, are you willing to accept the hand that fate dealt us?"

Jenny couldn't believe what she was hearing. More than anything in this world? Hardly. So he had obligations and commitments, but they were all to someone else. She'd heard a lot of loving words tonight. Obviously they hadn't meant a thing. They were merely the requisite sweet talk for the situation. "I see," she said, her anger as cold as the freezing chill that enveloped her. "You've made your priorities quite clear. For a little while tonight I was convinced that you truly loved me. But you haven't changed at all."

"Jenny, listen, you don't understand," he said frantically, and tried to reach for her hand.

She drew away and sat up, pulling the covers up to her chin to hide her nakedness, feeling herself drown in humiliation. *Can't I ever learn?* she silently cried, and felt her heart breaking. "I understand all too well. Leave now, Luke. I never want to see you again."

CHAPTER FIFTEEN

FOR THE NEXT FEW WEEKS Luke worked until midnight every night and accepted a three-week stint at the college to give an adult evening seminar on business, although he couldn't afford the time. He even let Stacy talk him into taking her to a cocktail party, *if* he got home from a San Francisco meeting in time. An evening with the nonstop-talking Stacy ought to keep his mind in neutral. Nothing else had worked. Jenny's accusing blue eyes haunted every minute of his days.

His rational self told him that he'd lost Jenny forever. Relentlessly he'd examined his goals, his work, his relationships with those around him and the direction his life was taking. No matter how he questioned each facet, the answer came out the same. It was as if he'd known all along and had deliberately worn blinders.

Every word that Jenny had spoken was true. She'd obviously lost all respect for him. Maybe he should honor her request and stay out of her life. Well, he would do that for the time being, but there had to be a way to redeem himself, and hopefully to win her back. It would take time, and perhaps he was even too late, but that wouldn't prevent him from trying.

Impatiently he polished his shoes, with one eye on the clock.

"I'll call you at six. If there's no answer, I'll go on without you," Stacy had said. "But try hard, Luke. I'm counting on you.'' She had a knack for building fences around him.

He despised cocktail parties with people he didn't know. He'd been softheaded to allow any chance of going tonight. A friend of Stacy's was introducing some new artist here in town to a, quote, ''handpicked group.'' Any excuse for a party. There would be the same people, the same boring conversation, the same overladen buffet of finger food.

He was going to have to do something about Stacy. There was no way he could imagine her in a serious relationship, but she had made it quite obvious of late, without putting it into words, that the matter had certainly occurred to her.

She managed her job and her life with admirable expertise, which was okay with him if she'd only stop trying to use her skills on him. She bought two tickets to everything that came to town and took it for granted he would take her.

Charles sang her praises often. ''I'd like to hire her away from this burg. She'd be a real asset to Beaumont Business Services. She's career-oriented. None of this dropping out to have babies. On top of that she's very attractive.''

Attractive? Yes, except that her perennial smile often got to Luke. Life wasn't continually so full of sunshine.

He pictured marriage to Stacy. In their brief acquaintance, she hadn't discussed it. Yet. He imagined any such conversation would be something like analyzing the Dow Jones averages. He didn't believe she would demand true emotional involvement as he knew it, maybe not even fidelity. Sex, yes, when she preferred it. What was important to Stacy was a man with the right job, the right social connections, who would be the right escort for the endless functions she considered a necessary part of her life.

Chemistry wasn't important in a relationship, Charles had told him. There was none of that between him and Stacy as far as he was concerned, and he suspected none on her part, either. Stacy would think exactly like Charles. Outward appearances, upward mobility, knowing the difference between a fine chardonnay and a common house wine were the criteria she sought in a man. If it weren't for their age difference, Charles and Stacy would be eminently suited to each other.

Well, neither Charles's parade of young women nor the willing Stacy ended his preoccupation with Jenny. There had to be some way to let go, but he hadn't found it yet. The kind of love he felt for Jenny, maybe always would feel, was dismissed by Charles as sheer sentimentality, a mere indulgence.

Luke shuddered, wondering if he actually fitted the mold into which Charles and Stacy sought to cast him. He slammed a fist on the table, making the telephone teeter. Here he was getting ready to jump to Stacy's command on cue and attend an affair for which he didn't have the time much less the slightest interest.

He would far rather spend any free time he snatched from his packed agenda with Eric Johansen. The old timber baron had become a good friend. Although he was worth millions, he lived up in the hills in a rambling log cabin above Woodhaven. He still dressed in khaki pants, plaid flannel shirts, logger's boots and a billed cap of indistinguishable color that he'd probably had for years. He wore the seasons of his life on his deeply tanned face, but his gray eyes were clear and youthful. Luke had never known a person who was as genuine and upfront. Except Jenny.

"Drop by soon, young feller," Johansen had said a few days ago when Luke had run into him at a local coffee shop. "Just made me a batch of applejack. Better'n anything you can get in the stores. Come on over and chew the fat and we'll test 'er out."

The telephone rang at six o'clock sharp, precisely as Stacy had promised. He reached for the receiver, then stopped midway and allowed the rings to echo in the silence, staining the air like streaks of black ink. He walked to his car with a light step, got inside, turned the key and took the road that led into the hills where Eric Johansen's cabin was located.

IT WAS THE LAST DAY of school before the two weeks of Christmas holidays. Joel and Beth had asked Jenny to spend Christmas with them, but she hadn't made up her mind about that yet. It was essentially a family time, and although her friends had enough love and hospitality for twice their numbers, she felt reticent about intruding.

Meanwhile, she tried to dismiss former dreams of the Christmas Luke and Jenny Beaumont would celebrate in their first home. She could see the twinkling lights on the tree they'd decorate together, the fat socks she'd knitted, hanging from the mantel. The house would be filled with the delectable aroma of all the goodies she'd baked to share with their friends during the holidays.

She banished the images and concentrated on getting dressed for the short hike to school. Walking had a way of recharging her batteries, and of late they seemed drained most of the time. A cold wintry light poured over the meadow this morning. Everything looked unnatural, the brown grass in the field laid low by recent storms, the log under the sugar pine where she often sat to read looked water-soaked, black and uninviting. Above, there seemed too much gray sky. It made her feel dull and insignificant.

The storm that had wreaked havoc weeks ago still raged inside her. The emotional assault of that night with Luke had been horrendous and lasting. She was the world's most gullible fool. She might have been forgiven once for trusting this man, for overlooking all the signals that were present, but twice! Well, there were reasons, weren't there? She had almost drowned and was out of her head with cold and shock. Rubbish! She knew exactly what was happening, and she'd done nothing, nothing to stop it.

For a few brief moments she'd believed Luke's tender talk, believed that he truly loved her, that he longed to try for new beginnings. Her joy had overflowed at being loved and cherished again, joy so overwhelming that it crowded out any doubts. He'd turned back into her caring Luke.

But, no. If he truly loved her, he'd drop Beaumont Business Services like a hot potato. It wasn't the only job in the world. So what if he took a lesser salary? They both knew how to economize. That tired old excuse for an absentee father was some line. He hadn't meant a word he'd said. Momentary lust had prompted the loving talk. All the ingredients had been present in the intimate situation.

As for herself, she had to admit that the depth of love she felt for Luke hadn't ended with the slash of the surgeon's knife. Rather it would have to be exorcised slowly and with great pain. Now she would have to pick her way among the mine fields of the humiliating memories.

At least Luke had taken her parting words to heart. She'd neither seen nor heard from him since. She'd pleaded illness so that she didn't have to attend the December school board meeting. Later she'd learned that Luke hadn't shown up, either.

Now that the school board had finally acted on her request for playground equipment, the grounds were too muddy to use it. The rainiest weather in fifty years, Amos Botts had told her. Well, at least the rain was good for the big trees.

Her pickup was in the garage for repairs again, so she took her bag lunch, put on her boots and raincoat and headed into the raw morning. She would do her best to get into the spirit of the season. The moment she reached the school and saw the children spilling from the bus, she straightened her posture and climbed the steps with a brisk stride.

Today the children would finish the presents they'd made for their families—a community recipe book. Each child had brought several of his family's favorite recipes. Robbie, the only child in the room who could type, had proudly and laboriously typed all the recipes as another pupil read them to him. She had run them off on the copy machine yesterday. Today they would make the covers and put them together. Every family had contributed. Her persevering students had coaxed Amos Botts's secret formula for his famous applejack and even Etta Mae had given up the secret for her sinfully rich triple chocolate cake.

The children had cut and decorated the tree with handmade ornaments, and underneath she would add a small gift for each of them—jacks for the girls and a bag of marbles for the boys, along with a candy cane for all of them. There had been no drawing of names for the festivity. Many of the fathers who held jobs in the woods had been out of work the past month because of heavy rain, so Jenny knew an exchange of gifts would have been a burden.

During the lunch hour, if the weather permitted, she'd walk the class down to the center of the village and sing some carols for the benefit of any noontime shoppers. Her pupils could barely contain their excitement. Christmas had never been celebrated at Woodhaven school with such extravagance.

JENNY HAD HEARD about cabin fever, and three days after school let out, she could have written a treatise on it. Rain had kept her inside. Never had she felt at such loose ends. It was totally unlike her. It was her earnest opinion that there would never be enough time to explore all that life held for her, but now she had to push herself to finish knitting sweaters for Beth and Joel's three little boys. Fixing meals proved a bore and she had no appetite for the endless pasta dishes she concocted, even though she had handpicked the huge mushrooms for the sauce.

So when Steve phoned that afternoon, asking for her advice on how to furnish the studio he'd just completed for his estranged wife, she felt as if she'd been rescued from a sinking ship.

"I'll be right over. If Corrie happens to be around, I'll bring her along. She's full of good ideas," she said with the most enthusiasm she'd felt in days.

A call to Etta Mae found Corrie there, and Jenny picked her up on the way to Steve's place. "I'll give you just one hour of my valuable time," Corrie said. "I came up to Granny's to avoid such interruptions."

"More likely to be pampered and dine upon Granny's good cooking."

"Oh, sure, some of that, too, but I have to write a paper on—would you believe?—the symbolism of a whale."

"On what?"

"Moby Dick, of course," she said with a superior lift of an eyebrow.

"I didn't realize you were taking English."

"Gotta clean up my language if I'm going to be a professional."

"So did you like the book?"

"Sure did, but it wasn't anything like *Hollywood Wives*. These books kinda remind me of the opera a guy once took me to. It takes forever for anything to happen and they can sing a twenty-five-minute aria describing a dandelion gone to seed. But let me tell you, there's plenty of meat along the way."

"You're going to do okay," Jenny said as they pulled into Steve's driveway. Etta Mae was ecstatic at Corrie's turnaround, proudly telling everyone she had a granddaughter "who was going to college!"

Steve met them, and they walked together to the adjacent studio. There had been a lot of conjecture in Woodhaven concerning the building. Steve merely mentioned that it was to be a getaway place for an important person from the city. Because he was so closemouthed about it, the rumors skyrocketed. A TV personality? No, a painter. More likely a screenwriter who wanted to soak in rural atmosphere for a movie. Maybe there would be a lot of parts for extras. The situation proved better than a steak with all the fancy side dishes for the local folks to chew on during the recent gloomy weather. Only Jenny knew the true hopes that were pinned on the place.

The open-beam ceilings made the studio look a lot more spacious than it appeared on the plans. Jenny noticed that a divider at one end of the room partitioned off a small area that had plumbing for a token kitchen. There was a bathroom and a cleverly concealed pullout bed, as well. Steve had hedged his hopes. If the building couldn't be put to the use for which it was intended, it could easily be turned into a studio apartment to be rented out. Jenny felt a poignant empathy for his hopes and dreams for the future.

She brushed a hand across her eyes and focused on the wide expanse of windows. "I'll volunteer to make the curtains."

"No curtains!" Corrie snapped, now the businesslike professional. "Get miniblinds for these windows. They're much more economical and give you better control of the light."

While Jenny found a razor blade and scraped paint that had spattered the windows, Corrie thoughtfully surveyed the room, then listed a few pieces of furniture and the color and placement of some throw rugs. "I'll choose them for you at the store where I work," she offered. "You can add a desk and some storage units later when you know the kind of equipment your tenant needs," she said, showing the best place to put them. "And for heaven's sake, don't go overboard and buy anything else."

"Not even a little knickknack shelf?" Steve asked with a grin.

"That's cause for murder, friend. In a room like this you avoid clutter." Corrie finished with some suggestions on where to place some plants and a couple of lamps.

"Thanks, Corrie. You're a wonder," Steve said.

"You're right. And if I had my shingle out, this would cost you. But since you're an old and trusted friend, I'll collect later, like maybe I'll let you treat me to dinner."

"How about right now?" Steve said. "All three of us. I hear that new seafood place in Cabrillo Cove is good."

She sighed. "Thanks, but I have to hit the books. Gotta refrain from all those *insouciant* type pleasures for the time being," she said casually, then looked out from under the sweep of her long lashes to see whether or not they were stunned by her ten-dollar word.

"Careful you don't dislocate your jaw, my girl," Steve said. "Well, Jenny, you and I can still go. How about it? That is, if we can stand to do without the company of this fugitive from the literati."

"Sure she'll go," Corrie said before Jenny could open her mouth to respond. "I'll drive her pickup home for her." She gave Jenny a broad wink as if to say she'd finally arranged this tête-à-tête. She'd tried hard enough, Jenny thought with some amusement. Corrie had resorted to any number of ruses to throw them together.

ON DECEMBER 24, Jenny packed her bag for her overnight stay with the Spencers and headed for Berkeley. After a few miles she almost turned back. The winding road made her nauseous, and she still wasn't sure she was up to projecting the lighthearted facade that would be expected of her. Her fervent wish was that the holidays were over and done with. Christmas wasn't made for people without families.

She recalled the dinner with Steve at Cabrillo Cove last night. In spite of the excellent food and the way both of them had gone all out to be bright and scintillating, the evening hadn't overcome the somber undercurrent. When the waiter served their cherries jubilee, Jenny had pointed to the brisk flame. "A symbol for a bright, happy future for Steve and Leah," she'd said with feeling.

He'd reached for her hand and had given it a squeeze. "And for you, too, Jenny."

At that moment they'd probably looked like a devoted couple, she thought. There had been a table of folks from Woodhaven across from them. Considering their nudges and knowing glances, the entire town would have them married and starting a family within the month. But Jenny knew she and Steve had eaten their rich dessert with their minds far away and on other people.

Several hours later she arrived at the Spencers. Beth and her three small sons welcomed her with exuberant hugs and at once led her in to admire the tree. She placed her gifts under it, allowing the children to feel the mysterious outlines. Then they pointed out the new sofa and chairs.

"How do you like them?" Beth asked.

"Perfect," Jenny said, looking at the sturdy, scuff-repellent pieces, and thought that as far as style and color were concerned, the Spencers could have done with a bit of advice from Corrie. But it didn't matter. The house was so full of love that cabbage roses on a sofa made not a dent in its ambience.

She and Beth caught up on all their news while Beth's sons behaved as though Amtrak was in the room. Every time Jenny looked at the three little boys she felt like bursting into tears. She might have had a dark curly-headed son.

"Are you all right?" Beth asked. "You look awfully thin. You must be working too hard."

Jenny flashed a brilliant smile. "Couldn't be better. Oh, I lost a few pounds last month when I suffered a nasty virus, and if you don't give me a plateful of whatever that delicious thing is that I smell, I'll perish on the spot."

"And how are things *otherwise*?" Beth asked, meaning, *Have you gotten over Luke yet?* Jenny supposed.

"Doing great," Jenny said.

"Well, at least you're way up there in the woods where you'd never run into him," Beth said, still looking concerned.

"I never expect to see him again."

Beth sighed. "I can't understand what happened. He was like a brother to Joel and me."

"How's the garage apartment coming?" Jenny asked, deliberately changing the subject. "If it'll be finished by February, I'd like to be your first tenant. I'll complete my term at the Woodhaven school the end of next month. Then I'll register at U.C. Berkeley so I can graduate in June."

"It would be wonderful to have you here! The apartment's almost finished. Things came to a sudden halt six weeks ago when Joel finally got a job with a law firm right here in Berkeley."

"I'm so happy for you!"

Beth nodded, her eyes shining. "There were a lot of times these past five years when our pantry was almost bare, but we finally made it."

Of course people could make it if they loved each other enough. Jenny wanted to go home that minute. She stayed for plum pudding and coffee, then in spite of a chorus of pleas, made excuses about delivering more presents and having to see someone about a part-time job and then stay the night with a cousin. "Remember, I'm moving down from the hinterlands the first Sunday in February, so tell Joel to get on the ball and finish the apartment."

Now why had she said a cousin? She had no such relative that she knew about, which Beth would realize if she took time to think of it, and only one other present to deliver—to Andy at the Little Super where she'd once worked as a cashier. Nor was Christmas Eve the time to look for a job, but any excuse would do. She couldn't stay with the Spencers when every part of their life reminded her of all that she had lost.

As for the job, even though she had substantial savings and a partial scholarship that would cover books and tuition, she still wanted to find a part-time position. At least stopping by the day-care center would make her excuse to Beth legitimate. It took only a few minutes to drive there. The children and teachers had already gone home, but there was still a light in the director's office.

As Jenny walked down the hall, a feeling of desolation swept over her. The place seemed cold and abandoned without the laughter and chatter of the small children.

"Jenny! How marvelous to see you!" the director cried, giving her a hug. Jenny forced a smile and explained how she was going back to the university for a term and wondered if there were any openings. According to the director, Jenny's appearance was nothing less than miraculous. It seemed that one of the afternoon teachers had given notice only yesterday that she would be taking a six-month maternity leave at the end of February. The job was Jenny's.

She should have walked out of that office full of elation, but she felt none. She left the present for Andy with a clerk at the store and headed home. Never in her entire life had she felt sorry for herself. What was the big deal now? Couldn't she have stayed with the Spencers without contrasting her own situation every minute with the love and happiness so evident in their family? Coward! What made her think that spending Christmas in her lonely cottage would be any easier?

It was midnight by the time she arrived home. A lovely potted poinsettia stood on her porch. A huge red bow almost hid the card. Her hands trembled as she opened the door, turned on the light and brought in the plant. From Luke? Maybe this was what she'd been waiting for—a graceful finale, something wise or witty that would smooth a final transition into their separate lives, something to help wipe out the night that should never have happened.

She set the poinsettia on the coffee table and admired the splash it made in the room, then took the card and held it a long time without opening it. Finally she pulled it from the envelope.

Dear Jenny,
Just want you to know how much I value your support, your insight and your chin-up way of dealing with life. Thanks to you, I'm finally getting my head on straight. Best wishes for a happy Christmas. I'll be spending a few days in San Francisco.

                                        Fondly,
                                        Steve

Too bad she couldn't snag some of that wonderful insight for herself. Nevertheless, it was a dear and thoughtful gesture. So why did she feel let down?

Christmas morning she opened presents from neighbors and friends who'd brought them earlier, then went for a walk in the woods, but had to return a few minutes later because it started to rain. Back at the cottage she baked a cake. When it didn't rise, she realized she'd left out the baking powder. Somehow she plodded through the rest of the day. She'd had several invitations for Christmas Day dinner, but she'd refused, believing she'd be spending Christmas with the Spencers.

The two-week vacation had never seemed so endless. Well, one way or another she would beat the lethargy she felt. For the rest of the week she cleaned house with a vengeance, washed windows, waxed floors and even painted the inside of the closets. She made lesson plans for her last month of teaching and prepared special seat work and tests. Then she tackled a large carton of miscellaneous belongings she'd hurriedly dumped into the box during the move to Woodhaven, intending to sort things out later. It would soon be time to move again. She'd better weed out any nonessentials.

That was when she came upon the cosmetic bag that contained the small plastic case. Half of the tiny tablets were still intact. Naturally. She hadn't used them since moving to Woodhaven.

A giant wave washed over her, and she gripped the sides of her chair to steady herself. The room lurched, and everything scuttled out of place, then slowly slid back. The world grew still.

Everything added up, all right, the physical signs as well as her biological calendar, the lethargy, the lack of appetite, the queasy middays instead of the traditional morning sickness, all blamed on uptight emotions.

It was going on two months since the stormy night when she and Luke had made love, and all she'd wanted to do since was to put the entire episode out of her mind. Somehow this consequence had seemed so remote she'd ignored it.

She was scared, frightened out of her wits! No she wasn't. She could handle it. And let no one even breathe the word, *abortion*.

Why was she jumping to conclusions? It wasn't necessarily true that she was pregnant. Signs could be deceiving. She couldn't know for sure until she visited a doctor.

But somehow she was certain. Irony almost smothered her. Endlessly she'd imagined the joy she would experience at the fulfillment of her dream for a family. Now this child she'd wanted so much would arrive without a father. Half a family! Was there no way to build happiness without sadness underneath?

If she was going to have a child, what about Luke? How would he react if he knew? He owned no poker face, though in his ruthless drive for success he'd better develop one. She tried to imagine his expression, but his features seemed to disintegrate, as if they'd been painted in watercolors and washed away by rain.

A fierce protectiveness surged through her. Never mind. She wouldn't allow any child of hers to think it was unwanted, much less a disaster. She had enough love for it and then some.

It had grown dark as she sat in the kitchen with the open carton still before her. A study in gray by Hogarth, she thought, and angrily dismissed any drift toward self-pity as she made herself a cup of tea. Nothing like a hot cup of strong tea to bolster one's sense of self-preservation.

She ought to stop thinking about it until she found out for certain. But how could she stop thinking about it? Anyway, if it was true, she would manage just fine. She'd taken charge of her life a long time ago, and she'd allow no interruption. Number one decision: Luke would never know. He'd made it more than plain that children would provide a stumbling block for years to come. She could imagine the trauma he'd feel if he found out he'd fathered a child.

Her mind raced ahead in spite of her resolve not to jump to conclusions. It would be easy to keep the secret from Luke. She would move to Berkeley in a few weeks, and even though he often was a part of social life in nearby San Francisco, their disparate paths would never cross.

Nor would she have to worry about adding to the Woodhaven gossip mill. She'd finish the term and move away before her condition was apparent. Meanwhile, in secret, she'd nourish her child with unflagging love, a child she believed even now rested close to her heart.

CHAPTER SIXTEEN

IN THE MORNING Jenny called one of the doctors listed in the Otter Bay yellow pages and made an appointment. He couldn't take her until five in the afternoon. She chose a general M.D. rather than a gynecologist in order to avoid any speculation in the event she might meet some acquaintance in the office.

She had to know the truth at once. There were certain rules pregnant women needed to follow for the good of their babies. If she was pregnant, she wanted to obey every one of them.

She pulled up to Woodhaven's one gas station to fill her empty tank. While the attendant serviced her pickup, Dirk McCleod got up from a chair where he'd been sitting inside the station and ambled out with his usual swagger. He leaned his arms against the open window and surveyed her. He needed a shave and his eyes were far too bloodshot for a twenty-year-old.

"Hi, teacher lady. Where are you off to all by your lonesome?"

"Just catching up on some errands before my vacation ends," Jenny said. "And how come you're not barreling down the road like Mario Andretti at the Indy 500 with your usual load of logs?"

His expression turned sullen. "I'm not hauling for that fink Douglas anymore."

So Steve had fired him. She wasn't surprised. Everyone knew he'd been spending time in the local bar when he was supposed to be working. "You're changing jobs? I thought you liked driving that big rig," she said. "Dirk McCleod, king of the road, left, right or dead center. I learned that my first day up here."

He grinned boyishly at the recollection. "Too bad you didn't learn to keep your mouth shut."

"Good heavens, that's asking a lot of a schoolteacher."

"You know what I mean. I'm talkin' about Corrie."

"Corrie and I are good friends."

"That's the problem. How come you had to give her all those highfalutin notions about goin' to college? She thinks she's too good for me now."

"Don't be greedy, Dirk. Leave one or two girls for the rest of the poor bachelors. The way I hear it, you have every young thing from here to Otter Bay panting for a kind glance from you."

For a moment his grin revealed the familiar cocky young turk. "Oh, yeah? Well I got to keep up my reputation, don't I?"

"Come on, Dirk, you ought to know by this time that Corrie is her own person. I have no influence whatsoever concerning her feelings about you. It's your technique that needs some adjustment. Like maybe you should act a little more like Robert Redford and a little less like Rambo."

"See, there you go tryin' to work some of that crap on me."

"Sorry, Dirk. I should know better. Just my compulsive schoolteacher habits. So now that you're no longer with the Douglas mill, what new vistas are you going to conquer?"

"Oh, I got a little unfinished business first, then I'll check out my list. There are probably a dozen mills up and down the coast that'll leap at the chance to have me haul for them."

"Well, don't let me detain you. If you'll just remove yourself from my door, I'll get on with my errands. Good luck, Dirk, and give your best to Corrie, this time along with a bouquet of roses, of course."

She pulled out of the station and drove the curving road to the coast. An hour later she walked into Dr. Griffith's office. A Dr. Morgan was the physician most people in Woodhaven patronized, so she'd deliberately avoided an appointment with him. She hoped she wasn't getting paranoid. No. Just prudent, she assured herself.

There were two other women waiting when she arrived, and she was glad to have a little time to get over the breathlessness she was beginning to feel. How many personal questions did a doctor ask? Well, patients' records were confidential, weren't they?

People in Woodhaven took such occurrences in stride if the gossip she heard was any indication. However, she felt certain that such news concerning the schoolteacher wouldn't be so casually dismissed, especially at the county office. In her wildest imaginings Jenny had never imagined herself a member of this particular sisterhood. Oh, no, she was far too wise and disciplined.

She caught one of the women looking at her oddly and realized she was clicking her purse open and shut with the persistence of a metronome beat. She set the purse on an adjacent chair, picked up a newspaper and tried to focus on the print. For a while the page blurred before her, then gradually she realized her attention was riveted on the society section of the *San Francisco Chronicle*.

She started to turn the page when her eye caught a picture of several dancing couples. In the article below the name Beaumont leaped out at her. "Gala Ball Climaxes the Holiday Season," the caption said. Below, an account named a few of the prominent people who had attended the benefit for the Children's Hospital held at the St. Francis Hotel. "An attractive twosome present at the event was Luke Beaumont, scion of the Charles Beaumont family, and Patricia Van Zale, lovely in a Pierre Cardin original." The print stretched across the page as tightly as her nerves, and the room seemed to turn strangely colorless like an exposed black-and-white negative. Anger and bitterness tread on each other's heels, and for a few seconds she felt the full stature of loneliness as she contemplated the years to come.

Stop it! You're not a tragic creature who whines at what life hands you. You are flesh and blood and fully in charge of your life.

At that moment a nurse called her to the desk and handed her a form to fill out. Under marital status she considered underlining widow for the benefit of any prying eyes, but she refrained.

The doctor acted coolly professional. "You are pregnant, and your body structure is ideally suited for bearing children," he said after the examination. She nodded. That latter fact was totally expected. He again glanced at the form she'd filled out. "*Miss* Valentine? You're not married?"

She nodded, resenting the question. He hesitated only a fraction. "I assume you intend to carry this pregnancy to term?"

She looked at him as if he'd lost his mind. "Of course," she snapped. "I didn't come to discuss anything else." She got up to leave.

"Most young women in your circumstances do," he said with a shrug. "Sit down. There are certain realities I like to discuss with the patient."

What realities? They seemed pretty clear to her. She supposed that he wanted to tell her about some fine family who yearned to adopt her child. He needn't assume such a fact. She rose, gave him a steely glance and willed him to shrivel. He merely shot her a cool smile and handed her several pamphlets on prenatal care, then told her to make an appointment for the following month. At the desk she paid her bill but made no appointment. She'd find a gynecologist in Berkeley as soon as she moved.

On the way home she found herself mentally talking to her baby. *Hey, little B, not to worry. You're just about the most wanted kid in history. I've planned on you for ages. So what if you arrive several years too early, you're going to have a fabulous welcome!*

Although by now she'd driven several miles out of town, she turned around and found a yarn shop where she dawdled over pattern books to choose the most beautiful baby afghan she could find, along with the finest yarn. Then she stopped at a bookstore and bought a copy of every paperback on prenatal care on the shelf and also *Baby's First Year* by a currently well-known pediatrician.

It was almost dark when she left the bookstore, and it had started to rain. Worriedly she scanned the downpour. The windshield wipers on the pickup worked so sporadically that she'd rather not drive in a storm. The pasta restaurant next door looked inviting. Perhaps by the time she ate dinner the weather would clear. If only she'd gone straight home after her appointment, she would have arrived by now. But how often did she have the opportunity to browse a favorite haunt like a bookstore?

She ordered linguine with a pesto sauce and ate with relish, refusing the glass of wine that came with the dinner. She'd seen the signs posted in numerous stores recently, warning of the danger of alcohol to unborn babies.

She would see to it that her child had everything going for it.

The rain was still coming down steadily as she walked to her car. But thank goodness, for a change, the windshield wipers worked well, although they complained with every arc. The drive along the winding coast highway seemed to take forever, and she met very few cars. Apparently most people had sense enough to stay home.

Rounding the curves, her headlights at times caught the spray of breakers, lighting them up like ghostly fireworks in the night. The hiss of her tires on the wet asphalt and the howl of the windshield wipers added to the eerie atmosphere and made her apprehensive, but she stoutly assured herself it was only a vagary of pregnancy.

Soon Jenny passed the small general store and café that she'd always regarded as a halfway marker. She'd gone barely a mile beyond when the pickup slowed and stopped. Frantically she shoved her foot against the gas pedal. Nothing. The car couldn't be out of gas. She'd filled it this afternoon. She checked. Not even a quarter down. She got out and lifted the hood. It wasn't the fan belt. The engine wasn't hot. In this old bucket of bolts it could be anything. Already her hair was sopping wet.

She peered up and down the highway. Not a single light in sight. The little store was probably closed, but she was certain she'd seen a pay phone outside.

She tied a scarf around her head and buttoned her coat all the way. It was heavy, but not rainproof. Her raingear was all at home. Head down against the deluge, she walked as fast as she was able. Whenever she spotted the distant lights of an occasional car, she walked as far from the edge of the road as she could. She'd rather get pneumonia than take a chance on accepting a ride with a stranger.

At last the light from the little store came into view. Weak with relief, she ran the rest of the way and up the steps to the wooden deck. A dim bulb burned in the booth. She looked in her purse and her heart sank. Two dimes and a few pennies were her total change. She'd have to make them count.

She dialed the number of Otter Bay's only towing service. A recorded message advising her to leave her telephone number and they would get back to her. How long would she have to wait? If the tow truck was out on another job, it could be midnight before they returned her call.

A fierce downpour battered the booth, and the cold wind from the ocean seemed to go right through her. She huddled against the rickety door of the booth and tried to rub some warmth into her fingers. It seemed she'd shivered for at least an hour in the breezy booth, but a glance at her watch showed a scant twenty minutes.

Dare she try Steve? She had only one dime left. She prayed that he hadn't gone to San Francisco this weekend. Endless rings verified the fear. She'd just pulled the dime from the return coin slot when she saw car lights weaving erratically from side to side on the highway, then suddenly turn into the store's circular driveway. Hope flared. Help could be here after all. She felt a rush of relief.

The driver careened up to the store, skidding and turning a complete circle followed by a volley of boisterous shouts. Relief turned to terror. No way she could risk asking that drunken bunch for help.

Darting around the corner of the building, she plunged into darkness. Male voices, coarse with oaths, filled the night. Fists banged on the locked door. "Open up, man! We want some beer!" the men shouted repeatedly, their words thick and slurred. They kept up the clamor, but no one responded.

"Give up, you guys," another one yelled.

Her nerves so tight that she could hardly move, Jenny slipped behind a big Douglas fir in back of the store and flattened herself against the far side of it, her heart beating violently. A moment later flashlights played all around her as the men continued to call out. Fear turned her so weak that she could hardly remain erect—fear for her child, fear for herself. She prayed the men would leave. What would she do if they found her cowering behind this tree? She would play dead. She would dart through the woods. Surely she could outrun the drunken louts. She would...

A loud crash interrupted her frantic conjecture, followed by the sound of tearing metal, then the click of coins. Were they robbing the change from the phone? What if they'd wrecked it? If anyone was inside the building, he wasn't answering.

With howls of drunken hilarity, the men sped away in their car. Jenny waited until the sounds of their departure faded, then slowly stole back toward the phone booth, feeling her way against the building. Suddenly she missed her footing and sprawled on the steps, her head hitting a railing. Stunned, she remained prone for a while until her head cleared, wondering if she'd broken any bones.

Her head ached unbearably, but she dragged herself a few inches at a time back onto the deck. The telephone was still intact, but the Coke machine was in shambles.

Inside the booth she pulled the door closed and sank to the floor to wait for the call from the towing company. No one could see her from the highway, but neither could she see an approaching car. It didn't seem to matter.

The rain had let up, but in her damp coat she was freezing. Then she saw the blood dripping into her lap. She clapped a hand to her head and felt the gash there, opened her purse and found a handkerchief, which she clapped hard against the wound. How did one make a pressure bandage on a head?

An eternity later the handkerchief was soaked, but the bleeding had stopped. Light-headed and unsteady on her feet, she managed to stand and reach again for the telephone book, thumbing through the pages to look up Etta Mae's number. Corrie nearly always came home on weekends. No answer. She tried Amos Botts's, then Mrs. Mallory's and, with increasing desperation, even Simon Flint's. Then it came to her. No wonder there were no answers in Woodhaven. On Saturday nights the community always turned out for the weekly potluck and dance. No one would be home before midnight.

Her hands shook as she again looked up the number of the towing service. Surely they would have called by now. Something must have happened to their message machine. Dare she try them again and risk losing the last of her change?

A cold wind whipped through the ill-fitting door. She considered her predicament. She could either return to her car and lock herself in until morning, or wait here and hope the towing service would call.

There was a third choice, of course. She still had one dime. She could call Luke. She'd told him she never wanted to see him again, but a helping hand was all she wanted tonight, regardless of its identity. If she had only herself to consider, the choice would have been simple: no way would she call him. But she had someone else to think about now.

After wrestling with herself for a while longer, she looked up his home number, dropped in the dime and dialed. Again no answer. Didn't anyone stay home on Saturday night? Luke was probably out squiring around one of the stable of society women he seemed to prefer. Still, if he adhered to his old habits, it was possible that even at this late hour he could still be working at his office. The gash in her head had begun to bleed again. She had never felt so helpless.

With scant hope, she dialed Luke's office number. "Hello?" Luke said after the first ring, and she could hear his surprise at the call.

"Luke, this is Jenny. I wouldn't call, but I need your help."

"My God, Jenny! What's wrong?"

"My car gave out on the way home from Otter Bay. I haven't been able to reach a towing service and I'm, well, I'm stranded."

"Where are you?"

"In the phone booth of Martin's Mini-Market and café on the highway about halfway home."

"Alone?"

"Yes."

"I know the store. I'll be there as soon as I can. Keep out of sight, and I'll give three quick toots of my horn when I arrive. I'm on my way."

She sank down in the booth again, her relief so intense that she felt drained. The signal from Luke's horn came less than a half hour later. She rose in the booth, opened the door and held on for support. He ran across the porch to meet her, and she fell forward against him. At that moment she desperately needed the feeling of security he could give her, the comfort of his arms, but he grabbed her shoulders and held her so that he could examine her face in the light from the booth.

"My God, Jenny, what happened? You're covered with blood!"

"I fell. I'm okay."

"I'm taking you to a doctor. You need stitches."

"No, take me home. Clumsy, I guess." She started to sway, and without hesitation Luke swung her up in his arms and carried her to the car. "You do get yourself into the damnedest scrapes."

"Sorry," she mumbled, and tried to dismiss some of the similarities of this occasion to the last time Luke came to her rescue. Well, any likeness ended now, this minute. "I apologize for bothering you," she said stiffly. "I called umpteen people. You were the only one I could reach. Don't know what happened to the towing service. Where are you going?" she asked as he turned the car around.

"To the emergency hospital in Otter Bay. Where else this late at night?"

She lacked the energy to protest, and rested her head against the back of the seat, absorbing the heavenly warmth of the car.

"Are you all right?" Luke asked periodically with a worried frown. Then he would reach over and squeeze her hand. It wouldn't matter if she reveled in the feel of his strong fingers, would it? She could do it and he'd never know.

The next hour passed in a daze as the doctor examined her, sewed a dozen stitches and announced that she had a slight concussion. "Get your wife to bed right away and see that she rests for the next day or two," the doctor said. She met Luke's eyes and saw a flicker of something desolate at the mention of the assumed relationship. How would Luke look if he were told that this was the second doctor she'd visited today?

Rest, the doctor said. That was fine with her. She felt as if she could rest for a year. He drove to his apartment. "You're staying here. The last thing you need is another hour's ride in the car."

"Take me home. Really, I'll be okay."

"You heard what the doctor said. I'm not allowing you to stay alone tonight in that isolated cottage of yours."

Too weary to argue, she followed him inside. Vaguely she was aware of thick carpets and sturdy oak furniture. He opened the door to what she supposed was the guest room; at least a glance showed no personal belongings.

He stood in the doorway as she took off her coat and sank down on the bed. "Give me your keys," he said brusquely. "I'll go to the garage and make arrangements for them to pick up your car."

She nodded, but he still remained, and she hated to admit that she didn't want him to leave. His lips moved silently, as if trying to form words that wouldn't come.

"And, Jenny," he said finally, "I won't blame you if you lock your door, but you needn't. I can't tell you how much I regret last November. I don't expect you ever to forgive me. All I can say is that it takes a long time for love to end, at least for me, but regardless of that, I won't hurt you again. That's a promise."

She tossed the keys to him, her eyes still on him. She ought to say something, some word of appreciation for taking such good care of her like, *Thanks for the rescue, not only for me, but especially for our child?* No, not that. Never that. "Thanks for everything, Luke. I'll try hard not to make this a habit."

"Considering your self-sufficiency, it's surprising that at times you do need a caretaker."

"You're right. Good night, caretaker."

He grinned, and for a moment the old banter between them flickered, then died as he grew serious again. He reached over from his stance at the door as if he dared not set foot any farther and laid a packet on a dresser. "The doctor gave me these pain pills for you. Take one now. Sleep in if you wish and I'll drive you home tomorrow anytime you say. Call out if you need anything," he said, and shut her door firmly.

She heard him leave. Five minutes later she was asleep. The bedside clock said 2:00 a.m. when she wakened, her head throbbing. She lay for a while, summoning the energy to get up and find the pain pills. Suddenly a movement, a breath, something, alerted her to a presence in the room. Except for snatching a quick glance from under her lashes, she remained rigidly still. Luke stood next to the bed, looking down at her. It was too dark to catch his expression. For minutes he stood motionless. Finally, with a sigh, he reached down and tucked the blanket over her shoulder, allowing his hand to rest on her forehead, as if he were testing for fever. Seemingly satisfied all was well, he removed his hand and walked so silently out of the room that it was a while before she realized he'd left.

Later she found the pills, took one and went back to bed. For as long as she remained awake, she saw the light under her door from the living room, and she wondered if he still hadn't gone to bed. She had a guardian angel tonight. Luke took the role as if made for it. She recalled all the ways he'd sought to protect her. Except for one notable exception.

The next morning she rose to the appetizing aroma of coffee and bacon. She showered, dressed and joined Luke for breakfast almost as of old, except for their stiff little freshets of words that adroitly covered what really went on in their heads. It was an odd feeling. They studiously avoided any movement where they might touch, and their conversation was strictly impersonal.

Later, when Luke took her home, he stopped along the side of the road at one end of Johansen Grove before reaching Woodhaven. "I want to show you something," he said. "It's only a short hike from the road. Feel up to it?"

"Of course. You needn't pamper me any longer."

They hiked through the woods along the brown compost carpet of the trail for perhaps a hundred feet and stopped beside a towering redwood. She gazed in awe. It had a cavity at least fifty feet high, forming a large room within the tree. She stepped inside and surveyed the interior. "I can't believe this. I could drive my car in here and still have space to seat all my pupils. But in this tranquil setting, it feels more like a cathedral."

"True. Would you believe the hollowed area is twenty by twenty-eight feet? Foresters have measured it. The tree's over a hundred feet in circumference, two hundred and fifty feet tall and two thousand years old."

"A terrible fire must have caused this."

"Probably not one fire but many, each one eating out a little more of the heartwood."

"But how can it survive?" she asked, staring up at the healthy green crown.

"Unless the fire completely circles a tree, it usually won't die. The nutrients and water from the roots flow through the outer sapwood, which is just beneath the bark, so the damage to the interior doesn't matter. These trees are able to heal their own wounds. Look here," he said, pointing to bark curling over the edges of the scar. "Given enough years, it will completely cover the wound."

"But I thought redwoods were immune to fire."

"Their bark is more fire resistant than any other tree, and they do survive most forest fires. Eric Johansen showed me a grove of fir and redwood that was swept by fire a few years ago. All the fir was destroyed, but every redwood is still standing."

They stood together and looked up at the blackened interior. The pleasing musty aroma of the redwood was tinged with the fragrance of a nearby bay tree. "This old giant makes one feel pretty humble the way it has survived. It makes a rather profound statement about life, doesn't it?" he asked.

She agreed. These woods always evoked lofty feelings. "Thanks for bringing me here."

"I've wanted to show it to you for a long time," he said. Then suddenly he took her face between his hands and stared down into her eyes. "If only..." he muttered, then kissed her. The kiss was sad, gentle and supremely sensual. His fingertips gently outlined the contours of her cheekbones and the faint hollow of her temple. Then he kissed her again. With a sigh he drew her to him and laid his face against her hair. A wild, intense hunger wrapped her in variable currents. She felt her body turn traitor, covetously longing for remembered intimacies.

Branches dappled his strong face in shadow, and she felt a pang of regret that shook her with its force. The only sounds came from a nearby rushing creek and the throaty call of a black-and-white spotted owl high above them. This day could be enough to break her heart.

He dropped his arms, took her hand in both of his and laid it against his cheek. "Oh, Jenny. I can't stop loving you. I was a fool to let you go."

She searched his face for honesty and caught her breath when she saw tears in his eyes. "I wonder if you really mean that, or if you're under the spell of this awesome place."

He shook his head. "I've never meant anything more in my entire life. Come back to me, Jenny, and I promise never to let anything come between us again, not my work, not Charles, not my confused thinking." He pulled her close, and she felt the tremor in his arms. "What I did to you was unforgivable, but I told myself I was doing it for you. Now I know that I put my career above everything in my life that mattered most."

"I was devastated," she said, but didn't move away from him.

"So was I. Can you forgive me?"

There was a breathless hush as they rocked together. She looked up to meet his eyes, and he seemed to gaze at her in a drinking-in way.

"Forgiveness is easy, Luke. It's love that's hard."

"You're wrong. It's easy to love you."

"Is it? I think love is a lot more than four little letters. It means truly caring about each other, trusting each other and being loyal. Mostly it means being there for each other, no matter what, so that we can deal with anything that comes along. Can you handle all that, Luke?"

"Oh, yes, Jenny. Love means the same to me. Please, allow me to give back your engagement ring. Wear it as a symbol of my promise."

"Promises don't need crutches, Luke. They should stand on their own."

"Then wear it just to let the world know we belong together."

"Not yet. We need more time."

"Time for what?"

"Time to see if we come first in each other's life. That's the crux of this whole matter, isn't it?" *Promises are easy. Show me, Luke. Show me!*

Could he handle knowing she was pregnant? That would put a completely different light on matters, as far as he was concerned. She knew only too well his attitude on that subject. One step at a time, she decided. There would be a right time to tell him.

He took both her hands. "Do you love me?"

She nodded, and with a sigh leaned her head against his shoulder.

"Say it. I need to hear you," he pleaded.

"I love you, Luke, but . . ."

His face clouded. "But?"

"I do want to believe you, but sometimes I think we move on separate tracks, that our words have two meanings, one for you and something entirely different for me. Do you understand what I'm trying to say?"

"So you need some time, right? Time for testing? Time for proving? If that will bring you back to me, I'll wait weeks, months, years," he said gravely.

"Don't make any rash vows, and don't think I mean that we should play a lot of giddy love games. I'm serious about us."

"And so am I, my dearest." Their eyes met in a silent pledge, and he bent to seal it with a kiss. Then in solemn cadence, he followed her back to the car.

On the way he plucked a little nosegay of trillium and handed it to her. "This occasion demands a glass of champagne or at least a fanfare of trumpets, but I guess this will have to do." She took the delicate flowers with sober thanks.

There came a clap of distant thunder as if to provide the missing fanfare. He looked up at the darkening sky. "I'd better take you home," he said. "It looks like rain any minute."

The mood abruptly dispelled, they drove to her cottage, discussing the heavy cloud cover like two avid meteorologists. The sudden turn to impersonal chatter didn't bother her. She could tell that he was aware of the depth of the commitment they'd made today, and so was she. They were also mindful that the new bond between them was so tenuous, that they couldn't risk severing it by examining it too closely.

CHAPTER SEVENTEEN

THE FOLLOWING WEEK Jenny and Luke saw each other almost every evening. At first their times together had no resemblance to the eager, falling-in-love weeks they'd spent when they first met. Instead, she sensed a delicate reticence in each of them. It was as if they sailed a familiar ship but needed to find their sea legs again.

And underneath, like the persistent drone bass of the bagpipes, was the secret she held from him. How could she tell him about their child until she convinced him to shed the image he had of himself as a reluctant parent? The subject had to be treated with rare skill. If only she could help him change the way he saw himself, she felt certain he would accept his new role with love and pride. There would be a right time to tell him, and she would recognize it when it arrived.

Luke must be thumbing his nose at Charles Beaumont. At least he spent very little time after normal work hours at his desk. Instead, he picked her up most evenings, and they had a lark trying out some of the wonderful seafood places in the area.

Once they drove south along the coast for an hour or so to Fort Ross. There they pictured the Russian fishermen who had built the fort in order to hunt sea otters for their pelts during the early 1880s, then left when the intensive hunting depleted the animals. "Now I know where your town got its name," Jenny said.

They walked among its weathered board buildings, visited the museum and held hands as they looked at the icons in the damp, austere, old Russian church. The compound was now a part of the state park system.

On a Saturday morning Luke rented wet suits for each of them and, armed with buckets and abalone irons, they took advantage of the unusually low tide in order to try the local sport of hunting the large shellfish. As playful as otters, she and Luke swam near cliffs and promontories and among the rocks, locating and prying loose the oval abalone that clung so tenaciously to underwater rocky surfaces. Legal keepers were seven inches. When they got their limit of four, they took them home, extracted the pure white meat and sliced it into steaks.

"Now we pound them, just a swift blow to release the muscle, or else the meat will be tough as leather," he said, wielding a vicious mallet. Then they fried the meat in butter.

"Mmm, food for the gods!" Luke said, tasting a bite of the tender meat and rolling his eyes heavenward.

She'd made a fruit salad and scones to complete the meal, and they proceeded to gorge themselves. "Tastes a lot like scallops, only better," she said, polishing off her second helping.

"Jenny girl, you're a wonderful cook," he said a little later with sigh of satisfaction. "This day will have to keep me going all next week. Would you believe I have to spend the next six days in Eureka?"

He'd be gone a week? At this point it loomed as a year. "Business?"

"Right. I'll be working out some tax problems with several clients I have there—court appearances and such. If all goes as planned, I'll return late Saturday night, so hold all day Sunday for us. You plan something. Surprise me."

They did the dishes then, chatting about the demands of their work. Her enthusiasm as always bubbled over.

"Would that every teacher showed such devotion!" he said. "Are you still planning to complete your credential?"

"Of course," she said, surprised. "Why would you even ask?"

"Oh, I'm all for it, but I thought you might like to wait for a while, relax for a change. Teaching sounds like pretty intensive stuff. The responsibility for seeing that all those kids meet the state standards in every subject must take a lot out of you."

"Are you the kind of man who carries off his beloved to some ivory tower and keeps her safe in his shadow but leaves her bereft of any identity of her own?"

"You make me sound like some dragon. You mean sitting around adoring me doesn't fulfill you?" he asked with a twinkle in his eyes.

"I'm glad you're teasing, or I'd give you my five-minute lecture. I need to have a creative outlet the same as you do."

"Yes, I know, and I didn't mean to cast any slurs."

He built a fire in the small fireplace, and they sat on the sofa, his arm around her, her head on his shoulder, drowsily basking in the firelight, savoring the satisfactions of the day. She looked at the flickering shadows mottling his strong features and saw the glow in his dark eyes.

"Please understand, Luke," she said as she considered what he'd just said. "I want more than to bask in your shadow. I want someone who knows that teaching is a significant part of me, something I've strived for over a lot of years."

"That's all you need?"

"You know that's not all."

"Then say it. What else?"

She reached for his hand. "I want that someone always be there for me through good times and bad. I want him to put his arms around me often and tell me that he loves me."

He laid his hand on her cheek. "My dearest girl, if you knew how much I want to do that, you'd marry me at once."

"I don't think we're quite ready for that step yet."

"Why? We're not exactly strangers."

"Yes, for a while you were. I still have a few hurdles. Let's take it slow and easy." She saw the stricken look on his face and reached over and squeezed his hand.

"What about now? Do I seem like a stranger now?" he asked.

She smiled up at him. "It's been like old times, hasn't it?"

He drew her to him with a kind of desperate gentleness and laid his cheek against her hair. It seemed as natural as breathing to wrap their arms around each other, and they clung together as if trying to make up for the months they had lost.

She felt their passion rise but knew that it was due as much to loneliness as desire. He asked with his eyes, and she silently answered with hers, letting him know that the right moment hadn't arrived.

After he left a little while later, she knew that she'd missed at least a half-dozen openings to tell him of her pregnancy. The day couldn't have provided a more loving ambience in which to divulge her secret. Why hadn't she?

she asked herself, and spent a fitful night trying to rationalize her answers.

EARLY THE NEXT MORNING Corrie dropped by. "Want to walk over to Steve's with me? I promised to give him the bill for the furniture I had delivered for the studio apartment. After sitting at a desk all week, you can use the exercise."

"I rarely sit at my desk. Keeping moving is the Valentine modus operandi," Jenny said. Then she added, "Want some lunch before we start?"

"Not enough time. Got to get going. I promised Granny I'd return soon to help her wash her windows. Again. They're so clean now you can't see the glass. Never mind that. She sets a time schedule for the chore, and whether needed or not, come storm, cyclone or tsunami, man, we wash windows." She aped her grandmother's grim expression and determined stance.

"Ah, discipline! It builds character," Jenny said dryly.

Corrie merely grunted. Jenny grabbed a jacket and the two set off through the woods. Since the creek was still too deep to cross without boots, Corrie took them on a little-used path unfamiliar to Jenny that cut immediately out of Johansen Grove and into a section owned by Steve.

They'd gone about halfway when Jenny knew she could no longer ignore the nausea that began to overtake her. Darn! If it persisted, she would have to make tracks back to her cottage. The booklet the doctor had given her said that nausea could end in as little as six weeks. So far she'd been lucky enough to be with Luke afternoons or evenings. She wondered if she would have been able to keep her problem from his sharp eyes had they been together when it happened.

Enough already. She took a few deep breaths and willed the feeling to go away. In spite of the chilly temperature, beads of perspiration formed on her forehead, and she tried inconspicuously to brush them away.

"Come on, old lady, pick up the tempo," Corrie called from far ahead as Jenny slowed down. "Hey, what's the matter? You look positively green."

"You go on. Must have been something in the tuna sandwich I ate. I'd better go back." She sank down on a log and put her head in her hands.

"For heaven's sakes, little B, pay attention to the book," she muttered. This so-called morning sickness was getting out of hand. She looked up as Corrie hurried to her side, frowning with concern.

"Hey, are you all right?"

"I'll be fine. I'll just sit here a moment and wait for my stomach to catch up with the rest of me."

"You're sure? Didn't get what you just said. Who's Bea?"

With effort Jenny managed a nonchalant shrug. "Oh, that. Just a little whimsy. Someone I consult on occasion, so to speak."

Corrie giggled. "I get it. Barry, Bob, Beaumont or how about *D* for Douglas?"

"Aren't you the wise one! If you don't mind, I think I'll start home after a bit."

"If you say so. I'll check on you on the way back." Corrie ran lightly down the path, her long dark hair swinging, and was soon out of sight.

A moment or two later Jenny stood up and tested her balance. Much better. As she started back over the trail, strident voices pierced the silence. "Stop!" a woman screamed. "Stop now!" Every nerve alert, Jenny listened to the prolonged cries. Oh, God! That had to be Corrie!

CHAPTER EIGHTEEN

JENNY FLEW along the path, listening to Corrie's screams grow louder. She tried to call out, but her mouth was so dry that she couldn't make a sound. In places the little-used path was overgrown with bracken, slowing her steps. Fir boughs needled her arms as she pushed them aside. Suddenly she turned her ankle on a half-hidden log and caught an arm around the trunk of a young madrone to prevent herself from pitching face first onto the ground. With a moan at her throbbing ankle, she sank down in a tangle of underbrush, shocked at the scene before her.

With powerful swings of a sledgehammer, Dirk McCleod was pounding a headless spike into a redwood. About as effective as an angry insect, Corrie beat her fists on his back, shouting at him to stop. Dirk drove the spike deeper into the tree until it disappeared from sight.

Fury turned Jenny livid. She'd recently read about this kind of vandalism. When the tree was cut and eventually found its way to the mill, the hidden spike would tear up the saw, shutting down the mill until a new saw could be installed—a costly and time-consuming procedure. Dirk had to be stopped. She tried to rise, but waves of pain radiated from her ankle, and she sank deep into the ferns again.

Dirk tossed the mallet high, catching it neatly as it whirled like a propeller beating the air. Corrie picked up a spike from the pile at his feet and shook it in his face. "How many have you used?" Her tone was scathing.

He folded his arms and grinned down at her. "Now that's a little secret I won't share."

"Can that minibrain of yours comprehend the damage you've caused?"

Dirk's expression grew surly. "Serves Douglas right. Firing the best hauler he ever had for no good reason."

"Goofing off at the bar during work hours is plenty of reason."

"Like hell it is. I get the work done, don't I?" He pulled a handful of red plastic ties from his pocket and dangled them in front of her. "I haven't nailed too many trees, but this will queer work in the woods for a while."

Corrie stared, her color rising. "You irresponsible idiot. Are you telling me you stripped off boundary tags, too?"

He tossed the tags into the air and batted them into the undergrowth. "Every one. That'll teach him."

"What will it teach all the guys out of work while the mill is shut down?"

"They won't mind a vacation."

"The kind without pay?"

"State unemployment insurance will get 'em by. So what if it takes a month to resurvey? What's it to you anyway? Say, you look real sexy when you get all steamed up." He reached for her, catching her in an embrace. "Let's have a kiss. You know you've been wanting one."

In a tornado of action, Corrie flailed her fists, kicked his shins and writhed out of his arms. Dirk rubbed his jaw and managed a grin. "Doesn't take much to wipe off those fancy airs you've been getting from your schoolteacher friend. Put her on a pedestal, didn't you? What would you say if I told you that Miss Pure and Perfect got herself knocked up recently?''

"Shut your mouth. How can you stoop so low?"

"Oh, she'll furnish proof soon enough."

Jenny gasped. Shock ran over her in waves of heat and cold. It had been barely a week since she'd been to the doctor. How could Dirk know? She sank further down into her prickly nest.

"You breathe a word of that vicious gossip, and you'll be sorry!" Corrie cried.

Dirk gripped her arm. "Won't have to. She'll take care of that little matter herself any day now, and you needn't run to report my spree in the forest. I'll be long gone before Sheriff Tucker can tool up the grade." Corrie slapped his face and pulled out of his grip. His face grew red, and his eyes narrowed. "Listen, baby, someday you're gonna stop going with those Otter Bay wimps and settle for a real honest-to-God man like me."

Corrie stood, hands on hips, cheeks flushed and hair disarrayed in a black cloud. "Now you listen to me, Dirk McCleod, and you listen good. I'll tell you the reason I can't stand the sight of you. You swagger around like you're God's gift to women, but the truth is, you act like a retarded adolescent. People around here have put up with your antics for years, hoping you'd mature. What's so brilliant about putting a whole crew of men out of work and costing Steve the best contract he's ever made? What's so honest to God manly about spreading vicious gossip about the best teacher and neatest flatlander Woodhaven has ever seen? This time you've gone too far. Grow up or get lost!"

With a curse, Dirk trudged off into the forest. Corrie followed, not letting up her tirade for a second. Unsure whether she was shadow or substance, Jenny crawled through the underbrush and somehow found the path.

She tested her weight on her foot. She could manage. Groggy and ill from the appalling scene she'd just witnessed, she stumbled back to her cottage and fell into bed. Eventually her inward quivering ceased, but now she felt as if her body were on remote control while her mind went off on tangents of its own, trying to deal with the vicious sabotage and the strangling loop Dirk had wound around her reputation.

Right this minute Corrie was undoubtedly alerting Steve concerning Dick's devilment. Her heart ached for Steve. By the time the tract was resurveyed and the spikes removed, it would be too late to deliver the lumber. He would lose the contract.

And what of the fallout over her own predicament? Tears started in Jenny's eyes as she remembered the way Corrie had defended her from Dirk's accusation. How would she react when she learned the truth? Jenny racked her brain, trying to figure how Dirk had so quickly learned of her condition. The only logical conclusion appeared to be that the doctor had violated patient confidence.

But other people would have access to the doctor's files. Suddenly she recalled the gossip about Dirk at Amos Botts's retirement dinner. Someone had offered the latest tidbit that an Otter Bay nurse was Dirk's latest conquest. Was that the answer? What twist of fate led her to the very office where the girl worked?

There was a knock and Corrie opened the door and poked her head inside. "Hey, old lady, feeling any better?" she called.

Jenny hurriedly got out of bed and went to the door. "I'm okay now," she said, forcing a smile. "Come on in."

"Thanks but I've got to get back to Granny's. You'll never believe what I caught that devil Dirk McCleod doing." She described the vandalism. "Man, I feel sorry for Steve. He was really counting on that contract. I went to his office, but he's in town getting a new bearing for the head-rig shaft. What a bummer to come home to! The sheriff will catch up with Dirk. No problem there, but that won't help Steve. Hey, I gotta go. Granny will kill me," she said, not waiting for a response.

Jenny wished she could talk the ugly affair over with Luke, but he'd left yesterday for some business in Eureka. He might know some way to help Steve.

Later that afternoon she roused herself to walk to Simon's market for a few groceries. As she climbed the steps, two young women sitting on the porch looked her way, whispered to each other and burst into giggles.

Inside Jenny spoke pleasantly to Mrs. Flint, who tended the store today. The woman pursed her lips and barely answered. Surely these women hadn't already heard about her visit to the doctor. Her imagination must be running wild.

She took her bag of groceries and, head held high, walked from the store. Yes, any number of persons could have heard, she realized. Dirk frequented the local bar, and he had a very loud mouth. Most likely he'd broadcasted the news at once. Considering the efficient local grapevine, there probably wasn't a single individual in town who hadn't heard it. Such news ordinarily caused little more than a ripple. But this time it concerned the schoolteacher. Her eyes filled with tears and her throat ached bitterly.

On Monday school went as usual until the close of the lunch hour. As she herded the children back into the classroom, she stooped to pick up a piece of paper. She started to wad it up when she caught her name. "Guess what?" it said. "Mr. Douglas got Miss Valentine in a family way, and he's not even divorced yet."

So that was what everyone thought. Well, it was a logical conclusion, wasn't it? People had seen her and Steve together often enough. How did one correct a rumor like that?

Well, let the rumormongers carry on. She would act as if they didn't exist. Moreover, she would refuse to succumb to raging attacks of self-pity, and she would keep on hand a supply of noncommittal answers for prying questioners. As for physical evidence, at least Dirk had got that wrong. She would be safely settled in Berkeley and back in classes before she started to show.

A FEW DAYS LATER Steve came by the school as Jenny was getting ready to go home. For the past week she'd listened for the whine of the chain saws and the blast of the whistle that would indicate the mill was sawing again, but all was silent. Steve's face was drawn into lines she'd never seen before, and circles under his eyes told of loss of sleep.

He set down a box of materials from the county office and slumped down onto one of the children's desks. "Picked up your order for you."

"Thanks. I appreciate that. Oh, Steve, how is the boundary survey going? I can't believe Dirk would be so vindictive."

"Going well but not well enough to meet the contract date. I'll lose it for sure. The forester is using a magnet to find the spiked trees and should finish tagging them in a few days, but the boundary survey is another matter."

"And Dirk?"

"He's apparently skipped the country. This whole thing has really got to me, Jenny. I was feeling on top of the world as I drove back from San Francisco. I hoped our rosy financial prospects might offer one more incentive for Leah to come back and live here. To make matters worse, on the strength of the contract, I went overboard and bought a lot of new equipment. Now I'll have to tighten the purse strings again."

"When she sees that wonderful studio, she'll know how much you care for her," Jenny said, and prayed that she was right. Leah's love must be pretty superficial if she allowed bad luck to come between them.

He shook his head. "I wanted to be able to give her whatever she wants, to show her how much I love her in as many ways as possible."

"The most important part of love is understanding the other person, accepting her for the kind of person she is." Her words gave her sudden pause. Fine sentiments, but had she practiced them? Had she really tried to understand Luke, or had she been so preoccupied with her own dreams that she'd completely ignored his? The sudden insight stunned her.

"Understanding? Accepting?" Steve asked. "Yes, you've shown me that. I'm trying, Jenny."

Jenny reached over and squeezed his hand. She wanted so much for things to turn out right for him. She wondered if he'd heard the rumor about her pregnancy, especially the suspicion that he was responsible. He'd only returned today, so maybe it hadn't reached him yet. Even though she'd never breathe a word about Luke, she wished she could talk over her situation with Steve. She could use some kind words after this dreadful week of rumor-mongering, but she refused to put one more burden on Steve now.

As he made ready to leave, he offered to take her to the store to get some groceries, since her pickup wasn't running again. When they walked in together, some women nodded and smiled and couldn't have acted more friendly, but Jenny didn't miss the knowing looks they cast at one another. She was furious that she'd been so unthinking as to add to the gossip about her and Steve. Now that he would be bringing his wife up soon, tongues would wag even more.

In spite of the excuses she gave about needing the exercise, Steve acted rebuffed when she refused to allow him to drive her home. Why did she want to walk a mile carrying a big load of groceries after a long day at school? Oh, Lord, Steve was the last person she wanted to hurt. Life had turned contrary beyond all belief.

SATURDAY MORNINGS it had become a kind of ritual for Corrie to drop by for a visit. Now that she worked and took classes in Otter Bay, she usually spent only weekends in Woodhaven with her grandmother. Today Jenny looked forward with more than usual eagerness to spending time with her good friend. This past torturous week had left her mentally exhausted, and she could use a generous dose of Corrie's feisty tonic, especially since Luke wouldn't return from Eureka until tomorrow.

Apparently Corrie's classes were going well at Otter Bay Community College, and she was enthralled with her job as junior decorator at Swanson's furniture store, according to her enthusiastic accounts.

Jenny picked a basket of the special mushrooms Amos Botts had taught her to recognize and made a mushroom quiche and a fruit salad, hoping Corrie would arrive for lunch.

She glanced frequently out the kitchen window, hoping to see Corrie swinging down the lane. However, the noon hour arrived without her. Jenny put on a sweater, fixed herself a plate and took it outside to sit on a log that edged the meadow. She could eat only small portions of the food and felt relieved that she wouldn't have to hide the telltale noonday signs from Corrie, after all.

Always the thought of her baby was with her. When would she feel it moving? she wondered, and knew it would be a precious time. Would it be blond like her, or would it have dark chestnut curls like its father? Probably any child of theirs would be too individual to remind her of anyone.

Jenny cast one more glance down the lane, sighed and went indoors. It appeared Corrie wouldn't be coming at all.

Jenny spent the rest of the day catching up on household chores and making the usual lesson plans for the coming week. Later she called Etta Mae to see if Corrie had come up this weekend, but there was no answer.

Maybe she would bake a cake for the Saturday night potluck at the community center and coax Corrie to go with her if she had no other plans. Usually there was dancing after dinner, or sometimes a movie was rented for the occasion. It was the only social entertainment this little town provided, and one could always count on a fun-filled evening.

January's early twilight had already darkened the cottage when Corrie finally arrived shortly after five. "I fixed your favorite quiche for lunch, hoping you would come."

"Yeah, I bet that you would, but Granny has been pestering me for ages to go to her sewing club. I finally ran out of excuses and went along. They sew all day and sometimes have a speaker. Today there was a representative from the county farm bureau, addressing the burning topic of how to cure and dry apples."

Corrie made a face. "Did you know that my greatest priority in life is to cure and dry apples? People up here have only been doing that for a hundred years. You can bet they could teach that county representative a thing or three. Mainly I think Granny wanted to exhibit her newly academic and highly respectable granddaughter." She went over to the refrigerator. "Any of that quiche left? The spit-and-gossip club seems to concentrate mainly on things drowned in whipped cream."

"Help yourself," Jenny said, and set out the remaining fruit salad. "So what's the latest hot item from your grandmother's club?" By the look on Corrie's face, Jenny knew exactly what the main topic of conversation had been the minute she asked the question. "Has anyone caught up with Dirk yet?" she hurriedly added.

Corrie took a bite of the quiche. "Mmm, delicious. Dirk, my friend, is a changed man."

"Tell me!"

"Would you believe he went to Steve and volunteered to work off the cost of the resurveying? He also went out with the foresters to help identify the trees he spiked. Of course he can never make up for the lost contract."

"I thought at the time that that was some lecture you gave him."

"You heard?"

"Yes, I did." Jenny described how she'd happened to eavesdrop. "When I heard you scream, I thought something awful was happening to you." She swallowed hard. "I truly appreciate your loyalty, Corrie. You're a good friend."

"That loudmouth waggled his tongue all over town. I'll never forgive him."

"I suppose you had to defend me at your grandmother's club?"

"Listen, Jenny, I positively know that you're the last person in the world who would get herself in this kind of fix. I told them and I told them good! That Dirk and his impeccable sources!" Her eyes snapped and her voice rose.

Tears smarted Jenny's eyes. Such loyalty was hard to come by. She wondered how she could find the courage to disillusion her good friend. She stared at the floor, as if it held some mysterious secret.

"Forget about him," Corrie said. "Lying is a way of life for that jerk. You ought to know by now that people take anything he says with a pound of salt. Anyway, you're bound to prove him wrong. Getting lizzied has a way of announcing itself without any help."

"Lizzied? Now there's a word for it. One of your grandmother's expressions? Well, Corrie, I'm afraid this is one time they can leave the salt on the shelf. I have no idea how Dirk discovered my secret, but it's true. I'm very much lizzied."

A heavy silence crowded the room, suffocating it with denial, disillusionment and shock. Corrie rose, planting her feet apart, hands on hips, her eyes smoldering. "Don't you dare kid about something like that!"

Jenny's chin trembled, but she met the girl's eyes without flinching. "I couldn't be more serious."

Corrie held a rigid pose while both disbelief and rage raced across her face. "You . . . you . . ." She struggled for words as her expression accused and condemned. "You sharked me!" she cried, again lapsing into the local jargon. "My God! I stood up for you against the whole damn bunch! You're the only person I've ever completely trusted, and look what you've done to me! Turned me into a fool and a liar! Miss Pure and Perfect! All that high-sounding palaver you spouted. And all the time you were carrying on with Steve Douglas!"

"Oh, no, Corrie. Not Steve. The father is no one in Woodhaven!" Jenny cried.

"Ha, don't put on any noble acts for me. You needn't protect him!"

"Not true! Believe me!"

Corrie began to pace the small kitchen, then stood before Jenny, hands on hips in her favorite posture. Her eyes were wide and bright with anger and tears. "I believed in you. I thought you were really somebody. And all the time you were playing dirty pool, pretending to help a nice guy like Steve, and instead you hustled him to cheat on his wife."

"You've got it all wrong," Jenny pleaded. "Steve isn't involved, I tell you. Even so, I'm surprised at your attitude. I seem to recall that not long ago you were making rather elaborate plans to take up with a married man."

"That's different. I don't make any bones about who I am. For all I care, you can have affairs with every guy in town, but what really gets me is the way you play Miss Goody Two Shoes in the meantime."

Jenny bowed her head. They were miles apart and there appeared to be no crossing. Finally she reached out a hand to Corrie. "Please. Sit down and let me explain."

"Thanks but no thanks. You're a fraud and a cheat. I'll never trust the likes of you again!" She marched out of the cottage, slamming the door hard behind her.

CHAPTER NINETEEN

As PROMISED, Luke returned on Sunday, and Jenny looked forward to escaping, at least for a day, from the emotional chaos in which she found herself. All she wanted was to go off to some never-never land and pretend that Saturday had never happened.

Luke picked her up around two, and they drove to one of the secluded coves along the beach. Although it was a winter day, the sky was clear. Gulls circled the shoreline, diving now and then for a luckless fish. Stick-legged sanderlings edged the beach, scampering and fluttering back and forth as they played hide-and-seek with the spent waves.

Jenny spread out the bountiful picnic lunch she had prepared, and after devouring every scrap of the food, they hiked hand in hand along the crescent beach, marveling at the wealth of life in the tidal pools, identifying the giant green anemones, the jellyfish and an occasional clumsy crab. Then they gathered driftwood, built a fire and hugged its warmth, watching the tide rise, its lace-edged waves splashing the shore with foam.

Neither of them mentioned their past week. She felt that Luke, too, wanted to escape from something. They hadn't talked a lot, but communicated more by the way they smiled at each other or the way they touched. Reluctant to leave, they remained until the moon rose and made a path to their Shangri-la, then took their picnic basket and drove home.

"This has been a perfect day. I needed it," Luke said as he walked her to the door of her cottage.

"We all need to get off the merry-go-round once in a while," she answered, and knew the day had nourished her, too. He held her shoulders and moved her over a little so that she stood in the moonlight.

"You're very beautiful, Jenny. I haven't told you enough, but I'm going to remedy that," he said as he kissed her good-night.

She reveled in the love she saw in his expression. "I think you're pretty handsome, too. If we have a son, I want him to look exactly like you."

"Hey, flattery will get you somewhere, but let's not talk about having kids yet. We need time for us. We'll get around to them someday."

Her mouth went dry. "Someday. When is that?"

"Well, for sure, we don't want children while you're going for your degree. A baby so soon would be damn inconvenient. Lots of couples don't have kids right away, if ever. We won't be oddballs." He pulled her into his arms and nuzzled her cheek.

She stiffened. He might as well have struck her. She turned away to fit her key in the lock. His response had been so unexpected that for a few moments she was mute with shock.

So he hadn't changed after all. He was still postponing having a family to some nebulous "someday." It wasn't hard to imagine how he could take the news she'd soon have to tell him. She wondered if she would be able to make it inside the house without stumbling.

"Come in. We have to talk," she said, averting her face so that he couldn't see her ravaged expression. She willed the huge lump in her throat to go away. "There are important things we need to discuss, and there's something I need to tell you."

"Darling, not tonight. I promised to see Eric Johansen no later than nine, so I'm due in about ten minutes. I'll come get you tomorrow evening after work and we'll go out to dinner. You can tell me all about everything then. I hope to have something special to share with you, too." He checked his watch, kissed her again and took off. Apparently her stunned reaction had in no way communicated itself to him.

She went inside the house and sat down, her knees too weak to hold her. Had he really said that? Supposedly her desire for a family was what their breakup had been all about, but now he'd promised not to allow anything to come between them. She hadn't heard any ifs, ands or buts recently. Something didn't add up. Yes, it did. He still believed a child would be "damn inconvenient."

Now that she thought about it, during these past weeks they had dwelled entirely in the present. Just being with each other again had been so satisfying that nothing else had seemed to matter. Anyway, at this point, they'd agreed to put their future on hold. It still was an unknown quantity.

She'd put off telling him about the baby endlessly because she'd wanted time to convince him that becoming a father wasn't the horrendous chore he seemed to think it was, that it wouldn't banish all their freedom and that he could stop worrying that he might follow his own father's pattern. So far she hadn't found the tact and skill to accomplish the task.

Luke would still feel incredible resentment at becoming an unwilling parent. His words tonight had made it clear he hadn't really changed—at least not in that respect. There would be no wedding now.

AFTER SCHOOL the next day as Jenny nervously waited for Luke to arrive, a call came from his secretary, advising her that Luke had left early that morning for an unexpected business appointment and would be out of town for several days. He'd call as soon as he returned. So what else was new? Not only had he not changed his view on having a family, but he was still dancing to Charles's tune.

For the next few days she saw no one but her pupils, and after school, she conjured up endless busywork for herself. A walk in the woods, her usual anodyne for problems, left her exhausted, as if she'd traveled for miles.

Life had turned unbelievably grim. She hadn't heard a word about Corrie. Had the angry girl quit her classes and headed back to San Francisco to hunt for an apartment? How much if any of the gossip had Steve heard about the two of them? And what if the rumormongering reached the county school office?

Or what if it reached Luke? Surely gossip from a little place like Woodhaven wouldn't stretch to Otter Bay. Luke was no longer on the school board, so he wouldn't have that contact. She should have told him at once. It was too late now.

Most of all, she wanted to be Jenny Valentine again, in charge of herself instead of being this witless zombie. She was one of the strong kind, wasn't she? Had been all her life. But right now she longed for someone to lean on, someone to share the downs of her life. She needed a kind, loving Luke.

At the afternoon recess at school she stood on a knoll above the playground, and watched her pupils playing, their energy seemingly inexhaustible. Thank God for these children. She'd be lost without them.

In her classroom there was no more note-passing or any suggestive remarks concerning her and Steve. Apparently the rumor had gotten replaced by the latest accident in the woods. The Douglas mill's most experienced driver had turned over his Caterpillar on a slope and would have to lie in traction for months to come. Already his girlfriend had been seen dating the sawyer. Even more a cause for discussion was the surprising news about the change in Dirk McCleod's behavior. It appeared to be the miracle of the season. Even the children discussed it.

"Pa says he probably ran into a tree and got teched. No other way to explain his actions," Earl Flint said—the ultimate authority as usual.

"Maybe he got bit by a sorry bug," suggested Robbie, who was currently working on an insect project. Jenny nudged his arm to show that she appreciated his joke but thought it more likely that Corrie's vitriolic lecture might have struck home at last.

After school Steve came by with several reams of paper she'd ordered for the copier. "Thanks, Steve. That was thoughtful of you. I know how busy you are." He looked so weary that her heart ached for him. "How are things going?"

He shook his head. "I've lost, Jenny. There's no way to meet the deadline."

"No chance of an extension?"

"None. The time is spelled out in the contract. A damnable time for it to happen. Leah will be coming up this weekend. It meant a lot to me to show her a flourishing business.

"Surely if the company knew the circumstances, they might give you more time."

He shook his head. "Business doesn't work that way. My signature guaranteed delivery beginning next week."

"But there are logs in your pond."

"All fir. The Richter company wants redwood."

"There has to be a way. Why don't you talk to Luke Beaumont? He might know some angle."

"I haven't seen him for a while. Did you know that he resigned from the school board?"

"It didn't take him long to bypass our little burg, did it?"

He gave her a sharp glance. "You've got him all wrong. He's a square shooter if I ever saw one. Odd that you never cottoned to him."

"Oh, he's a whiz at business. I hear he's out of town a lot, but why don't you call his office and get an appointment?"

"I don't like to take advantage of a friendship."

"You'd do the same for him. Go for it, Steve. At this point, what have you got to lose? Call now before the office closes. Here's his number." She noted earlier that except for the area code and the first digit, it was the same as theirs in Berkeley. She jotted it on a slip of paper for him.

He looked amazed. "You have some head for numbers!"

"Yes," she said. "Math is one of my better subjects."

While he made the call, she debated whether to tell him the gossip about the two of them. He'd given no indication that he'd heard it yet. Perhaps the preoccupation with the latest scuttlebutt would override anything else. Anyway, she hated to dump more worries on him now.

A few minutes later he returned from his phone conversation in the coatroom wearing an enigmatic expression.

"So what happened? Did you get an appointment?" Jenny asked.

"Sure did. Said he'd see me tonight."

"You say you talked to him in person?" Ice slid down her spine. When had he returned, and why hadn't he called?

"He said to come over this evening and we'd talk about it, but . . ." He left the sentence hanging.

"But what?"

"Well, he didn't sound like his normal self, if you know what I mean. Damn abrupt. I got the feeling he was annoyed with me. Still, he insisted that I come. I don't get it."

"Go. He was probably tired or something."

"I'll go, all right. At this point I'm snatching at straws. If it isn't too late when I return, I'll drop by and let you know what happened."

"I'll keep the coffee hot," she said with an effort, trying to keep her voice normal. With a sinking feeling, she watched Steve go. Why hadn't Luke called? Somehow he must have heard the gossip. What kind of maze had she gotten herself into?

LUKE STARED at the phone on his desk. Ever since he'd overheard the talk about Jenny and Steve, he'd been out of his mind. Then a minute ago, right out of the blue, Steve had called wanting to see him. The confrontation couldn't come too quickly. He couldn't stand living with this news much longer.

He'd arrived in San Francisco from Seattle that morning, and after a big brouhaha with his uncle, he'd driven straight to Otter Bay. He couldn't wait to see Jenny. Full of plans for their weekend, he wanted to surprise her and whisk her away the minute school was out. They would drive up the coast, have dinner at the beautiful Heritage Inn and spend the weekend there. It would be a perfect place to reveal that he would soon quit Beaumont Business Services, and to tell her about his new job possibility. Johansen had made it clear that it was a long shot, but they could dream, couldn't they? Then maybe he could convince her to set a wedding date. As far as he was concerned, it was long overdue.

When he'd arrived in Otter Bay, Luke had found a list of directives a mile long that Charles had sent—enough to keep Luke at his desk the entire weekend. Well, to hell with the list. The guy must stay up nights, Luke thought. How else could he dream up all that busywork, most of it unnecessary paper pushing.

For some time Luke had known that he could no longer work for Charles. He now saw that Charles played on his nephew's fears of repeating his father's mistakes in order to manipulate him. Charles implied that he promised Luke such an exciting future because he loved him and thought of him as a son. But the only person who truly loved him was Jenny, Luke realized. Not Charles. Not Stacy. They were users.

The recent days he'd spent with Jenny showed him in no uncertain terms all that he was missing. His determination to quit his uncle's employ had been too long coming, but since he'd made up his mind, he'd felt like a new man.

A week ago he'd applied for a position in Eureka and another in Reno. He'd learned that the owner of one of the companies was a close friend of Charles, so he'd immediately withdrawn his application, and for the other position, someone else was hired.

It went against his grain to offer himself to Jenny without a job just as they planned to get married. He knew that Eric Johansen had numerous business interests, so he'd decided to explore that possibility. After he took Jenny home following their wonderful day at the beach, he'd headed for Eric's hilltop log cabin.

"Wondered how long it would take before you left the Beaumont bailiwick, young feller," Johansen said when Luke asked if there were openings in the Johansen empire. He poured glasses of his homemade applejack for the two of them. "Figured you had guts enough to get out sooner or later. Saw you strainin' at the reins from the time you arrived."

"I have a thick skull, but I've learned my lesson," Luke answered.

"Glad to hear it. As a matter of fact, I've been watchin' you, and I have something in mind that's right down your alley, if it isn't too late."

He explained that he was a member of a corporation that owned international timber holdings. They were opening a West Coast office in Seattle as soon as they lined up a staff. "I hear they're looking for an aggressive, creative manager. I figure you might stand a chance. Interviews are going on in Portland right now," he continued. "I understand they're talking to about ten candidates. If you care to fly up and bowl 'em over, I'll call and put in a good word for you—that is, if it isn't too late to get an appointment and if you want to take a crack at it."

Luke's spirits soared. "If they'll see me, I'll take the first flight I can get in the morning!" The job sounded ideal, but what kind of chance would he have? He'd been head of a relatively small office for only six months. He knew quite well he'd be up against men with years of experience. Would a reference from Johansen mean anything to an international corporation, even though Eric was one of the stockholders?

Eric called the next morning. "I got you an appointment in the nick of time. Tomorrow's the last day they're holding interviews. Better fly up tonight."

The interview went well, Luke believed. But who knew what went on behind the poker faces of the men on the hiring committee. A decision wouldn't be made until the end of the month. He knew he ought to forget about it until then, but he couldn't. The job had enormous potential. Even though he knew his chances were slim, his mind continued to seethe with ideas that he could implement in this international business.

This morning after he'd flown back to San Francisco, he'd headed first to the Beaumont Building. The secretary had ushered him into Charles's office. Charles rose and extended his hand, then clapped Luke on the shoulder. "An unexpected pleasure. May I fix you a drink?"

Luke thought he could use one, but refrained. He needed to keep a clear head. "Thanks, no," he said, his tone brusque.

Charles frowned and scanned his nephew closely. "I gather you've got something on your mind."

"Well, Uncle Charles, there's no use beating around the bush. The fact is, I'm handing in my resignation."

Charles stiffened and his profile grew taut, as if hastily hacked out of a piece of cardboard. "I hope I didn't hear you correctly," he snapped. "Would you mind repeating that?"

"You heard me."

"That's ridiculous. Don't tell me you're on coke or something."

"No way. For the first time in months I'm doing some straight thinking."

"What's the matter? You want more salary? Hell, you're the highest paid employee I have."

"Pay has nothing to do with it. First of all, you almost lost me the woman I love."

"Good Lord! Don't tell me you're still drooling over that ragtag what's-her-name."

"Jenny," Luke said, thrusting out his chin. "You know her name, all right. How can I work for someone who twists me around his little finger? It took me a while to see how subtly you accomplished this and I hate myself for falling for it, but that doesn't mean I don't blame you, too," he said, bitterness coating every word.

"Sit down, damn it!" Charles thundered. "You're giving me the jitters the way you're ranting and raving. I can't believe a man of your intelligence would act such a fool. I suppose you've been seeing that woman again."

"Positively and I hope she'll marry me soon."

Charles slammed a fist on his desk. "You fool! You crazy fool! Didn't you listen to one word of my advice?"

"I listened, all right, and it almost did me in. There's no way I can work with a man who deliberately set out to con me out of marrying the girl I love."

"That can't be all that's sticking in your craw. Out with it!"

"Jenny is the single most important reason. Alongside of that, anything else is meaningless."

"So there *is* more! Spill it!"

"You asked for it," Luke said. "I'm sick and tired of acting as your pawn. You have my future blueprinted for the rest of my life, regardless of my own goals and opinions. You even try to choose the people I should meet and those I should ignore."

"My God, man, up there in the boondocks, hours away from my office, you're damn well on your own!"

"And more than that, I don't like some of the ways you do business. Making a buck comes first with you, regardless of any consideration."

Charles gave a derisive laugh. "Listen to the young turk telling off one of California's top ten business men, will you! It must be wonderful to be so brilliant. I've seen your kind before. They all want to start at the top."

"So it's best for both of us if I quit now."

Charles's face grew red. "You idiot! Every M.B.A. graduate in the entire world would kill for the opportunity I've handed you. I'll give you a scant year before you crawl back on your knees begging me to take you back."

"Don't count on it!" Luke snapped.

"And if you don't," he paused, and his eyes narrowed. "I'll have to change my will."

Luke had expected that trump card a lot sooner. "Sorry, Uncle, I'm not for sale. But I won't leave you high and dry. I'll stick with the job until you find someone to replace me."

"Damn you, you're just like your lily-livered father after all!" Charles shouted, and his curses filled the room.

Luke turned on his heel and walked out of the office, venom following him like a cloud of poison gas. His step was light as he walked to his car. For a man who had no job, he felt downright exuberant. Even if he starved, he would never work for Charles again. This time he'd do the job-hunting himself. Silver platters weren't all they were cracked up to be.

He got into his car and drove straight to Woodhaven. He could hardly wait to tell Jenny about the events that had been crammed into the past three days. What would she think of his resignation? He could almost see the sparkle in her eyes.

To fill in time until her school let out, he went into the town's one bar and grill for a leisurely lunch. As he ate his sandwich, he couldn't help overhearing the strident voice of a waitress talking with a young woman at the next table. The conversation seemed to concern some serious vandalism in the woods committed by a guy named Dirk something or other. He listened indifferently until he heard Jenny's name mentioned.

"Can't feel too sorry for that Miss Valentine," the waitress said. "Steve Douglas is the best-looking thing around."

"You better believe it," the other young woman agreed. "Even I wouldn't mind getting pregnant if I thought I could snag him. But you'd think a schoolteacher would be more discreet."

Luke left his sandwich half-eaten, put some change on the table and took off, feeling as stunned as if someone had punched him. He got into his car and drove to his office where he sat immobile, staring at the walls.

An affair with Steve? When had that happened? Well, Luke shouldn't be too surprised. She'd raved often enough about how supportive the fellow had been.

Luke cursed himself for the thousandth time for the crass way he'd broken up with her. She must have been very vulnerable during that period. Still, he couldn't imagine Jenny getting involved in an affair that soon. Damn that guy, letting her in for that unsavory gossip! Making her risk her reputation! How in the devil did such information get started, anyhow?

Just then Steve called. After Luke got off the phone with him, he thought to himself, *Now I'll get to the bottom of this or kill the guy. Cut it out, Beaumont. Maybe, after all, this whole issue is nothing more than rumor.*

Jenny certainly didn't look pregnant. If she was, she couldn't be more than two or three months along. It had to be a rumor. She would never have reconciled with him that day in the woods if she were pregnant with another man's child. Jenny was too honest for that.

Another man? My God! If she really was pregnant, it was far more likely that the child was his. He counted the weeks and months since that stormy night early last November. It could be true, all right. So why hadn't she told him? He started to call her, but he didn't want to ask questions until after he'd talked to Steve. People must know something he didn't, or Steve's name wouldn't be linked to Jenny's in this quagmire.

Steve arrived about forty minutes later. "Good of you to see me so soon. I appreciate it," he began, taking the chair across from Luke's desk.

Luke took in the tall, well-built fellow and strove to relax muscle by muscle, nerve by nerve. Could he deal with it if Jenny's child belonged to this man? "Glad you called," Luke said. "As a matter of fact, I had something I wanted to discuss with you, too."

"Shoot," Steve said. "Mine can wait."

Luke fiddled with his top desk drawer, opening and closing it, then shut it firmly, none too quietly. "Well, I might as well say it straight out. I'm more than a little concerned about this talk about you and Jenny."

Steve's mouth dropped open. "What talk?"

Luke eyed him warily. "I'm sure you know exactly what I mean."

"No, I don't. Explain yourself, man," Steve demanded. His jutting chin seemed to dare Luke to come up with a single derogatory statement.

"Well, the information I've received isn't exactly a secret."

"What information? Whatever it is, I can't see that it's any of your business."

Luke gave him a level look. "I'm making it my business," he said in a tone that got Steve's attention.

"Listen," Steve said, "I don't know what this is all about, but I can tell you for certain there's not a damn thing between Jenny and me except friendship."

"That's not what I heard," Luke snapped.

Steve gave him a hard look. "You should now by this time that gossip is a way of life around here. If nothing's happening, someone makes up a thrill or two. For the life of me, I can't see what it is to you! Listen, I'm trying my best to get my own marriage back together, and Jenny has given me a lot of insights to help make it happen."

"The way I hear it, Jenny is pregnant and you're the father."

"Pregnant! My God, what are you talking about? Jenny pregnant! That's a lie. Who told you that? Jenny and I have never slept together. I'm still in love with my wife, and Jenny is still hung up on some creep who promised to marry her, then jilted her. I'd like to get my hands on the guy."

Luke sat back in his chair and felt a series of dark waves wash away every blindfold he'd hung on to. He admitted that he'd relentlessly blocked out that night last November when he'd found Jenny half drowned. His love for her had escaped every boundary he'd built, superseded all reason. He hadn't wanted to deal with the way his actions might have affected *her*. He swallowed hard and brushed his hand against his damp brow.

"Hey, are you okay?" Steve asked.

So his agitation showed. How much could one person hold until it spilled over? "Sorry," Luke said. "I guess I owe you an apology. Ever since I knew Jenny at Berkeley, I've wanted to look out for her.''

"I can understand that," Steve said. "If I hadn't met my wife first, I'd probably have fallen for her like a ton of bricks myself. Too bad she got hung up on that no-account jerk. Maybe you'd have stood a chance."

"I doubt it," Luke said quickly. "I can see that this talk about you adds up to rumor, obviously untrue. I apologize for jumping all over you, and please don't tell Jenny I mentioned it. She's so damn independent that she'd resent my interference." Although his body felt as if it were filled with lead, he managed to open his desk drawer and take out pad and pen. "Now let's get to the reason you wished to see me."

Steve explained his predicament. "Jenny thought you might have a suggestion. She seems to have a lot of admiration for your business know-how. I'm afraid I came up short on that score."

Luke saw at once the depth of Steve's frustration. Luke wasn't certain if he could twist anyone's arm, but he would try. For no reason at all he felt as if he owed Steve a mint. "I know Richter," he said. "He's a client of our San Francisco office. I'll give him a call. I can't promise anything, but I'll be glad to see what I can do." The two men shook hands, with thanks on both sides. Luke shut the door and paced his office.

"Creep? No-account jerk?" Luke had never thought of himself in those terms. He'd told himself that he wanted to free her. Instead he'd wrapped Jenny in chains that could affect her entire life.

He recalled the last exchange they'd had the evening he'd brought her home from the beach. If she actually was pregnant, his careless words must have devastated her! *My*

God! What kind of man am I? Would she ever forgive him?

He wasn't certain how long he sat at his desk, questioning his sanity, his integrity, his courage to face the truth. It could have been noon or midnight. He had no conception of time. At least he knew what he must do, and he'd waste no time getting at it.

CHAPTER TWENTY

IT WAS ALMOST MIDNIGHT when Luke reached Jenny's cottage, but her light was still on. For a minute he stood on the porch and watched her through the window, her cat curled up like a puffball at her side. The stupid girl still didn't pull the blinds, and he would bet the door was unlocked. Still, he was glad for a private moment to watch her.

She sat on the sofa in avid concentration, apparently correcting papers, one foot tucked under her. The lamplight rested softly on the sweet curve of her cheek. A lump formed in his throat. After a few moments he took a deep breath and knocked.

She looked up, then walked to the door, but didn't open it. "Steve?" she asked.

Steve! Had they planned to meet? "It's Luke," he said sharply.

She opened the door. "Luke! What are you doing here?" She beckoned him inside and they sat down on opposite ends of the sofa.

"You were expecting Steve?"

"He said he might stop by after his appointment with you. He did see you, didn't he?"

"Yes. I'll do what I can for him."

"I told him that you would. He deserves any help you can give. He's been snowed under with bad luck recently."

"You're really concerned, aren't you?"

"Yes, I am. He's been a wonderful friend. I don't know what I would have done without him."

"So I gathered," Luke said wryly. "He mentioned that some creep had jilted you."

Jenny caught her breath. "Oh, no, you didn't tell him about us, did you?"

"No, I didn't tell him, coward that I am. I think he would have beaten me to a pulp on the spot, not that I would have blamed him."

"What's done is done. Now tell me what you're doing here at this hour. I thought you were going to call me."

He calculated his next words with care. "I had a change of plans after I heard something that set me back on my heels. It seems that a lot of folks in these parts seem to think you and Steve are a lot more than friends, although he convinced me otherwise." His hands automatically curled in tight fists.

Jenny caught her breath. "So you're heard the rumor?"

"Not from him."

"Well, it's gossip, I tell you. There's nothing between us but friendship," she said with some heat. "He loves his wife. In fact, she'll be here next weekend."

"Yes, I believe that. But, Jenny, I also believe that you and I, that is . . ." His voice broke. "If you really are pregnant, I know that I could be responsible."

Her expression flattened, revealing nothing. "And what difference would that make?"

He felt as if she'd struck him. "A hell of a lot!"

"Well, if this is what you're all steamed up about, I suggest you go home and forget about it. You needn't worry about rumors, remorse or regrets."

He felt dented, as if she'd pounded him with a hammer. "I'm not talking about rumors. There aren't any about you and me. I want the truth. Answer yes or no, are you pregnant?" he demanded.

"Luke," she said coolly, "I don't have to answer to you for anything. I'd appreciate it if you'd gather up your unrighteous indignation and leave."

He gripped her shoulders. "Not until you answer me!"

She jerked away. "You have no right to such information!"

He reached for her again. "The hell I haven't! If what I suspect is true, I'm the father of this child. I have plenty of say."

She got up and moved to another chair. "Oh, no, you don't. Not a syllable, not a word. You don't want children. You made that exceedingly plain last summer and again last week!"

"I made a stupid remark. I want to be involved now that I might be a parent. I mean that!"

"Hah! What kind of father would you make? You rejected this baby before it was ever conceived!" she cried with more fire than he'd ever seen in her.

He felt as if he were falling, as if he were somehow ricocheting down a series of cliffs. "So, it's true!"

"Yes, it's true," she said so softly that he scarcely heard, her expression so bleak that he wanted to take her in his arms at once. He reached out to her, but she ignored him. It was as if a powerful ocean wave were forcing them apart, leaving each one on a separate island.

"Oh, God, I'm sorry. We were always so careful, but that time was different. Marry me now, Jenny. I want to give our child a name. I want to take care of you. I can't allow you to go through this alone."

"Oh, sure," she cried with scorn. "The honorable gentleman sees his duty, and he'll do it come hell or high water. Well, don't worry. I know exactly how you feel. You told me last week."

He stepped back as if licked by flames. "That's not fair. I didn't know you were pregnant when I said that. Why didn't you tell me?"

"Would it have made any difference? I doubt it. Listen, Luke, feeling bound by a sense of duty is no way to enter into a lifelong commitment. I'm not interested. You'd resent this baby. What would that do to our marriage? A child needs to be loved, not resented."

"My God, Jenny, doesn't anything that happened between us these past few weeks mean anything to you? Can't you tell how much you mean to me?"

"What about our baby, Luke? I haven't heard a word about how much *it* means to you. I'm afraid the two of us come in one package. Thanks, but no thanks. I can take care of both of us."

"But how will you manage? Think about it."

"Oh, I've thought plenty. Believe it or not, I have my life under control. I'll manage just fine. Keep your money. It must cost a bundle to wine and dine all those Patricia Van Zales. I wouldn't know."

"That's a low blow. You remember how poor we were. It's a lot different now. Besides, it was Charles who kept producing women for me to squire around."

"Stacy, too, I suppose."

"Stacy's a business colleague. What is this, a grilling session? Jenny, please, it will be a lot different when the baby comes. I know all about that. Remember, I was the oldest in a large family. We can get married right away. Babies come a month or two early all the time. As long as we're married, no one will lift an eyebrow."

"Oh, is that what you're concerned about, appearances?" she asked with contempt.

"No, damn it!" He gave a helpless gesture. "You take everything the wrong way."

"Relax. I have plenty saved. You should remember how well I can stretch a dollar."

"I never thought that you of all people would deny a child its father!"

"I plan to give this child the image of a father who was the most caring, loving man I've ever known. You were that once, Luke. Then you turned into a stranger, a man programmed to prosper, a different Luke who prized the promise of a glorious future and a glittering social life above family and love. I'll never break our child's heart by revealing that."

A shudder of panic ran through him, and he could no longer conceal the frantic edge of his concern. "My God, Jenny, do I have to draw you a picture? Can't you understand that I love you? That above all else I want to marry you, whether you're pregnant or not?"

"I don't believe you, Luke. You've shown me plenty that gives the lie to those fine sentiments. Run along on your merry way. I mean it. This discussion is wearing me out. I have to teach tomorrow."

She walked to the door and held it open. Her ridiculous cat headed out, waving his tail in wide arcs as if to lead the way. The silence between them was thick with pain. There seemed nothing to say that could penetrate it. Without a word, he strode out of the cottage and got into his car.

His mind and body heavy with defeat, he drove down the dark, winding road in a kind of stupor. When he arrived at Otter Bay, instead of going home, he parked near the shore and stared blindly through the fog now swirling in from the bay. Maybe he could shut out the world and make some sense of all that had happened this evening.

He'd really blown it. The whole evening was so charged with emotion that he hadn't been able to think straight, much less articulate his feelings. Even though these past few weeks with Jenny had been heaven as far as he was concerned, obviously she'd never really forgiven him for losing sight of what really counted in life. Well, he couldn't blame her for that.

And now he'd thoughtlessly compounded her resentment just when he'd been about to show her that he'd finally straightened out his life. He clenched his fists as if to ready himself for an assailant. How could he have been so stupid? As for their child, the sudden confusing emotions that flooded him were far too new to put into words. If only he could make her understand that. He'd been through worse hours in their relationship, but this one would haunt him forever.

CHAPTER TWENTY-ONE

AN UNEASY CALM filled Jenny's days now. It was as if she'd weathered a fierce storm, but she still wallowed far from shore in a lifeboat. The longing for what might have been would fade, wouldn't it? Maybe. Eventually.

She was proud of her strength in taking responsibility for her life. What kind of marriage could they have had with Luke squirming under the harness of obligation? How could they have achieved a loving relationship, with him resenting the child she carried? She was resigned to their breakup at last; resignation was always superior to such conditions.

Only two more weeks remained before she left Woodhaven. She would register for classes at the university on the first Monday in February and would move to Berkeley the day before. Leaving wouldn't be easy. She would miss her good friends, and teaching in this one-room school had been far more wonderful and satisfying than she'd ever dreamed.

Today after school Robbie had asked if she would teach him a spiritual he'd heard on his radio. Now, while he was running home to get his guitar, she sat on the schoolhouse steps, tuning her own instrument and reviewing several of the more difficult chords. Then she sang the song and realized the words weren't exactly the kind she cared to sing right now.

"Nobody knows the trouble I see, nobody knows the sorrow," the first phrase went. "Sometimes I'm up, sometimes I'm down," it continued in a too-accurate description of her present moods.

After the first verse, she ignored the words and sang the plaintive tune on a neutral syllable. The chord changes between major and minor would be difficult for Robbie, but she had no doubt he would master them. She leaned back against the railing, closed her eyes and sang the song once more.

When she finished, she opened her eyes and almost dropped her guitar. Luke stood looking up at her from his stance at the foot of the steps, his jacket slung over one shoulder. He had appeared without warning. For a second she wondered if she were dreaming.

"That's lovely, Jenny. I haven't heard you sing for a long time."

How long had he been listening? Darn! If only she hadn't been singing *that* song. She probably sounded like some self-pitying wimp. She lifted her chin. "I was just going over a song Robbie wants to learn. He'll be here soon for a music lesson," she said with a stab at nonchalance.

"Lucky Robbie." Luke moved a step closer, and the late-afternoon sunshine highlighted the deep lines on his forehead, accenting his sudden frown. He planted a foot on the first step and leaned forward. "Why didn't you tell me?" he demanded.

The way it burst from him, he must have been seething with the question ever since he'd learned she was pregnant. "Tell you what?" she parried, playing for time.

"Don't play games with me. You know what I'm talking about. I feel like a damn fool."

"Considering the way you feel about having children, what difference would it have made? I know I was wrong not to tell you, and I'm sorry. But I still say it wouldn't have mattered. Our blowup would have just come a lot sooner.''

"Or it wouldn't have come at all. Why can't you trust me?''

"You ought to know the answer to that.''

A slow flush rose in his cheeks. "What do you want from me? Sackcloth and ashes? I was blind and stupid, and I'll always regret it, but a man can change when he sees his errors. I know this whole thing is my fault, and maybe I'm crazy to expect you to change your mind, but I still think we could make it together.''

She was so taut that she ached all over. "Maybe we expect too much from each other, Luke.''

"And maybe we don't expect enough. I think I'll make a damn good father. I'd feel a lot better if you'd expect that of me, too, instead of mouthing all that negative stuff. You and I could be a real team, but apart we turn every molehill into a Mount Everest.''

"I don't know, Luke. Maybe we would be a real team. And maybe we'd set off a nuclear blast.''

"It would be better than what I'm going through. Listen, I won't bother you for the next couple of weeks. Anyway, I'll be in and out of the office a lot. I understand that the school board is honoring you with a luncheon the day after school is out. Steve called yesterday and invited me. I'll be there for sure. Wouldn't miss it for anything.''

"Yes, I just received the invitation.''

"In the meantime, why not recall the wonderful months we spent together after we first met? I know it can be like that again. Total up some points in my favor. Surely you can find one or two,'' he said with his crooked grin.

"You're proposing a balance sheet?''

"Something like that. You might discover that we're not in the red after all. I'm asking you, no, begging you, to reconsider. I'll be at the luncheon—that's a promise—and we'll talk about it afterward, and, well, I'll accept whatever you decide." His last words came so haltingly that it must have cost him to say them.

"And if I decide that it won't work?" She met his eyes and looked away first. She couldn't bear the desolation she saw there.

"I promise not to bother you or to ask you again," he said.

An osprey swung above in the wind, and the young emerald-green pines so lustrous among their elders all seemed to grow twice their size as the silence lengthened.

So he was suggesting a deadline. Perhaps that was best. She'd been positive that anything between them was over, but at the moment she was a quivering mass of indecision. Maybe a deadline would force some clarity into her thinking. "All right, Luke. We'll talk then," she said finally.

Robbie came loping up, clinging to Rosie's leash with one hand and barely managed his guitar with the other. Luke gave a goodbye salute and walked quickly down the path to his car.

Robbie turned his head back and forth as was his habit when he tried to identify a sound. "Is someone else here?" he asked.

"Just a former member of the school board. But he's gone now."

"What did he want?"

"I guess you'd call it a bookkeeping assignment."

"Yeah, I know. My dad told me all about it. If you're going to succeed in business, your books have to show more pluses than minuses."

She smiled. That about summed it up, she thought. If a relationship is going to work, there'd better be more positives than negatives.

THE FOLLOWING FRIDAY EVENING Steve stopped by her cottage, as nervous as a boy on a first date. "Leah will be driving up Saturday afternoon. Robbie can hardly wait for us to take her on a tour of the mill. She'll never recognize it, what with all the improvements. Then we'll barbecue steaks. I can manage that and a salad, and I'd sure like to top off the meal with her favorite dessert. I wouldn't dare attempt a pumpkin pie though."

She looked at his eager face and said a little prayer that things would turn out right for him. "I'll be happy to make one. Anything else?"

"Just your good wishes, Jenny."

"You have all of those and then some," she said, and never meant anything more sincerely. "Have you heard anything from Luke Beaumont yet?"

"Not a word. His secretary says he's out of town, but that he'll get back to me after the weekend. Looks as if the next few days hold the clue to my future. You don't own any crystal balls, do you?"

"Not one, but if I can think up some good-luck potions, I'll put 'em into effect."

He laughed, but it wasn't hearty. "I'm anxious for you to meet Leah, but I'll have to play things by ear."

"I understand. Bring her by for coffee if there's time."

"I'd like her to get acquainted with Corrie, too. Those two with their artistic talent have a lot in common. I can't believe how Corrie turned the place into a classy studio. Where is the girl, by the way? Haven't seen her around recently."

"Busy with her job and classes, I assume. I haven't seen her, either," Jenny said, and fervently hoped she was right, hoped the volatile girl hadn't thrown away the start she'd made. She'd had Corrie on her conscience continually since their blowup. It wasn't that Jenny hadn't experienced failure. God knows she'd had plenty of that, but never had she failed someone's trust. It was a raw wound that wouldn't heal.

Steve said no more for a moment or two and seemed to be involved with some inner debate. "Jenny," he said finally, "I hope all this recent gossip about us hasn't hurt you too deeply."

"So you finally heard."

"Well, you know Woodhaven. People around here conjure up an affair if a couple even nods at each other. I suppose it wasn't too hard to believe in a romance between two lonely people like ourselves. The funny thing is that from all I hear, everyone approves."

Everyone but Corrie and Luke, Jenny thought. "Thank goodness the rumors have died down. There's never a dearth of such talk around here, is there? I just hope the ridiculous gossip never reaches Leah. If it does, you must allow me to talk to her. I know positively I can convince her of the truth of the matter."

SHE MADE THE PIE early the next morning, and as she got ready to deliver it, the pickup wouldn't start. She'd already spent a bundle at Joe's Garage with all the things that had gone wrong lately. When she moved back to Berkeley, she was going to take a course in auto mechanics. There was no reason why she couldn't learn to take care of her own repairs.

She set out to walk the mile on the main road, the pie in a covered basket over her arm. The path through the woods was impassable because recent rains kept the creek too high to cross on foot. She met a few cars, and whether folks knew her or not, they never failed to wave a greeting. It was pleasant to receive their salutes. In the city she didn't know the people across the street much less to say a friendly hello.

Amos Botts came along and turned his car around so abruptly when he recognized her that it was a wonder he didn't tip over. "Where you headed, Little Miss Riding Hood?" he yelled as he skidded up along side her. "Hop in. Wherever, I'll take you."

"Dangerous offer, Amos. But you lucked out this time. I'm only headed for the mill. Steve is having company, and I promised him a pie. And where are you going with this car jammed full of supplies? Looks like enough to furnish a house."

"That's what I'm gonna do. Hank Porter's cabin burned down yesterday, so I collected a few things to help him out."

"Burned down completely? How awful."

"Yep. Lost every durn thing but his workbench."

"Workbench?"

He gave her a broad wink. "His bed."

She laughed. Amos had a heart of gold. It didn't matter if old Hank was the laziest man in town and that he lived up in the woods far off the beaten track. If he was in need, he could count on Amos.

"Well, hurry back," she said as he dropped her off. "I think those dark clouds mean rain."

"Hey, don't worry about me. I'm too old to melt." He gave her a cheery wave, and she held her breath as he skidded back around and peeled off.

She was going to miss Amos and his plump little wife. They gave the phrase "salt of the earth," a matchless meaning. If only... Well, not to speculate. She already owned too many "if onlys."

Steve wasn't at his house, but the door was open, so she set the pie on the kitchen counter and had just turned to leave when she saw a couple come out of the studio. Steve and Leah. Leah must have arrived a lot earlier than expected. Should she greet them? Something about the way they spoke to each other, so earnest and intense, warned that this was a very private moment.

She quickly stepped back into the kitchen. The girl wasn't at all as she had imagined. Jenny had expected to see a tall, sophisticated, intense young woman. This girl was tiny, and even from this distance, she looked vulnerable. Maybe it was the way she'd tied back her hair with a lavender ribbon. It was plain to see where Robbie got his fine-featured, angelic face.

Suddenly Steve put his arms around the young woman, and she seemed to melt into his embrace. Reproving herself for witnessing the intimate moment, Jenny hurried out the front door, scurrying around the far side of the house and up the slope to the main road, chiding herself with every step.

Even so, she couldn't stop herself from stealing one last glimpse as she slipped back onto the road. The sight held such intolerable perfection that she stood glued to the spot. Steve and Leah stood hand in hand, their arms outstretched toward Robbie who strained at Rosie's leash as he raced up the hill to join them.

CHAPTER TWENTY-TWO

STACY POKED HER HEAD into Luke's office. "Where shall we have dinner tonight? I have some exciting news for you," she said, her smile as sparkling as ever. He wondered if she even sparkled when she slept.

He hadn't asked her to dinner, but that was the way it was with Stacy. Anyway, the occasion would provide the opportunity to tell her of his future plans. Considering her ongoing possessive actions, he could predict her response. She could parry an argument with the zeal of a swarm of bees. Well, if he could prevail against Charles, he ought to be able to take on Stacy.

"How about Perrino's? I have news for you, too."

She beamed. "Going classy tonight! Your tidings must be pretty special. Well, so are mine."

He put on his overcoat and found his umbrella. She chattered nonstop on the way to the restaurant, something about knowing the harpist who played at Perrino's.

"My news first," Stacy said after they'd been seated at a window table. "Would you believe my surprise is located just a block or two above this restaurant?" That remark grabbed his attention. She leaned forward, bright-eyed with excitement. "Listen, today I learned that the Bourke place is going on the market. You know it, of course."

Yes, he knew it. It was a huge colonial home where the society queen of Otter Bay, Ethel Bourke, reigned in all her regal splendor. It seemed Mrs. Bourke, now a widow, was going to move to New York, and she was giving Stacy first crack at the house before putting it on the market.

"We'd save the Realtor's fee, which would be considerable. It's a dream of a place. The living room will hold half of Otter Bay!"

True. He'd been there for a cocktail party. "My God, that house is at least as big as Mount Vernon!"

"That's just the point, darling. In both our careers entertaining is essential. Not only that, one wing has a library, plus double offices just made for us."

Good Lord! He'd never even kissed this woman, much less gotten engaged to her, and already she was choosing their house! The waiter interrupted their discussion as he took their orders, then brought them gin and tonics.

"So what do you think?" she said, her face glowing. "I have the key. Why don't we look at it after dinner? I know you'll love it."

Luke took in her eager expression. Stacy was used to making plans and implementing them with dispatch. He could see that in her mind the imminent purchase of the house was a fact, and they need only move in. "Stacy, before you go any farther, I think I ought to tell you that I'm going to be leaving Otter Bay soon."

It was the first time he'd ever seen Stacy's poise teeter. She bit her lip, and for a moment she seemed at a loss for words. "Leaving Otter Bay! What on earth are you saying?" she asked finally.

"Yes, matters aren't firmed up completely, but I expect to leave within six weeks."

"Where?" she demanded. She seemed to bristle, as if to fend off any negative pronouncements.

"I'm not sure yet. Maybe back to the city. Possibly out of state."

"Luke, no! Why didn't you tell me earlier?"

"I only recently made the decision."

"Luke, you can't do this to me. I mean, you know how well I'm established here, and so are you."

Yes, he was quite aware of how much Stacy relished her role as a big duck in a little pond. "My plans are firm."

"Are you saying Charles is opening a new office somewhere? I'll talk to him."

"He's not opening another office, Stacy."

"Explain then!" She sounded as if he'd taken leave of his senses. "Surely you're not splitting from the Beaumont business?"

"Yes, I am."

"But why would you do such a thing? You have everything going for you! You'll own it someday. Charles told me all about it. Your future is set!"

"That's true. Set in concrete."

"Luke Beaumont, you're crazy!"

"I think it's the most sensible thing I've ever done."

"And I think you're out of your mind! There's no way I'd leave Otter Bay to go to the big city at this point. Of course, by the time you replace Charles, I'd be willing to move, but we both know that won't be for years. You need to go home and sleep off this wild idea."

"Stacy, listen. I have to point out that you and I have never mentioned marriage."

Her smile grew tight. "But I thought we had an understanding."

"I'm sorry. It seems more like a misunderstanding."

"Is there anything at all that might change your mind?"

"Not a thing." Yes, one. If Jenny has asked it of him, he'd stay.

She looked at him for a long time. "You mean that, don't you?"

"Absolutely." He'd never meant anything more sincerely. If she felt rebuffed, she hid her feelings well.

"I'm sorry then. We could have made beautiful music together, and the Bourke place would have been a perfect place to start. But I have to tell you that I would never leave Otter Bay, even for someone like you. Don't worry. We don't have to make excuses to anyone, do we? After all," she said, allowing only a slight tinge of bitterness, "we never were officially engaged."

They finished their dinner in silence, an entirely new experience for the two of them, and not all that unpleasant. He felt a certain amount of guilt. He hadn't encouraged or led her on. Far from it. He'd refused so many invitations it had become embarrassing, and he'd avoided every intimate situation she'd provided. Still, he would have been sorry to hurt her.

Letting her be the one to end their relationship made it easier on her. For certainly there would be no grieving.

JENNY'S LAST DAY of teaching was over, and her classroom was empty. Her pupils had helped her pack away everything that had stamped Jenny Valentine's identity on this school. Blackboards were clean and bulletin boards and counters were free from artwork and projects, all of which had been sent home. The batch of library books she checked out monthly were boxed, ready to be picked up by the county truck, along with the movie projector, slide machine and phonograph records. The room looked as bare as when she had arrived. Captain Fussbudget Ballard should be relieved, not to mention Etta Mae, who could dust freely again without all those encumbrances.

She scanned the room, then winked at George Washington and Abraham Lincoln in their solemn portraits. *Haven't I left a single imprint on this school?* Only the bookcases she'd built from orange crates remained. Some legacy!

Well, maybe she'd instilled a love of reading in some of them. "That's something, isn't it, Mr. Lincoln and Mr. Washington?" she asked aloud.

"There she goes, talking to herself again," a vibrant young voice said, and Corrie came bouncing into the room.

"Corrie!" Jenny didn't know what else to say. It seemed an aeon since the night Corrie had walked out after her bitter indictment.

The young woman stood politely as if waiting for permission to sit down. "So you're pulling out of the woods come Sunday."

"That's right. Back to Berkeley to finish up my units. Sit down. I've missed you."

Corrie plopped down on top of one of the desks and wrestled her short denim skirt over her knees. "I'll come on Sunday and help you move," she said, and had to clear her throat as she said it.

An olive branch, Jenny realized. *Seize it*. "That would be great. My old truck finally gave up the ghost and had to be towed to the junkyard. Steve can get most of my stuff in his pickup. I'd love it if you could help with the rest and drive me down."

"Can't imagine why. As Granny would say, I've been a damn serowlsh. Why didn't you shake me up or beat me over the head?"

Jenny smiled. "I guess I prefer light to heat. I don't blame you for your reaction, Corrie. I'm sorry you misunderstood about Steve's involvement, but it doesn't change the basic issue."

"Hey, remember me? Act first, think later. Anyway, it's your business. I was a prize dope for shooting off my mouth like that. I'm sorry."

"Considering my own five-cent comments on your affairs, I think you deserve an explanation. You see, this whole situation arose because in a single brief moment I had the magnificent illusion that things were going to be right again between my former fiancé and me. Unfortunately that didn't happen."

"*That* guy!" she said with venom. "I'd like to give him a piece of my mind!"

"Oh, he has a conscience. When he found out, he offered to marry me."

"So what did you say?"

"What do you think?"

Corrie gave her a long look. "I think you told him to get lost."

Jenny laughed but knew she was closer to tears. Did pregnancy keep one's emotions so close to the surface? "Ah, Corrie, you know me well, after all."

"I hear you're getting a send-off tomorrow afternoon."

"The board is meeting for lunch and I've been invited. I understand that Steve's wife is in charge. It's sure to be special."

"Good for her. Granny tells me she's back to stay. I'm glad someone's finally doing well in the romance department," Corrie said. "Mine has been null and void recently."

Jenny didn't care to dwell on that subject. "How about helping me carry these cartons out to the car? I'd leave most of my material here, but Captain Ballard doesn't approve of all that folderol.''

"Ha. If you ask me, Captain Ballard got cold feet when he suddenly learned what big shoes he was going to have to fill.''

"What do you mean?''

"Boy, you always were the last one to tap into the grapevine. The way I hear it, the old codger got a sudden urge to retire to Florida. He saw that your class had increased to over thirty kids, so he had second thoughts about handling that many in all six grades. He also made a lot of noise about not willing to compromise his standards with so-called modern education. Some smoke screen! People around here aren't that dumb!''

"So who will teach at Woodhaven?''

"I hear they've lined up a married couple. Hey, that ought to stroke your ego! Takes two people to replace you! The board figures a couple will be more likely to stay put. The kids will be split into two groups: primary grades and upper ones. The old church next door will be used for one class until a survey verifies the need for building a new school.''

"Good heavens, when did all this happen?''

"At the emergency board meeting last night. Granny Etta Mae is better than any snoopy reporter.''

"A new school? Simon will have apoplexy!''

"Listen, the board was all for requesting you to stay. Would you believe that even Simon didn't object? But Steve insisted that you were determined to go back to university to finish your credential.''

"I would have loved to stay.'' Yes, she would have leaped at the chance to stay another semester. But she needed the anonymity of a big city now. Little B deserved that, and maybe, so did she. "Well, Corrie, it's just as well that I'm leaving, considering..."

"Yeah, I suppose so," Corrie said with a a deep sigh. "Considering..."

CHAPTER TWENTY-THREE

JENNY WAS WAITING for Steve and Leah to arrive to take her to the luncheon the members of the school board were having for her. She'd been breathless all morning. No one in her entire life had ever held a party for her. Maybe it didn't qualify as such since it technically was a board meeting, but as far as she was concerned it was *a party*.

Corrie had insisted that she buy a new dress for the occasion and had driven her to Otter Bay to shop yesterday after school. The sea-foam green gown with its dropped waistline looked smart and feminine, and besides it would hide her condition for a long time, not that she needed a maternity dress yet.

"Hey, old lady, you look smashing. Every guy at the party will want to sit by you."

Jenny laughed. "All four?" There was only one of them she would favor. True to his word, she hadn't heard from Luke, but she knew he would be there. Breathless with anticipation, she listened for Steve's car and knew the feeling wasn't all due to the party. She was glad she'd bought a new dress. She wanted to look special today.

Steve had picked her up at noon. "Leah went early," he said. "Seems she wanted to pretty up the table and whatever else you ladies do for a luncheon. She's having a ball." His eyes shone with exhilaration he felt at Leah's participation.

As they drove down the rutted road, Jenny realized this would be the last time she would see the old log building. Never would she forget the mouth-watering spreads at the Saturday night potlucks, the lively dances with hometown musicians. Sometimes the band only had an accordion, a fiddle and a drum, but no one at the most lavish party could have had more fun.

"Good heavens!" Jenny cried as they wound their way down the final hill to the flats where the center was located. "Something else must be going on here!" Cars filled the meadow, but no one was in sight.

"Maybe the county farm bureau is having one of their demonstrations today. We may be relegated to the small private room," he said as they walked to the entrance. He pulled open the heavy door of the building, and they were blasted by a mighty shout.

"Surprise!" everyone cried. The place was packed. She recognized her pupils scattered throughout the hall with their parents. They clapped and called out her name. Jenny was speechless. She met Steve's eyes and silently begged an explanation.

"Yes, it's all for you," Steve said, enjoying her bewilderment, and seated her at the head table.

"I can't believe this!"

"Believe it," he said. "We were going to keep it exclusive, for the board only, but the community wouldn't hear of it."

All the members along with their spouses were at the head table. All except Luke. Well, he'd be here soon. "I won't miss it for anything," he'd promised.

As she looked at the cheering crowd, she was afraid she wouldn't be able to hold back tears. After this last nightmarish month, a party honoring Jenny Valentine was past imagining. She wondered if everyone assumed that the gossip about her and Steve was another incident in Dirk's mischief-making. Truth was dull. It was more fun to put two and two together and get five.

Amos Botts at once took the floor and gave a witty speech on the "Education of Jenny Valentine." He said that Woodhaven very much appreciated the learnin' she'd given their kids, but Woodhaven deserved the major credit for turning this green flatlander into one of their own. He presented her with a large certificate, verifying that she was a "Genuine Woodhaven Citizen." In her heart she knew it was one of the highest honors she would ever receive.

Jenny noted that Leah's hand was visible everywhere in the hall, from the garlands of pine boughs draped over the doors and windows to individual favors of little red schoolhouses fashioned from milk cartons, cleverly painted and filled with candy and nuts. She must have spent hours.

"It's fabulous, Leah. This old place has never looked so festive," Jenny told her later, and was pleased to note that many others complimented Leah, as well. It looked as if she were getting off to a good start. Trying to understand each other's needs had brought understanding between Leah and Steve, and between Leah and the community, too.

The thought spawned a wrenching insight. Had she failed in understanding Luke's needs? She realized now that what Luke felt wasn't a need to excel in the fast track, but the need to be his own person. She hadn't taken into account how deeply his father's failure as a husband and parent had affected him. No wonder he set impossible goals for himself.

She scanned the room again to see if Luke had finally put in an appearance. He hadn't.

Later, when the tables were folded away and the dance music started, Jenny had no lack of partners. Behind a smiling mask, she chatted gaily and tried to leave each man feeling as if he were the best dancer in the hall.

When at last Steve asked her to dance, she told him how much the party meant to her. "I can't believe this big turnout! I suppose Luke Beaumont was too busy to come," she added nonchalantly.

"Yes, you wouldn't believe how disappointed he sounded."

"You mean he told you he wouldn't be here? When?"

Steve missed a step and stopped dancing for a moment. "Are you saying that you didn't get the message?"

"What message?" Her head swam and the room blurred as if infiltrated by mist.

"He called last night and said he'd been unable to reach you, so he asked me to let you know. I thought your phone might be out of order, so I went to your place, but you weren't there."

"Corrie and I went to Otter Bay after school yesterday. We stayed for dinner, shopped until the stores closed and didn't get home until rather late."

"I wedged a note in the door. You didn't find it?"

"It wasn't there. I'm positive."

"That's strange. Maybe it fell off. Take a look when you go home. It seems Luke is tied up in Seattle. He really poured it on about how sorry he was to miss your party. Said he'd call you as soon as he got home." Steve grinned. *So you two are getting together at last,* he seemed to say.

"Oh, I expect he exaggerated. I'll probably never see him again," she said. Anger choked her. So much for his promises. Charles was still manipulating him. Luke was probably off on another project for Beaumont Business

Services, maybe even opening a new office. Another step up the corporate ladder. *There he goes again!*

They finished the dance and Jenny hurried to the ladies' room. She poured cold water in her cupped hands and tried to cool her burning cheeks. Why couldn't she accept that Luke wouldn't change? She stared in the mirror at her ravaged face. *Calm down. You're so consumed with your bruised ego that you've completely forgotten all the grand people who are here for your party.*

Hastily she repaired her makeup, straightened her shoulders and went back into the hall, where for a while she joined some of her pupils who gathered around her in a fit of giggling.

She was startled to spot Corrie dancing with Dirk. It was the first time she'd ever seen him dressed up. He cut quite a figure. Although the music was an old-fashioned two-step, their movements were more appropriate to a current rock number.

A few days ago Jenny had found a freshly picked bunch of watercress on her porch. On top was a laboriously printed note:

I'm sorry for all the mean things I said about you. I was off my rocker. No more cockamamied tricks. That's a promise.

Yours truly,
Dirk McCleod

She'd had to smile. Even the long word was correctly spelled. From all she'd heard about his efforts to reform, the sentiments may have been sincere enough, but she couldn't imagine Dirk writing the note without some zealous persuasion, no doubt from Corrie. She'd probably even corrected the spelling. Good for her. Corrie might prod the young fellow into a civilized specimen yet.

During an intermission she ran into the girl. The Gypsy in the tangerine skirt and purple sunglasses Jenny had met the day she arrived was no more. Corrie, her makeup discreet, wearing a smart navy knit suit, could have passed for a young professional woman in any city. Still, Jenny was relieved to note that Corrie's wildly colorful scarf and matching earrings left some remnant of her beguiling flamboyance.

"You and Dirk are the best dancers in the crowd," Jenny told her.

"Surprised to see my partner? Would you believe he swears he's turned over a new leaf? Don't know how long the miraculous transformation will last, but I figure giving him a dance or two is the best way to encourage him." After noting Dirk's ecstatic expression as the two danced together, Jenny agreed.

As the day ended, people gathered their children and surrounded her to say a last goodbye and to wish her well. To her amazement even Simon Flint extended his hand. "I guess you and I won't ever see eye to eye on this education business, but I wish you good luck anyway," Simon said. It was probably the most magnanimous statement he would ever make. It had been a day to remember.

THE FOLLOWING MORNING Jenny rose early in order to give the finishing touches to the cottage, making it ready for the new teachers who were due to arrive before noon. The night before she'd waxed the floors to a high gleam and cleaned the windows until they'd sparkled. As a final touch, she'd set a sprouting redwood burl with lavish feathery shoots on the kitchen table.

Now Jenny sat on the front porch steps, watching the sun come up and waiting for Steve and Corrie to arrive to help her move. She'd be in Berkeley for lunch.

She'd found the brief note Steve had left on Friday with Luke's excuse for not arriving at the party. It had fallen down and wedged under a window box. Another broken promise. She didn't want to think about it.

She drew deep breaths of the cool, damp air and heard the soft twittering of a song sparrow in some nearby tree. She would never forget this little cottage in the woods. Its simple beauty and comfort had been like a mantle slipped over her shoulders. Trading these fog-draped forests and lush meadows for the noise and density of the city would come as a challenge.

All her things were packed in cartons stacked on the front porch. Most would fit into Steve's pickup. The rest would go in Corrie's car.

Earlier she had taken Fat Cat's basket from the closet and had gone to call him. He sat grooming himself on a nearby log, took one look at the basket and streaked into the forest. No amount of pleading coaxed him to return.

Fat Cat was no longer fat. Jenny had noted often of late how his flanks rippled with muscle, how his yellow coat shone as tawny as a lion's. For some time he'd disavowed juvenile capers in favor of stalking through the giant trees. She couldn't blame him for wanting to stay here. Life in a small apartment posed a pretty meager alternative, but considering the food and warm quarters she'd supplied him through the years, she couldn't believe he would abandon her this way. It lent a sour note to the day, and she was glad she and Corrie were riding together.

Steve had called a few days before her party, elated with the news that Luke had arranged a new contract. It seemed that the Richter Corporation was a long-standing client of the Beaumont San Francisco firm. At the moment the Richter operation was tied up by a carpenters' strike, so the late delivery of the lumber would pose no delay after all. Steve had been on top of the world with the good news and had sung Luke's praises until Jenny wanted to tell him to get lost.

She mulled over Luke's confusing behavior for the zillionth time. Well, she couldn't exactly claim perfection in this duo. Maybe she'd raved so continually over the family she wanted that Luke decided he'd be reduced to a mere figurehead. She'd known women who ignored their husbands when the children came.

Not Joel and Beth Spencer. Perhaps that was one reason they had such a good marriage. Whenever Jenny had been with them and their family, she couldn't help but notice their loving reaction. When Joel came home from work, he'd go first to Beth, give her a hug and a kiss, then turn to his sons. Whenever the two of them were in a group, Jenny noticed that their eyes often met, as if to enjoy a little silent communication concerning whatever was happening. They let each other know who came first in their lives without in any way taking love away from their children.

If she and Luke had only listened, really listened to each other, maybe the outcome would have been different. But the time for meaningful communication had passed. Any further speculation was redundant.

Corrie drove up then with Steve close behind. Leah and Robbie were with him. "I'm taking the family for an outing after we move you. It's time Robbie got to visit the petting zoo in San Francisco. Then we'll go out to dinner in some classy place. This girl of mine has been working like a beaver all week. She deserves a treat." Leah reached over and squeezed his hand.

They all helped to pile Jenny's cartons in Steve's pickup, and when Jenny's cat was still missing when they were ready to leave, Robbie promised to find and adopt him. Jenny and Corrie got into Corrie's car to lead the way to the Spencers' garage apartment in Berkeley.

Beth had called last week to let her know the place was ready. "We haven't had time to furnish it yet, but I rounded up a cot and a card table for the time being," she'd said. Jenny was so thrilled to have four walls and friends around her that the lack of furniture was the least of her worries.

Corrie jerked a thumb back at Steve's pickup. "So those two got back together after all. You were right all along. I always thought she was too snooty to mingle with us hill-billies, but she's not like that at all. Just shows how you shouldn't go on first impressions."

They were quiet for a while as Jenny concentrated on the winding road down to the coast highway.

"So what's ahead for the unsinkable J. Valentine? I'm sure you have plan A. Also plans B and C."

"So far things are working out. I register tomorrow morning, and my part-time job at the day-care center begins in March. The baby will arrive the end of July, which will give me over a month before I start teaching in September. I learned that I was eligible for a scholarship from a women's reentry program. So, with my savings, I'm all set."

"You mean you're going to work and go to school up until the last minute?"

"Why not? I'm positively glowing with health, and pregnant students aren't all that unusual."

Corrie gave a low whistle. "You really plan ahead."

"Hardly, or I wouldn't have ended up being a pregnant student," she said dryly.

"So you already have a teaching job lined up for next fall?"

"No, but I'll get one."

"And if you don't?"

"I won't consider that possibility."

"Look out, folks! Here comes a steamroller with bells on! Count on me to take a week off to help you out when the baby comes."

Jenny could hardly swallow. "Thanks, Corrie, you're a real friend. I'll let you know. Beth says she'll help, too. She ought to be an authority, what with those three boys."

"So you've told her?"

"Figured I should, considering it will be evident soon. Just you and Beth and Joel, though."

"Not Steve?"

"Not Steve. Believe me, at this point, he'd never understand. I'll find the words when the time comes." Steve would not only be astounded to learn that Luke had fathered this child, but would be at a loss to understand the entire situation, as, no doubt, would Corrie.

Corrie looked dubious. "If you say so, but I think you underestimate him."

"Just call me a coward."

"Not so I've noticed," Corrie said with emphasis.

It was noon before they arrived at the Spencers'. Following introductions, everyone helped carry Jenny's things up to the little apartment. As Steve handed Jenny a carton of bedding, a sleek calico cat jumped out and landed on her shoulder, giving her cheek a swipe with his sandpaper tongue.

"Fat Cat!" everyone cried. He must have sneaked into the truck when no one was looking. He raced up the stairs into the apartment and planted himself in front of the small refrigerator, yowling like a despot.

Jenny hurriedly brushed away the sudden moisture in her eyes. She would never be able to explain why she was moved to tears merely because her old cat had decided to stay with her after all.

CHAPTER TWENTY-FOUR

LUKE ARRIVED at the San Francisco airport at seven in the morning and rented a car. He'd sold his VW and would buy something new as soon as he got settled. Things had moved so fast this past week that he could scarcely contain his elation. A spokesman from the board of directors at the Wharton Timber Corporation had called him four days ago to tell him he'd won the job and had asked him to fly up to Seattle immediately. He felt downright frustrated about missing Jenny's party yesterday, but now that he finally had some great news to share, he knew she'd understand.

He pressed the speed limit all the way. Even if there were no traffic, he wouldn't get to Woodhaven before noon. He'd already turned the Otter Bay office over to his replacement. All he had to do was to pack up his clothes and other personal belongings from his apartment and ship them up to Seattle. He had to fly back tomorrow night, so he had exactly thirty-four hours to convince Jenny to come with him.

He couldn't wait to see her. He recalled their last meeting with no little apprehension. He'd better consider the distinct possibility that she would have none of him. He tried not to think about it and knew he mustn't feel too optimistic. Just because *he* was rolling along with glorious momentum didn't mean Jenny would want any part of it. God knows she was more than capable of making it on her own.

He couldn't help a figurative lick of his chops when he thought of his uncle's reaction to his new job. It had been wonderful irony that Charles had telephoned less than five minutes after the favorable call from Seattle. He'd wondered how long Charles would keep his silence.

Charles's tone had been mellow. One would never have thought they'd parted in anger a few weeks ago. It seemed that a Senator Ellis was in town for a few days with an offer that was almost too good to be true.

"It's tailor-made for you, Luke. You've got to hear it to believe it, and the salary is equal to what you earned with me," he said, his enthusiasm charming over the wire. "I've set up a luncheon meeting at the Fairmont on Wednesday. I'll have the company pilot fly you down. In fact—"

"Hold on," Luke interrupted. "I've already accepted a job in Seattle. I'm pulling out tomorrow."

"What in hell did you do that for? Chuck it! This is the best offer you'll ever receive, bar none."

"I don't think so, Uncle Charles. I'll be managing the Wharton Corporation's international West Coast office opening soon in Seattle." Luke smiled at his uncle's silence. They both knew the senator's offer would have to be pretty sensational to top that.

"I see. Well, congratulations," Charles said stiffly. "Perhaps I should congratulate myself for the excellent training you received from Beaumont Enterprises, enabling you to earn such a position."

"Perhaps you should. I consider the experience invaluable."

"Well, you'd better think it over. I can't imagine a single soul foolhardy enough to ignore an offer from Senator Ellis."

No doubt Senator Ellis owed Charles any number of plums for Charles's generous political contributions. His uncle had managed to dredge up a few amenities, then rang off.

Luke wondered how many more attempts Charles would make to woo him back under his control. Well, Luke would undertake to instruct Charles about the meaning of a simple no.

As he had done often lately, he thought about their association. Luke knew he had no right to blame his uncle for his own errors. Charles never tried to hide who he was. In fact, he was quite blatant about it. No, the truth was that the starry-eyed nephew had been bowled over by Charles, the oracle, his opinions inviolable, his knowledge and experience unrivaled. Anyone who'd achieved all that success had to be right, didn't he? What naiveté! What a fool he'd been!

Luke reached Woodhaven a little after noon. As he drove down Jenny's lane, he saw a man and woman unloading a truck, and carrying boxes inside the cottage. What was going on? He thought Jenny wasn't leaving until next week, but obviously someone was moving in. How could she have left so soon? Her party had only been yesterday. But, yes she could have left, all right, a fact he soon learned from the busy young couple.

"We understand she moved to Berkeley this morning," the fellow said. "She didn't leave an address or phone number."

Luke thanked them and headed for the gas station where he used a pay phone to call the Spencers. Jenny had mentioned sometime ago that she planned to rent their garage apartment if it was ready. But there was no answer. He rang every few minutes for the next half hour, hoping that sheer persistence would force the call through.

Finally he gave up and drove directly to Berkeley. He hadn't seen the Spencers since moving to Otter Bay, except for a brief hello at Christmas when he'd dropped off some presents for their three little boys. It struck him that they might not be too cordial. In fact, they probably considered him a prize heel. He was fond of Joel and his family and hoped he could mend their friendship.

Life without Jenny loomed too empty to contemplate. And now that there would be a child, he wanted them together with a longing that almost overwhelmed him. The thought of his very own son or daughter had been with him continually ever since he'd learned of it. He'd been astonished at the emotion he felt. Jenny believed he didn't want children. If only he could make her understand how mistaken she was.

The Spencers' home was located just down the block from the apartment where he and Jenny used to live. He parked, hurried to the door and knocked.

Beth opened it at once, reached for his arm and pulled him inside. The gesture, cordial as it was, lacked the spontaneity of her usual hug and kiss. "Come in, stranger," she said, and gestured to a chair. "Sit down and I'll get Joel. He came home for lunch and is fixing a blind in the new apartment. You arrived just in time."

"It's all finished then?"

"Yes—" she hesitated "—and rented."

"To Jenny, right?"

"Yes, but she's not there now," Beth said hurriedly, and went to get her husband.

Joel came striding in a few moments later. They shook hands and for a few minutes caught up on the specifics of Joel's new job and the improvements in the house.

Luke turned to Beth. "Sounds like you two have been busy, but what else is new? Where are your three little bombshells? I suppose they've grown a foot. Anything in that cookie jar I used to raid?'' He hoped it wasn't acting too hearty, but he felt a wall between them ten feet high.

"Just filled it this morning," she said, and hurried into the kitchen.

Luke fidgeted impatiently. "Look, Joel, I want to see Jenny, and I haven't much time. Do you have any idea when she'll return?"

Joel looked uneasy. "Not really."

"What's all this about opening another branch office for your uncle?" Beth asked as she returned with coffee and a plate of cookies.

"I'm not. I've changed jobs. I'm going to work for the Wharton Timber Corporation in Seattle. I have a flight out tomorrow night. That's why I'm so anxious to get in touch with Jenny this afternoon."

They looked startled. "Does this move have anything to do with you two? We never could figure out what happened," Beth said.

"It has a lot to do with both of us, and I can't tell you how important it is that I see her. My God! You must have some idea where she is or when she'll be home."

"Listen, Luke," Beth said after an awkward pause. "Do you think it's wise for you to meet her? After what you did to her, we don't want to let her in for more hurt."

Luke slumped back in his chair. "So you know about the baby?"

"We know," Joel snapped, and Luke felt as if a fist had slammed into his chin. "My God, man, what's with you anyway? Why won't you marry her?"

"That's what I'm trying to do! I've pleaded and begged but I've messed up royally. I love Jenny. I've never stopped loving her. I want to take care of her and be a real father to our child. I'll do anything for another chance. Damn it, if our friendship means anything at all, tell me where I can find her!'' Luke tried to discover an iota of compassion in their austere faces. "Did *she* tell you she didn't want to see me?''

"She didn't have to,'' Joel said. "Your actions told us all we needed to know.''

Luke's anger flared. "Playing God isn't like you, Joel. What makes you think you have the right to mess with our future?''

A long look passed between husband and wife, and Beth mutely nodded. "You'll find her with the boys at the park.''

Luke leaped up and had one foot out the door before Beth stopped him. "The neighborhood park. You know which one we mean?''

Yes, he did. It was the one where last June he and Jenny had celebrated his graduation and planned their wedding. They'd held the world in their hands then. He ran to the car and started it. Jenny was a mere three blocks away.

When he arrived, he drove slowly around until he spotted her with the three boys, then parked and found a secluded table under the familiar gnarled sycamore. Although it was an unseasonably sunny day, the temperature was cool and Jenny and her charges were the only ones in sight.

He granted himself a few minutes to sit and watch, time to assemble the words he needed so desperately. Picking up a discarded newspaper, he pretended to read as he took in the scene before him. His eyes blurred and his throat constricted.

A still-slim Jenny played follow-the-leader with the three children. She wore a full-skirted cotton dress with a ruffled collar that recalled the endearing, unique garb Jenny had worn the day he'd met her. Her blue eyes sparkled and her cheeks were pink with exertion.

He watched as she scaled imaginary mountains, leaped across wild rivers, then, arms spread wide, soared like a gull. The three little boys shouted in delight and followed close behind in spirited mimicry. Blue sky and sunlight highlighted the eager faces, and the joyous communication between Jenny and the children fused into a moment of perfection.

Luke had to look away. He put his head in his hands and saw himself tossing a ball to his own little son, loping around the park with his tiny daughter on his back, and tried to deal with the new emotions that pulsed inside him.

A few second later a tug on his arm broke his reverie. "Uncle Luke! Come have some ice cream with us." The child pointed to an old-fashioned hand-cranked freezer. "We made it!" No surprise at Luke's presence. Just acceptance. That was the way it was with kids. But would it be so with Jenny?

She hadn't joined the boys in their invitation, but stood some distance away. Her smile had vanished. He couldn't read her expression. Mutely their eyes met, knowing they couldn't help but recall that day months ago they'd spent here together, the joy they'd felt, the plans they'd made, the promises spoken. If only the aftermath didn't form too great a bridge to cross.

"Jenny?" The name contained the question he feared to ask. By the set of her mouth, forgiveness would be too formidable a task. He felt a tightening along his spine and across his jaw, but the words that stayed ever fresh in his mind came firmly now. "I've made a lot of mistakes, and I guess deceiving myself was the worst of them."

"What about broken promises, Luke? Where were you Saturday?"

"My God, didn't you get my message? I've quit my uncle's business for good, and I just got the nod for a great new job. It's been hanging fire all month, but I didn't want to tell you unless it came through. That's why I was in Seattle—sewing up my new job so that we'd have Charles out of our life for good."

The fifteen feet of grass that separated them might as well have been the Sahara Desert. She stood incredibly still. After an eternity she spoke, and her eyes shone. "Say that again. Tell me you really left Beaumont Business Services. Say it!"

"It's true. I've been dying to tell you."

"Oh, my darling, forgive me for not trusting you."

"Jenny, what was that you called me?"

A pixie smile lit up her face. "I said, *my darling*." She held out her arms to him. His heart gave a joyful leap. It took only a half-dozen strides to reach her, to catch her up and enfold her tightly in his arms, feeling her slender frame through her dress. With one hand he tipped up her chin. "Oh, Jenny. Jenny." He took her face gently between his hands. "Marry me. I want us to raise our child, our children together."

She searched his expression, then placed a hand against his chest to feel the steady beat of his heart. "All our children?"

"The entire basketball team. I'll have enough love for all of them."

She burrowed her head against his shoulder. "You weren't the only muddlehead in this outfit. I was so caught up in my dreams, I ignored yours. I blabbed so much about having a family that you probably thought I would draw a circle around me and the children and leave you standing outside."

"Sometimes I wondered," he said.

"But I never would, and that's my promise to you. I'll adore our children, but you'll always come first in my life."

"And you in mine," he said, and they smiled at each other unsteadily.

"That's settled, then, so kiss me like you mean it." He complied at once, wholeheartedly and with abandon.

They rocked together in each other's arms, and it seemed for a while as if their entire world had diminished to the confines of the tight circle they formed. They were scarcely conscious of the children consuming the ice cream in vast quantities, leaving a generous amount smeared on faces and clothing.

"And all the time I thought you'd taken off on another errand for your uncle," she said when at last he released her.

"Never again!" he sang out. "We can start over, my love. Thank God for the chance."

"Not start over," Jenny replied with conviction. "True love is like that giant burned-out redwood—split by lightning, gutted by fire, yet it survived and grew taller than any tree in the forest."

Their eyes met in a solemn vow, and they wrapped their arms around each other, putting themselves into each other's keeping for all time.

Harlequin Superromance.

COMING NEXT MONTH

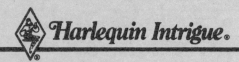

Indulge a Little, Give a Lot

To receive your free gift send us the required number of proofs-of-purchase from any specially marked "Indulge A Little" Harlequin or Silhouette book with the Offer Certificate properly completed, plus a cheque or money order (do not send cash) to cover postage and handling payable to Harlequin/Silhouette "Indulge A Little, Give A Lot" Offer. We will send you the specified gift.

Mail-in-Offer

OFFER CERTIFICATE

Item	A. Collector's Doll	B. Soaps in a Basket	C. Potpourri Sachet	D. Scented Hangers
# of Proofs-of -Purchase	18	12	6	4
Postage & Handling	$3.25	$2.75	$2.25	$2.00
Check One				

Name _____

Address _____ Apt # _____

City _____ State _____ Zip _____

ONE PROOF OF PURCHASE

To collect your free gift by mail you must include the necessary number of proofs-of-purchase plus postage and handling with offer certificate.

HS-1

Harlequin®/Silhouette®

Mail this certificate, designated number of proofs-of-purchase and check or money order for postage and handling to:

INDULGE A LITTLE
P.O. Box 9055 Buffalo, N.Y. 14269-9055